Something Like REDEMPTION

International Bestselling Author

MONICA JAMES

THE MONSTERS WITHIN DUET
Bullseye
Blowback

DELIVER US FROM EVIL TRILOGY
Thy Kingdom Come
Into Temptation
Deliver Us From Evil

IN LOVE AND WAR
North of the Stars
Fall of the Stars

REVENGE IS SWEET SERIES
Crybaby

HEART MEMORY TRANSFER DUET
Heart Sick
Love Sick

STANDALONE
Mr. Write
Chase the Butterflies
Beyond the Roses
Someone Else's Shadow

"It is not in the stars to hold our destiny but in ourselves."

— *William Shakespeare*

It's been said that before you die, your life flashes before your eyes. All the good, all the bad, all the significant, or the nonsignificant flicker before you, presenting you with an epiphany. And then in turn, you're supposed to embrace death and accept it's your time.

But what happens if you're not ready to die? What happens if your life is snatched out from under you, with no real say as to why it ended so suddenly?

If that's the case, do those who meet a tragic demise not have the luxury of this magical epiphany? Is it fated for those who fight death with their last dying breath to just burn out and…fade?

If this is so, then my quest for revenge and redemption will be filled with nothing but bloodshed.

An eye for an eye, the Bible says. Well, I'll settle for anything so long as the result is the same.

My dad and Phil are already dead…they just don't know it yet.

One

"**R**ed, are you awake?"

No!

My sense of hearing is finely tuned as my eyes have been shut for the past three hours, refusing to open because once they do, the events of why I'm here will become real.

I don't want to believe that my dad, who I put a bullet into, is not really dead. Nor do I want to believe that he and his drug dealer, my former "boss" Big Phil, shot a man in cold blood, ending his life like it never mattered.

But it did matter.

It matters to me.

He mattered to me.

And because of me, he's dead.

Hank protected me until the very end. He could have

ratted me out, but he didn't. He faced my dad head-on, proving to be more of a parent than my own biological father. So where's the justice in him being dead while his murderers roam free?

There isn't any.

When I jumped on a bus close to three months ago, headed for the sleepy town of South Boston, Virginia, I never imagined the harm I would cause so many people I came to care for.

Especially not the man sitting beside me.

Nothing about Quinn Berkeley is simple, and from the get-go, I knew he would change my life forever. But I never foresaw just how much so. Nor did I ever predict that his brother, Tristan, would do the same.

Tristan, who Quinn and I left unconscious and bleeding to death on his hallway floor, is the reason Quinn and I are alive.

Yes, we're on the run from the police, as we're both prime suspects in Hank's murder, but we're alive.

And we're together.

But I don't blame Quinn for resenting or even hating me. I mean, I'm the reason his brother was coughing up his own blood, thanks to a stab wound my dad and Phil inflicted on him.

I hate myself for it, and I will continue to do so for all the days of my life.

But that's good.

All that hate and anger will fuel me to rid this earth of two assholes, ensuring they never hurt another living soul again.

I tell myself to open my eyes, as Quinn just asked me a question.

Yet my eyes remain closed.

How am I supposed to open them and face the eyes of the man whose life I have just destroyed? Because of me, Quinn's life is one big fucked-up mess, and I can't do anything about it. Or is there?

"I know you're not sleeping."

"How do you know?" I ask, cracking open an eye, only able to take him in this way.

Step by step with Quinn—I've learned the hard way. If I overindulge too fast, he's proven to be hazardous to my health.

"Because I know you," he replies plainly, his face inches from mine. His weary eyes reveal how our messed-up situation weighs heavily upon him.

"Where are we?" I ask, looking around at our unfamiliar surroundings, seeing a strip of derelict shops and lots of greenery.

"Someplace in North Carolina. Thought we could get something to eat and withdraw some cash," he replies, muffling a yawn with the back of his hand.

"Sure." I unbuckle my seat belt.

My Border Collie pup, Lucky, likes the sound of that, as he sits up, wagging his tail excitedly. Patting between his ears, I'm so happy he's in better condition than when I first found him. "Okay, buddy, you're coming too."

Quinn exits the cab, and I take a minute to admire him.

He stretches his long arms above his head, which results in a sliver of his hardened stomach becoming exposed. My eyes drop to his ink, which I only know is there because I've been lucky enough to see him topless.

I know what lies underneath that plain, simple T-shirt, and nothing is plain or simple about it. I berate myself to stop checking him out because one, he's cocky enough, and two, I need to ween myself off him because three hours is a long time to plot and plan.

I'm certain of a few things. It goes without saying my need for revenge animates me to survive. But I'm not selfish enough to drag Quinn down with me.

I've done enough of that.

No, what I have planned will *save* Quinn. It will clear his name, and in time, this will all be a distant memory for him.

But to do that, I have to *sacrifice* myself to *save* him.

I have no doubt that at the end of all of this, Quinn will hate me with every fiber of his being. And you know what? I can live with that.

I can live with that fact because I can live with anything as long as he's happy and free.

"Did you want me to drive for a bit?" I ask, looking down at Quinn, who nurses his third cup of black coffee.

We're sitting in a roadside diner called Yo-Yo's, and it's nothing like Bobby Joe's, the diner I worked at back home.

Home.

It's funny how I don't consider LA my home anymore even though I grew up there. But when was it really my home? It stopped being my home the day my mother up and left, moving to Canada. I was three when it happened, and I haven't heard from her since.

It was my mission before all this shit happened to find her and ask her to fill in the blanks because my father sure as hell didn't. I was prepared to beg for an explanation as to why she left because, how could a mother abandon her three-year-old child? Was I a disappointment in her eyes? Is that why she left?

But now, my priorities have changed.

I've found my mother. I know where she lives. But nowadays, that doesn't seem as important as it once was to me.

Granted, things have turned to shit, but deep down, it was never really a priority. If it were, I would have left the moment I found out where she was. But I didn't. I stayed in South Boston because I had found the place I wanted to call home.

It's too bad because if I had left, Hank would still be alive, and Tristan wouldn't have gotten hurt.

"Nope, it's fine. But I think we should crash. We've got to figure out what the hell to do next," Quinn says, interrupting my what-ifs.

Rubbing my temples, hoping to soothe my pounding headache, proves futile. "Okay, good idea," I reply, looking down at my untouched burger.

The thought of eating turns my stomach, so I slide it over to Quinn. "Here. I don't want it to go to waste."

As Quinn accepts, his long fingers brush over mine accidentally, and I pull away like I've been burned. He eyes me strangely but doesn't question it, as we both know where that conversation will lead. For now, it seems we both want to live in denial.

I peer around the quiet diner and take in my surroundings because, this time, I really am just passing through a quiet, sleepy town.

"Can I get you another cup of coffee?" the server asks, clearly eyeing Quinn as she wiggles the glass coffeepot, blatantly flirting with him.

I've tried to ignore her because this has been going on since we first sat down. She looks like the girl-next-door type, and I already know she's a better match for Quinn than I am.

And that's because she doesn't have a fuckload of baggage coming out of her ass, which won't remain dead and buried.

"I'm good, thanks. Red?" He looks at me, and I shake my head in response because the next word to come out of my mouth will be a curse word.

"What brings you to North Carolina?" she purrs, leaning in unnecessarily close to collect Quinn's dirty plate.

I don't blame her for flirting because Quinn is hot and never short of female attention. But I need to get out of here, as the images of throttling this girl are becoming way too vivid.

"I'll meet you outside," I snap while reaching into the back pocket of my jeans and throwing some money onto the table.

Quinn looks up at me, puzzled, while the server looks relieved I'm leaving.

"Red, wait, I'll…" he says, half standing.

But I don't give him a chance to finish his sentence because I'm charging toward the exit.

Shouldering the door open, I welcome the cool breeze that slaps me in the face and mercifully cools me the hell down. I need to put a lid on my possessive, irrational feelings for Quinn. We haven't even established what we are.

And besides, I'm supposed to be weening myself off him.

Thankfully, I find a distraction in the form of an ATM across the road, so I quickly run over to the quiet strip of shops with Tabitha's credit card.

Tabitha Henderson.

Another friend I collected along the way who showed nothing but loyalty till the very end. It's only because of Tabitha's generosity that we could afford to do any of this. Otherwise, we'd be on the run and broke.

I intend to pay her back every penny even though I know

it'll take me my whole life to do so, as Tabitha comes from money. Not that you'd guess, seeing as Tabitha worked with me at Bobby Joe's. That's how we met.

With her fiery-red hair, warm eyes, and welcoming smile, I didn't stand a chance at not being her friend—her best friend.

Trying not to look too suspicious, I flip my hand over to where I've written down Tabitha's PIN numbers for each card in blue ink. As the machine reveals just how much money is available to withdraw, I have to take a closer look because I've never seen so many zeros before.

I feel awful, but I withdraw it all and do the same with the other two cards she so generously gave me.

As I quickly stuff the money into my backpack, in fear I'll get mugged on the way back to Quinn's truck, I wish I had my flick knife for protection. But I lost that in a scuffle with Brad, the sheriff's son. But kicking that bastard's ass was so worth it.

Thinking back to how different things would have turned out if not for Quinn saving my ass, I realize how much he's done for me. Time and time again, Quinn has saved me and my ass. And all I've done is get his ass into trouble.

"There you are," Quinn says when he sees me leaning against the hood of the truck.

"Here I am."

He raises his eyebrow, confused by my behavior.

"Let's go find somewhere to stay. I've withdrawn some money."

Quinn nods but wisely doesn't make a big deal about it because we don't know who may be listening.

"Cool, let's split," he says, walking over to the passenger door to open it for me, but I pop off the hood and get there first.

Again, he raises his dark eyebrow and chews on the silver hoop in his lip, but he thankfully lets it go.

This is all part of my plan for him to hate me.

In the words of Quinn Berkeley, "It's for the best."

We find the perfect little motel hidden along the highway a few miles out of town. My heart breaks as I see its condition is similar to Night Cats, the motel that Hank owned and I worked at. It didn't take long for it to become my home.

"You okay?" Quinn asks as he switches off the truck and catches me staring vacantly at the motel.

"Never better," I blankly reply, not making eye contact as I reach for my backpack off the floor.

"Red." Quinn sighs, and I can clearly hear the exhaustion in his voice, but I ignore him and push open my door before he can corner me and make me crack.

Finding the office, I barge through the front glass door, needing to get away from Quinn. But the pang of guilt as I step into the small room hits me straight in the guts, and I want to head back out the way I came.

Nothing in this cold, sterile, and unfriendly room resembles Night Cats. But I still can't stop my heart from pounding out of my chest and my breaths from leaving me in loud, anxious pants.

"Miss? You okay?" a nasally voice asks, snapping me out of my blackout.

"What?" I ask, looking up at the lady in front of me. She has cold eyes, unlike Hank, who always greeted me with a smile.

"She's fine," Quinn answers as he winds his arm around

my waist to stop me from collapsing.

The lady looks from me to Quinn, pursing her thin lips. "What can I get for you, then?"

"A room, please," Quinn replies, stepping toward the counter while softly releasing me.

Surprisingly, my feet hold me up.

"How long for?"

"Just a night," Quinn says, pulling out his wallet.

Reaching for her silver-rimmed glasses from where they're tangled in her wiry gray hair, she perches them on the tip of her skinny nose and begins tapping away on a computer.

"Two single beds or a double?" she asks, looking at the screen.

"Double," Quinn says

I say, "Single."

We reply at the same time, which is not at all awkward.

Quinn glares at me, his nostrils flaring slightly, and when we're asked again, double or single, he replies, "Double," without breaking eye contact with me.

I lower my eyes, unable to maintain contact. I know I'm being a total bitch to him, but I have no other choice.

"You're in room 14. And *no* pets," she barks, curling her lip. "I saw you pull up with that *dog*."

She didn't dare refer to Lucky in such a derogatory manner, did she?

I lean forward, bracing my hands on the counter and getting into her personal space while she leans back nervously. "The only *dog* around here is yo—"

But I'm rudely cut off by Quinn when he yanks on my arm, talking over me.

"Thanks," he says quickly while grabbing the key card and escorting me out the door.

"Let me go!" I demand, attempting to shake myself free. But it's pointless, as Quinn drags me toward our room without loosening his grip.

My boots drag on the gravel as I attempt to kick my heels in, but I have no doubt Quinn will drag me, kicking and screaming if need be, so I let him lead me. He unlocks our door and hurls me into the room, slamming the door shut behind him. The walls rattle with the force, and I know he's pissed.

"What is the matter with you?" he shouts, dropping our bags onto the carpet.

"I don't know what you're talking about," I smugly reply, sitting on the end of the bed.

"Bullshit, you don't," he huffs, stalking over to me, his huge frame dwarfing mine. "You do remember we're on the run, right? Trying to keep a low profile is kind of imperative. But you insulting everyone you come across is not really low-profile material."

He drops to his knees, crouching in front of me.

"I know this is hard, but…"

"I'm going to take a shower," I snap, standing up and stepping around him, as I'm in no mood for a lecture or pep talk.

Nothing he says will change the fact that Hank is dead, and Tristan is hurt, and it's all my fault.

"Red!" I slam the bathroom door shut, wishing I could do the same with Quinn.

But somehow, I don't think it'll be that easy.

So this is what guilt feels like.

Staring at my reflection in the foggy bathroom mirror, I have an urge to smash my fist through the glass, shattering the appearance before me because I hate what I see.

I have destroyed so many people's lives—good people.

I'd do anything to trade places with Hank because he deserves to be alive, not me. As for Quinn, he deserves to be free. And I plan on setting that one thing right because that's the only thing I can control.

"Red?" Quinn knocks softly. "Everything okay?"

I sigh. He should hate me for everything I've done. But he doesn't.

But he will.

"I'm fine, Quinn. I'll be out in a minute."

With my hands braced on the edge of the sink, I take a deep breath, needing a sea of courage for what I have planned. I step out wearing my pj's. I'm beat and want to catch up on a little sleep before I make good on my plan.

However, all plans of sleep are thrown out the window when I see Quinn slumped forward on the end of the bed, head cradled in his hands, his foot tapping frantically.

"Quinn?" I ask, rushing over to him, my heart in my throat.

As he lifts his head, his bright emerald eyes peek out from under his long, messy bangs. "He's going to be okay," he says, a breath leaving his chest in a whoosh of relief.

"Oh, thank God."

Quinn nods, holding up Tabitha's iPhone.

"Abi just texted. Said it was a close call, but he's just come out of surgery and the doctor said he's going to be fine."

I step toward Quinn, embracing him.

He wraps his warm arms around my waist and presses his head to my belly. We stay this way for a while, both needing the comfort of this connection.

And I need it because it'll be the last time I hug him.

I'm trying to feign sleep while Quinn is in the shower because tonight is when I make things right. Knowing that Tristan will be okay is a small weight lifted off my shoulders, but it's still not enough.

When I hear the shower switch off, I shut my eyes, hoping sleep will be kind to me—but it's not. My eyes snap open, and no matter how tired I am, I don't think I will ever be able to get a sound night's sleep ever again.

Quinn strolls out of the bathroom, switching off the lights. It's dark out, so the only light illuminating the room is from a dim streetlight just outside our window. I beg my eyes to shut, but as soon as they fall onto Quinn's bare, chiseled chest, they do the opposite and open wider. He's a work of art, which is funny, considering he's the artist.

I've seen his work, and it should be hanging in a gallery somewhere. I think about the sketchbook he showed me all those nights ago and remember the sketch of Hank. His kind gray eyes came alive onto paper, Quinn capturing him perfectly.

But now, I'll never see his light ever again.

I don't realize I'm crying until Quinn slips under the covers and pulls me against his warm chest.

"Shh," he soothes while brushing the tendrils of hair off my face that are sticking to my fallen tears. "It'll be okay."

This just makes me cry harder because it'll never be okay. But I allow this one moment of vulnerability because there will be no more after it.

I can't stop the avalanche of tears, and when Quinn pulls away, kissing them softly, more follow in their place. His lip ring caresses my cheeks, sending chills down my spine, and a warmth pools in my belly.

He senses my desperate need to wash away this hollowing pain and softly pulls my lips toward his, kissing me with a deep longing. I moan the moment my lips meet his, tangling with his tongue as he slips it into my welcoming mouth. His barbell gets me so hot, and as our tongues move wildly, devouring each other, the cool metal piercing only adds to the pleasure of kissing Quinn.

Before long, we're pulling at one another frantically as the space between us, which is mere inches, is too far. Quinn hitches up my leg, wrapping it around him, and slides me onto him with ease.

As I lean up on my knees, my hair comes loose, sheltering us from the real world. Our lips move frantically, trying to kiss away the events that led us here, as we both want to feel anything but pain, and for now, this is the best distraction.

Before I leave him, however, I want to touch him…taste him in the flesh—just once. I quickly break the kiss, my teeth tugging at his lip ring and sucking it into my mouth with a soft pull. Planting soft kisses down his chin, his light stubble tickles my lips, and I can't help myself as I bite down on his strong jaw.

"Fuck," he hisses, his hands squeezing my waist firmly while his body shivers from my assault.

Knowing I can draw this response from him turns me on because God knows he does so for me. I may be a virgin, but I do know what desire and want is, and I know I want and desire Quinn.

I've seen Quinn lost to passion, and it's a sight that has

been burned into my brain for an eternity. Quinn engages in that how he does with everything else in his life—with dominance and complete control.

Kissing lazily down his chest, I trace the tattoo he has inked down his side as I latch onto his left nipple, sucking the piercing into my mouth with a deep, long drag.

Quinn curses, then exhales loudly, and his hands move down to my ass, squeezing feverishly. I want into his pants, but I'm scared since I've never touched him in the flesh before. And under the thin material of his sweatpants, I can feel his hard-on.

My hands slowly slide down his defined abs and are just about to slip under the waistband of his sweats when his fingers still mine. I look up to meet his wild green eyes.

"You've got plenty of time for that, Red," he says, his hands slowly resting at the small of my back. "We should get some sleep."

Chewing on my lip, I feel rejected and shyly shift off his body, embarrassed I have done something wrong. But his large hand grasps my hip and the other clutches the back of my neck, stilling me.

"I want you. Don't think that I don't."

"Then why did you stop me?"

"Not now. Not like this," he replies, his clever eyes watching me closely.

I understand his reasoning, but I begrudgingly slip off him, turning onto my side, feeling heated and unsatisfied. Quinn slides in behind me, slipping his hands around me and cradling me to his chest.

"Good night, Red," he whispers, kissing my neck, his exhaustion apparent in his voice.

"Good night, Quinn," I reply, closing my eyes as a silent

tear slips down my cheek, afraid of what comes next.

I wake, checking the clock to see how much time has passed. Four hours of sleep is pretty good for me, seeing as I usually rouse from a nightmare, dripping in a cold sweat.

But tonight, I haven't dreamed, and I know it's because I'm wrapped in Quinn's arms.

I look upon his face, his chest rising and falling softly, his sinful lips parted. The slight exhalations he's taking lull me back to sleep, but as I tenderly brush back wisps of dark hair off his brow, I chew the inside of my cheek to stop the tears because I know it's time.

Slipping out of bed silently, I shrug into my jeans and tee, which lie on the carpeted floor near me. Reaching for my backpack and pulling out the money I withdrew, I place it all onto the kitchen table and then creep toward the front door. Grabbing Quinn's black hoodie off the back of the sofa, I pause when I hear him stir.

As his light breathing starts up again, I let out a deep breath and continue. My boots are by the door, and I bend low, picking them up without a sound. With a muted mouthful of air, I give Quinn one last look, my heart breaking with the departure as I shut the door behind me.

I slip Quinn's hoodie on, tucking in my hair, wanting to shroud as much of myself as possible. I walk away quickly, trying to make my exit as speedy and as quiet as possible. However, I'm glad no one can hear my beating heart because it would wake the whole damn neighborhood.

Wiping my sweaty palms onto my jeans, I'm so relieved when I see the truck. Lucky lies in the bed and sits up excitedly when he sees me.

"C'mon, boy," I whisper as I open the gate for him, and he jumps down, ready to follow.

Gently opening the unlocked driver's door, Lucky jumps in, settling on the passenger seat while looking at me unhappily.

"Don't look at me like that." I sigh, springing into the driver's seat. "I have to." And he drops down low with an unimpressed gruff.

I madly search through Quinn's hoodie pockets for his truck keys, but they're not there.

"Fuck," I curse, hunting through them a second time, but still nothing.

Panic seizes my gut, and I flip down the visor, hoping he keeps a spare set here. But he doesn't. Frantically rummaging through the console and glove compartment, I toss everything onto the floor, but it's fruitless because I'm still keyless.

"Looking for these?" a deep voice asks by my window as I hear the distinctive sound of keys jingling lightly.

Jumping so high and letting out a startled yelp, I hit my head on the truck roof with a loud, painful thwack. But ignoring the pain, I look over my shoulder at Quinn. He stands outside my window, dangling the keys from his index finger.

"Get out," he commands.

But I stubbornly reply, "No," and stupidly lock the door, as he has the keys.

His mouth twitches slightly as he folds his arms over his broad chest. However, he looks menacing out here in the shadowy night, all tousled hair, hard eyes, and dominating stance.

"I can do this all night," he says, sucking on his lip ring.

"So can I," I retort, staring back at him, mimicking his pose.

He suddenly lunges for the door, unlocking it quickly, but I read his apparent ploy and relock it just as fast.

He grins, the moonlight reflecting off his perfect white teeth. "You're going to stay in the truck all night?"

"Sure, why not? You'll have to go inside eventually, and when you do, I'll just hot-wire your truck." I smirk at him smugly.

Quinn chuckles, which infuriates me, and my cheeks heat.

"Do you know how to do that?"

"Did you forget what I used to do for a living?" I snap, sitting up and making a face at him through the window.

Quinn smirks, brushing his hair out of his eyes. "Good point." He casually strolls toward the back of the truck with his hands dug deep in his pockets.

Looking out the back window, I wonder what he's up to. When I see him reach into a toolbox, pulling out a screwdriver and Zippo lighter, I know this won't end well. He flips the screwdriver and begins whistling as he taps the handle on the driver's window arrogantly while giving me a lopsided grin.

I watch him curiously through the windshield as he jimmies the hood open with the screwdriver. It opens with a loud pop, and as he whistles the tune to "Highway to Hell" by AC/DC, he begins tinkering under the hood.

Even though I can't see him because the hood is up, obscuring the entire windshield, I know whatever he's doing under there can't be good. I try to shuffle up in my seat but give up and slump low, crossing my arms over my chest in a huff.

After a minute, he closes the hood and winks while

holding up some wires. "Now you're not going anywhere."

"Oh, that's real clever!" I shout to be heard through the windshield. "You've just defaced your truck."

"Oh well. You can just hot-wire me another," he replies nonchalantly.

I should have known his mechanical knowledge would beat me at my own game.

"Are you going to get out? Or am I going to have to smoke you out?" he asks, flipping the Zippo lid open.

With no other choice, I unlock the door because we've gained an audience. A few guests have come out of their rooms to see what the ruckus is all about. Lucky follows as I storm out of the truck, marching toward our room, and when I barge through the door, I look for something to throw at Quinn.

Quinn locks the door behind him when I throw the Bible at him. It thuds against the door, narrowly missing his stubborn head.

"You should have let me leave."

"No," he replies, tossing his useless keys onto the small wooden table.

"Why not?" I exclaim, stalking toward him and shoving him in the chest.

"Because that's not the way to solve this. You think I'll just stand by and let you take the blame?"

He knew all along that I planned to go to the police.

I was going to tell them all about my dad and Phil, and what we did back in LA, hoping they would believe me. But deep down, I knew they wouldn't because Phil was smart. He never left a trail. Unlike me, he paid his taxes and was the perfect American citizen with no rap sheet.

They would pin Hank's murder on me, so then I would

confess and take the blame. But I couldn't do that if Quinn was with me. He would never allow that, so I had to leave him behind.

"How did you know?" I ask, looking at him guiltily.

"Because I would do the same for you," he replies, grabbing my upper arms firmly.

However, I shrug out of his hold and take a step back, shocked by his confession.

"So how could you stand in my way?" I ask, trying to understand his reasoning.

"Because I won't let you throw your life away."

"But you will yours?"

"My fate is already decided for me," he replies, turning to look out the window.

"What's that supposed to mean?"

Quinn shakes his head stubbornly, turning to face me. "It doesn't matter."

"Like hell it doesn't!" I yell, storming over to him and squaring off with him.

"You know all my secrets," I say, hands out wide.

"My secrets are the ones better left buried," he answers, and I can see a hint of regret in his eyes.

"And mine aren't?"

"That's different. You never had a choice, whereas I did."

He is so goddamn stubborn. I open my mouth, ready to argue, but he clamps a hand over my lips.

"You will not run. So help me God, if you try to run, I will tie you to that bed and gag you. We clear?" His eyes search mine, making sure I understand.

The hard set of his strong jawline and his fierce exhalations indicate just how serious he is.

Well, *fuck* him.

I bite his fingers, and he pulls them away, hissing.

"We're clear," I reply, walking into the bathroom and slamming the door shut behind me.

Fisting my hair in frustration, I pace the tiny room. Plan A didn't work. But lucky for me, I have a plan B.

Two

I wake, thankfully not gagged or tied to the bed.

Quinn has every right to be mad at me. But I don't regret my decision. I'm just disappointed I got caught.

I stretch and yawn, still exhausted, but I doubt a week of sleep would be enough rest.

I'm alone in bed, and as I peek out the window, I see it's still dark out. I wonder what time it is and where Quinn is. Panic seizes me, thinking he may have left, but as I sit up quickly, I see him hunched over the table, studying a map.

"Mornin'," he says sleepily, not making eye contact but sensing I'm awake.

"Hey," I reply hoarsely, brushing the hair off my face.

As Quinn raises a paper coffee cup above his head, his eyes still glued to the map in front of him, I quickly slip out of bed and throw on a sweater because it's freezing. I graciously accept the coffee and take a seat near him at the tiny table. I cringe as I sip the bitter black coffee, but it's better than nothing.

"Whatcha doing?" I ask, looking at the road map spread out in front of us.

Quinn finally meets my eyes, tapping a pen on the table, deep in thought. "Trying to figure out where to go next."

"Oh," I reply, sipping my coffee quietly and lowering my eyes. "We're going to have to ditch the truck. The cops will be all over it by now."

Quinn nods, dropping the pen onto the table and running both hands through his disheveled hair.

"I was hoping you wouldn't say that," he says.

Knowing how much he loves his truck, I bite my lip remorsefully. "Sorry."

He sighs, shaking his head.

"Any ideas?" I ask, jutting my chin out toward the map.

He rubs his weary eyes, sliding Tabitha's phone over to me. "I got that a couple of hours ago."

Reaching for the phone, I glance at the screen and realize it's just after three o'clock.

```
Keep moving.
Got someone to help.
Will text when I have more info. DO NOT
go to the police. T x
```

"Someone to help?" I ask, looking at Quinn, confused.

But he only shrugs. "No clue. But I agree with the keep moving part."

"To where?" I question, leaning in closer to see the routes he's marked.

I trace my finger along the line he's drawn, following the state lines that lead into Mexico.

"It's the long, most indirect way, as we'll need to take the back roads. But it'll certainly keep the cops off our tails instead of taking a direct route."

My eyes flick north, however, zeroing in on one particular place.

"Is there anywhere specific you wanted to go?" he asks as my finger circles around Alberta, Canada.

"Anywhere that serves better coffee than this," I tease, making a pained face as I take another sip, still tracing over the location where my mom lives. "Do you want to know why I came to South Boston?"

Quinn waits for me to continue.

"To find my mom," I whisper, my eyes meeting his. "After I shot my dad, I needed to leave LA. I wanted to get as far away from my past as possible, and it was pure luck I ended up where I did."

Quinn knows I mean it was pure luck that I found *him*. Out of all the places I could have gone to, I ended up discovering this amazing man before me in South Boston. But I've had to pay a price for my fortune and so have others.

"So she's in Canada?" he questions, though it's pretty apparent as my finger has circled the same spot for the past few minutes.

"Yes," I reply, nodding. "I found out within the first few days of being in South Boston."

"So why did you stay?"

"Because of the people I met. Because of the friends I made. Because of…you," I reply softly, hoping that doesn't sound weird.

"Me?" he asks, taken aback by my confession.

"Yes."

Thankfully, he doesn't ask me to explain because I'm not

sure I could clarify what I mean without freaking him out.

"Well, I'm glad you did."

I'm well aware of his fingers grazing over my knuckles affectionately, and the gesture warms me all over. His long fingers envelop my wrist, pulling me toward him, and I quickly comply as he settles me onto his lap.

I'm sitting sideways, his long legs offering me all the support I need.

"Do you want to go to Canada?" he questions, his hand resting at the back of my nape, toying with my hair.

"It was so important to me, but now...I don't know," I confess as his fingers trail down my neck and across to my collarbone.

"What's important now?" he asks, his breath fanning out across my cheeks.

I don't reply as I lose myself to his touch.

"How about we just go wherever the road takes us?" he suggests, placing a soft kiss on the corner of my mouth.

"I like the sound of that. And besides, who knows what Tabitha has planned. She did say to keep moving."

"Then it's settled."

"I've never really been anywhere. I'm sorry we're seeing the sights of America as fugitives," I add sadly.

Quinn inches his face toward mine, mere inches separating us as he whispers, "I'd go anywhere with you, Red. It wouldn't matter where. Just as long as you were with me, nothing else would matter."

"Even if we're Bonnie and Clyde?" I ask, trying to make light of our situation.

Quinn nods, a small smile tugging at his sinful lips. "We could be Thelma and Louise, for all I care. Just promise me no more running away from me. We do this *together*. Promise me."

I bridge the gap between us, pressing my lips to his before I whisper, "I promise."

It's day two, and we need a car. We ditched Quinn's truck a few miles down the road, hiding it as best we could in a dense area of trees.

"I'm sorry," I mumble for the tenth time as we walk alongside the road, the early morning sun leading us toward our journey to nowhere.

Quinn walks Lucky on a short leash while he enjoys sniffing everything in sight. "It's fine, Red. It's just a truck," he says, adjusting his black baseball cap to block out the sun reflecting off the pavement.

He only says that to make me feel better, but it's not working.

"I know you're lying. So, to make it up to you, I'm going to steal you a hot-ass car," I reply loudly when a semi roars past us, my hair whipping into my face from the momentum.

Quinn chuckles, his lips tipping up into a heart-stopping smile. "Oh yeah?"

"Yup."

"I don't think you'll find anything but tractors out here, Red," Quinn teases as we walk past a few farms.

"Why does it smell so bad out here?" I ask, covering my nose as I keep getting wafts of…something.

Quinn chuckles and waves his hand out toward the sky. "That would be the fresh country air you smell, city slicker."

"Well, if that's what fresh country air smells like, give me pollution any day."

That earns me another laugh from Quinn, who finds this simply hilarious. After we decided to go wherever the road took us, we both lightened up a bit, but every so often, I could see his thoughts drifting back home and, no doubt, to Tristan.

I find myself doing the same, but after Tabitha's ambiguous text message, I try not to think too much about it all because I know she has something up her sleeve. And so do I.

"Red, I think we're going to have to hitchhike," Quinn says, placing his hand over his brow and looking from left to right at the vast nothingness before us.

I'm not sure where we are, as we've driven for about an hour and dumped the truck in some creepy, remote forest. I shiver when thinking about the desolate, insect-infected spot. I'm trying to keep my cool and not envision every bug known to humankind coming out and eating my face off. We've walked a couple of miles into, well, nowhere, so I hate to say it, but I think he's right.

"Do you think that's safe?" I ask, swatting a fly away from my face.

Quinn smirks. "As opposed to walking out here, in the middle of nowhere, waiting for a crazy man wielding a chainsaw to attack us?"

"Good point. I wish I had my knife," I say, reminiscing about the days when all the safety I needed lay in my boot.

"Such a boss," Quinn comments, winking playfully at me.

"I'd feel better if I had my Colt. Where did that end up?" I remember him confiscating it when I pulled it on him.

"It's in my backpack," he replies, but thankfully doesn't mention why he has it.

I nod and let it go, realizing he won't return it, which troubles me. Does he not trust me? I promised him that I wouldn't run, and I meant it. Plan B doesn't require me to run, so that's why I was able to make that promise to him.

"Hey, up ahead," Quinn says, nodding toward the road.

Squinting, I make out a bright orange VW camper van driving at a steady pace down the hill. "You think they're nice?" I ask, hooking out my thumb while walking backward.

Quinn follows my motion and chuckles. "Probably not."

The van sees us, and surprisingly, it pulls over a few feet away from us.

"I am so going to regret this," I mumble as Quinn and I approach the passenger window.

Quinn throws me a carefree grin, and when we're inches away from the van, he mutters, "Whatever happens, just roll with it, okay?"

I cock my eyebrow, puzzled. "Why—" I stop midsentence as I hear him address the van's occupants.

"Thanks for stopping, y'all," he says in a thick Southern accent.

I nearly fall over my feet when I hear him speak because, yes, Quinn has a *slight*, almost nonexistent Southern twang, which becomes somewhat stronger when he's tired or angry, but I'm presuming he's now neither, so I wonder what the hell he's playing at.

"That's okay," says the young brunette female driver while checking Quinn out.

"Where're you headed?" pipes up the passenger, also giving him the once-over.

"Wherever you're willing to take us," he replies in that ridiculous fake accent.

These girls will undoubtedly see through his bullshit and drive off, thankful they didn't pick up two strangers.

But they don't.

"We're headed into South Carolina to see The Blizzards.

27

We can take you that far?" says yet another eager brunette from the back seat as she leans between the two front seats, eyeing Quinn.

Great.

Quinn looks at me as I stand behind him, totally against getting into the van. But what choice do I have? This might be the last car we see for hours, and the prospect of being out here with all this country air and country...bugs has me taking a step toward Quinn.

"Whatcha think, Mabel?" Quinn asks, his mouth twitching as I take a visible breath.

Mabel? *Really?*

"I think that's a peachy idea, *Theodore*," I reply in an accent that is just as bad as his.

"Well, all right then," Quinn replies, and he has the gall to tip his baseball cap at them in gratitude.

All the girls giggle and flutter their eyelashes while I'm about to puke in my mouth. I'm pretty sure that only works if one is wearing a cowboy hat.

The side door squeaks open, and the eager brunette from the back seat greets us. "Welcome aboard. I'm Bridgette," she says, gesturing for us to enter.

"Thanks," I mumble while stepping into the bordello on wheels and sitting in the back.

Quinn steps in behind me, and just as he is about to sit near me, Bridgette corners him. "Come sit here, Theo," she purrs, patting the seat near her, leaning forward so her boobs are on display.

I clench the leather seat underneath me, my fingers about to tear through the fabric. But I quickly remind myself to chill out. Quinn looks at me awkwardly, and I roll my eyes, snatching Lucky's lead from his hand and positioning him near me.

"I hope you guys like eighties music!" shouts the driver, taking off while Bon Jovi's "Bad Medicine" drowns out my curses.

"They won't know," I whisper to my only companion in the car who feels my pain.

Lucky gazes up at me, looking as pained as I do, and as we're being subjected to Bret Michaels for the fifth time, I revisit my idea of banging my head repeatedly on the window, hoping to knock myself unconscious.

We've been in the car for nearly two hours. The whole trip, Quinn has received the complete, undivided attention of his fans—Bridgette, Tonya, and Pippa—who have fawned over his accent, asked repeatedly what he likes doing, did his piercings hurt, does he have any unseen piercings, what's his favorite food, who is his favorite *Sesame Street* character. The list goes on and on…and on.

Quinn is uncomfortable with their attention and only playing along, but I still hate it. However, deep down, I know that I'm jealous.

But Quinn isn't mine, per se. We've fooled around and made out but haven't spoken about where we stand. And who knows if we even *stand* anywhere. It was complicated enough before all this shit happened, but now, I don't even want to think about what this means for "us."

Our kiss yesterday was filled with desperation, two inconsolable people trying to make the pain go away. I won't read into our reckless union because what kind of life can I offer Quinn?

A life of crime and that's about it.

Looks like plan B with a twist will be set into motion earlier than I planned.

My decision made, I'm going to encourage Quinn to flirt and hook up. God knows he won't have to try very hard. I'd rather eat glass than do this, but it's for the best.

I'm really starting to understand the meaning behind that phrase now.

"Everything okay?" Quinn asks softly, turning toward me as Bridgette whispers with her partners in crime through the gap in the front seats.

I give him the best fake smile that I can and reply a little too happily. "Never better."

His eyes narrow, not believing a word, but he turns back around as Bridgette passes her hand over his thigh, making him jump in surprise at how forward she's being.

As I envision cutting off her fingers, I remember the promise I made to myself thirty seconds ago and take a deep, calming breath.

"So, Mabel..." Pippa, the driver, looks at me in the rearview mirror. "How do you know Theo?"

I'm surprised that after two hours, they remember my name, as none of them have spoken a word to me.

Quinn begins without pause, "I'm her bo—"

"He's my brother," I cut him off, disregarding the dirty look he gives me.

I ignore the satisfaction I feel at the fact that Quinn was about to refer to himself as my boyfriend. And under any other circumstance, I would be thrilled, but now, now I just feel undeserving.

Three sets of shoulders depress, thankful I'm not a threat.

"Oh, that's awesome," purrs Bridgette, running a long

fingernail along Quinn's bicep, which is poking out of his gray T-shirt.

I try not to scowl, but my heart is ready to explode. But as Quinn subtly pulls back his arm, not at all impressed with her touching him, my lips tip up into a small smirk.

"Woo-hoo!" yells Tonya, sticking her head out the window. "We're here!"

My eyes snap up to witness what Tonya hollers about, and I see the blue Welcome to South Carolina sign.

Woo-hoo! I internally cheer. I can finally get out of this suffocating environment, which has just become a lot more uncomfortable when I see Quinn mulling over my comment.

We roll into town, and Pippa finds a parking lot. She spins around to face us. "So did you wanna tag along? Come see the band with us?" she asks, looking at Quinn, not really caring if I go or not.

"Sure thang," I reply before Quinn can decline.

He twists around to face me, tilting his head to the side and giving me big eyes. "Mabel, we got that *thing*, remember?" he says, nodding so I'll agree.

But I shake my head, scrunching my face. "No, we don't. And besides, *Theo*, I'm sure the girls are just dying to have you all to themselves without your little *sister* tagging along."

My whole speech is tongue-in-cheek, dripping with sarcasm, but the trio believes it, clapping their hands excitedly at the prospect of spending some one-on-one time with Theo.

The worst part about hitching a ride with fellow travelers is that you're both looking for a place to crash. I bet Quinn doesn't think his little country twang was such a good idea now that he's being grilled by three very pushy girls.

It's all fun and games until someone loses an eye. In Quinn's case, I bet he wishes he could lose both eyes so he doesn't have to watch Tonya demonstrate why she was head cheerleader one last time.

We're sitting in a small bar across the road from where we're all crashing for the night. The girls decided spending even more time with Theo by staying at the same hotel as him would be fun. Looks like my plan of getting Quinn laid will be easier than anticipated.

The bar is small and cozy, and I feel my eyes droop shut as the second beer I just downed goes straight to my head.

"I'm going to go crash," I announce, tossing a few bills onto the table to pay for my beer.

Quinn also stands, but Bridgette pulls on his arm, and he loses his balance, plonking back down.

"You're not going anywhere, are you, Theo?" pouts Pippa, licking her lips, which still resemble a disco ball.

"No, Theo is staying here," I reply, looking at Quinn smugly, who's baffled by what the hell is going on.

The girls squeal and continue fawning over Quinn as I turn my back and exit, looking forward to some peace and quiet. In my travels, I see an army disposals store and decide a new flick knife is in order. And maybe some new combat boots, as my soles are nearly worn down.

I enter the store and keep my head down. I want to be in and out. That's my motto from now on, as I'm sure my face can be found on wanted posters from here to New York.

The glass cabinet contains sexy-looking weaponry, but I want something I can conceal. My eyes skim over a blade with a deep mahogany handle. It's small and sleek, and I want it.

I practically squish my face against the glass cabinet as I

hungrily eye the knife. However, I nearly headbutt the display case when I hear my real name called out loudly. Who would know *me* in South Carolina?

"Mia? Mia Lee?"

I turn my head cautiously, afraid to see who's standing near me. But the person staring back at me is someone I never thought I'd see again.

"Justin? Justin *Miller*?" I release the deep breath I was holding as I stand to full height.

"It *is* you!" Justin says, giving me a big hug while I stand awkwardly.

Justin Miller was a fellow freak and the only guy in high school who was ridiculed as much as I was. He's also the only guy I've ever kissed more than once. However, neither time was earth-shattering or mind-blowing, like it is with Quinn.

I can't believe Justin Miller is here in South Carolina. Seriously, what are the odds?

"What are you doing here?" we both question each other at the same time, and he laughs, thankfully letting me go.

The store clerk looks back and forth between us, unenthused by our reunion because we're blocking the counter. Stepping aside, Justin looks at me, waiting for me to explain. But all I can do is stare at him because I feel like I've just taken a trip down memory lane.

Justin's head is still shaved, and his huge brown eyes gawk at me with a disbelieving look. His guarded, dimpled smile hasn't changed since I saw it last, and it beams down at me as he takes in my appearance.

His sculptured right eyebrow now dons a barbell piercing, but that's the only thing that's changed about him. My gaze quickly drops to his lips as I recall kissing him behind the gymnasium before fifth period when I was fifteen, and once again, two years later, when I delivered dope to a party. Both times were big mistakes. And both times I felt vulnerable and sad, and Justin was just…there.

"I can't believe you're here," he says, making it more than obvious he's checking me out.

"I know, right? Small world," I reply, shuffling uncomfortably as seeing him again brings back memories I wish I could forget.

"So…tell me, what brings you here?" he asks, crossing his arms over his lean chest.

I can't help but compare his stature to Quinn's. He isn't as tall or muscled as Quinn, but he certainly carries himself with an air of confidence.

"Just here with a friend," I reply lamely, reaching for a combat boot that catches my eye. "You?"

"Just here on business."

"What do you do?" I take a seat on the small bench seat and slip off my boot when he makes it clear he's not leaving.

He sits near me, a move I wasn't expecting, and turns to look at me as he replies, "Just tying up some loose ends."

I nod but have no idea what that means as I try on the boots, bending forward to lace them up.

Justin laughs, his deep, throaty cackle making me feel like I'm fifteen again. "I'm still as vague as ever," he teases when I cock my eyebrow at his unusual response.

I smile because he *is* just as vague as he was in high school. But I liked that about him. He wasn't your typical teenage boy. He was different.

"Do you live here?" I ask, feeling obligated to make small talk because he's still looking at me.

"No, I—"

"Red?"

34

My palms sweat, and my mouth dries up when I see Quinn openly eyeballing Justin.

"Who's this?"

"This is Justin," I reply in a small voice. "We went to high school together."

Quinn crosses his arms over his chest, and suddenly, the room becomes very, very small as Justin and Quinn glare at each other.

Leaning back uncomfortably, I quickly slip my boots back on and stand by Quinn. "You ready to go?"

Quinn nods, but his body does anything *but* move. I slip my fingers through his and squeeze lightly, attempting to get his attention. Thankfully, it does.

"Yeah, sure. Let's split."

Attempting to remove my hand from Quinn's to say goodbye to Justin proves futile since Quinn holds my hand in a death grip.

"See you, Justin," I say with a small smile. "It was nice seeing you again."

"See you around, Mia," Justin replies, but I nod nervously, hoping he goes away.

When the bell chimes above the door, announcing his departure, I let out a deep breath, thankful that didn't end in bloodshed. My hand is still enclosed in Quinn's, so I shake it out of his grip to pay for my goods.

After asking the store clerk for the flick knife I was eyeing earlier, I quickly hand over a wad of cash, telling him to keep the change. I want to get out of here before Quinn explodes. As soon as I push open the door and step out onto the sidewalk, Quinn follows in hot pursuit, quickly grabbing my elbow and spinning me around to face him.

"What do you need a knife for?"

"For protection," I retort, yanking my arm out of his grasp.

"That's what I'm for," he snarls, following me down the street when I turn my back to him and walk away.

"You can't be with me all the time," I reply over my shoulder.

"Like hell I can't."

I cross the road, jogging over to our hotel, which is a tiny, inconspicuous place tucked away in an alleyway. Trudging up the stairs, Quinn trails me loudly as I pull the key out of my back pocket, unlocking the yellow door and shoving it open angrily.

Quinn slams it behind him, and I turn around to face him. "What is your problem?"

"My problem is you!" he replies, pacing the room.

"Yeah, I can see that. Care to tell me why?"

Quinn takes a deep breath, his broad chest rising. "What are you playing at by trying to pawn me off to those girls? And to make matters worse, I find you chatting up some asshole the minute my back is turned! What's the story between you two? Have you *kissed* him?" he questions, disgusted. He stops pacing as he stands in front of me, waiting for an explanation.

"First," I bite back, poking my finger into his firm chest, "I was *not* chatting Justin up. I was simply talking to someone I knew. And our 'story,' is none of your business, seeing as your 'story' could go on for a trilogy with all the girls you've been with."

Quinn's nostrils flare, and I dare him to continue because I sure as hell won't shy away from bringing up Amber.

However, now that I've started, I can't seem to stop. "And second, you weren't complaining when you were sandwiched between those girls."

Quinn's mouth parts, surprised by my admission. And

so am I. Wasn't that what I wanted? Isn't that why I called Quinn my brother? So those girls would make their best play for him, and Quinn would fall for it.

I should have known better.

"You think I *liked* being around those girls? How could you think I was interested in any of them?" he asks, taken aback.

I shrug.

"Red?"

"Because you didn't seem to shy away from their advances."

Quinn's eyes narrow, clearly frustrated. "I'm doing all of this...for you. I don't *want* anyone but you," he finishes, imploring me to believe him.

And I do.

His admission touches me because he wants me. He really wants me. But I don't reply because if I do, I know I'll break down, forgetting the reason I'm being so horrible to him in the first place.

"Just in case you've forgotten," Quinn says when I stand quiet, sounding hurt that I haven't replied. "We're on the run. I'm just trying to blend in and not cause a scene."

What I'm about to do next will haunt me for the rest of my life. My heart breaks as I'm about to shoot him down after he confessed he wanted no one other than me.

But I have to.

"Oh, so using a lame accent is a way *not* to stand out?" I question sarcastically, my heart shattering as the venom spills from me.

Quinn sighs, rubbing a hand down his face. "Okay, the accent was a dumb idea. I was just trying to make you smile. After everything that's happened..."

"I don't *need* you to make me smile or protect me, Quinn. I've survived a long time on my own, and I can take care of myself!"

Quinn steps back, looking as if I've slapped him. "You're so fucking stubborn. I thought we were past this bullshit!"

I hate myself. I hate myself for what I'm about to say.

"Why? Because you got me off? You thought I would just back down and let you boss me around. It wasn't a big deal. So get over yourself."

Plan B has been put into full swing, and I want to be sick.

Quinn chuckles, but it's not a pleasant sound. "Well, it was a big deal to me," he says before storming out the door, it rattling off its rusty hinges when he slams it shut.

I rub my forehead, a headache pounding at my temples, but I deserve it. I hurt Quinn, and although it was intentional, it still sucks.

Plonking down onto the mattress, I raise my eyes to the water-stained ceiling, questioning whether plan B was a good idea.

Quinn made me promise to never run from him again, and I intend to stick to my word.

I promised not to run from *him*, but I can't promise he won't run from *me*.

Three

So plan B was a terrible idea.

But Quinn won't let me go to the police, and my dad is no doubt still looking for me, forcing us to run, and therefore putting Quinn's life in danger. I know he has some fucked-up notion that he has to protect me, and I'd be lying if I didn't admit it feels nice to have someone watch my back. But how can I live with myself, knowing yet another innocent person has given up their life…their freedom, to protect me.

I can't.

So plan B, no matter how hard it may be, no matter how much it breaks my heart to hurt him, it's for him in the end. I hope he will get sick of me and leave. Turn his back on me and go back home. And when he does, *then* I will go to the police.

I know what Tabitha said, but I have no doubt she's putting herself in danger for me. And I can't do that to her either.

I know my altercation with Brad is the reason I'm in this mess. In hindsight, picking a fight with the sheriff's son was probably not the smartest thing to do, but I wasn't thinking clearly at the time. That fucker drugged my best friend, most likely intending to do unspeakable things to her.

So I don't regret my decision. I'm just sorry Quinn got caught up in all my baggage.

In a way, I wish I'd never met Quinn, Tabitha, Tristan, or Hank, and that's not because I regret a second spent with them. No. The only thing I regret is lugging my shit onto their doorsteps.

If I were a believer in fate and kismet, then I may be fooled into believing that destiny sent me to South Boston. But how can I believe that when Hank is dead? And that's why I'm a realist. I know fate, destiny, whatever you want to call it, had no hand in my life.

Only I did.

The clock reads 9:00 p.m., and Quinn has been gone since he stormed out of here over three hours ago.

I wonder where he is.

Is he with someone?

That's what I wanted, right? At the moment, that's the *last* thing I want.

Kicking off the bed, I decide to stop tormenting myself and go find him. Lucky follows me into the bathroom, sitting by the door, watching me as I attempt to make myself look human.

As I strip out of my clothes, stepping over the lip of the bath and into the shower, I sigh. "We might be here for a while, buddy."

What is it about a shower that always makes me feel better? It could be the fact I usually shower under a spray of boiling water. It burns my skin, making me feel human again.

Only when the water runs cold do I step out.

I dry off with the little yellow towel that barely covers me and wipe down the bathroom mirror to look at my reflection.

I look and feel like shit. But I don't really care what I look like, unlike most on a Saturday night who are letting loose.

Me?

I'm sitting around on a Saturday night, wondering if my dad and the police are getting closer to finding us.

At times like these, I wish I could drown my sorrows in a bottle of tequila, but after living the life that I've lived, I know that's just a short-term solution. In the morning when I'm nursing a nasty hangover, hating myself for having that "one last shot," all my problems will still be there.

But I guess being a drug dealer at age eight and having a crackhead for a father changes your opinion on addiction. So maybe I'm just biased.

My new combat boots sit in a heap in the corner of the room where I dumped them, and I decide to wear them with my ripped black jeans. I slip on my Harley Davidson T-shirt, and although it is too big and slips off one shoulder, it's the only clean thing I have. I don't leave the room without tucking my new blade into my boot, feeling safer with it on me. Giving Lucky a pat between the ears, I head down the stairs, crossing my fingers I don't trip over Quinn and some random girl along the way.

South Carolina is actually a pretty cool place. And it turns out that wherever the hell we are has a vigorous nightlife. The area where we're staying has enough bars and nightspots to keep the population happy.

Walking past a pizza place, which smells amazing, I know I really should eat something because I can't remember when my last meal was. However, the thought of eating sends a wave of nausea through me, and I'd rather have that feeling without food in my stomach. Because if I ate, I would puke it all back up.

As I pass partygoers on the busy street, I can see they're dressed to impress and ready to have a good time. I see an old-school sign buzzing up ahead, announcing The Blizzards are playing in the next fifteen minutes. Maybe Quinn is here. He certainly wouldn't have to look far for some female company to forget all about me.

"Five dollars," the girl at the door barks, extending her hand my way, totally uninterested.

I pull out a five from the back pocket of my jeans and try not to recoil when she grabs my arm and stamps my wrist with a happy face, which sits just above my moon tattoo.

So there is no way I will be able to see if Quinn is in here. The small place, which looks like a run-down coffee shop, is packed. Fortunately, I score a table at the back of the room, out of sight of everyone, which suits me just fine. I perch upon the stool and instantly gain three feet. Swiveling the chair from left to right, I'm attentively looking for Quinn, but I still can't see him.

Once the band finishes, they pack up their gear in no real hurry.

"Are you here all by yourself, sweetheart?"

And my night just got a whole lot worse.

"Can I buy you a drink?" a man asks, his hot breath caressing my neck.

"Nope, all good. Thanks," I reply, looking up at the huge jock standing too close for comfort.

He's in a gold-and-blue varsity jacket with the number one printed on the front, right-hand side. I'm thinking that maybe he plays for the local football team. And from his size and overwhelming ego, I'd say he's the quarterback. No doubt he's accustomed to girls swooning over him, dropping their panties before he even says hello. But I'm not most girls.

"Aw, c'mon, darlin'. One drink ain't gonna hurt," he slurs, placing his beer on the table and reaching for a vacant stool to pull up next to me.

"I'm good, thanks," I casually reply, trying to appear occupied while staring up at the stage.

Varsity Jacket moves closer to me while I shift away, repulsed by the smell of beer and his heavy-handed cologne. But his hand slaps onto my knee, stopping me from moving another inch.

My body recoils, and he's about two seconds away from being headbutted in the stupid face if he doesn't move his hand.

"She's spoken for."

I would know that voice anywhere. And in this instance, it's music to my ears.

Raising my eyes, I meet Quinn's heated gaze, and oh my God, how is it even possible that I have desperately missed him in such a short timeframe apart. He looks, as per usual, hotter than all hell, mixed with a dash of devilish rebellion. His lengthy hair is blanketing his large emerald eyes, but I can see they are dangerously narrowed, as they have dropped to where the asshole's hand currently paws at my leg.

I move it away, but his hand is like a magnet and just goes with me.

"If you don't move your hand," Quinn snarls, still eyeballing it, "you and I will have a problem."

But Varsity Jacket is obviously getting off on the exchange as he tightens his hand on my leg, shifting it higher up my thigh.

I'm just about to headbutt him, but Quinn gets there first as he reaches over the small table, yanks the lapels of his jacket, and connects with his face.

I gasp as the big brute drops to the ground with a thud. Tumbling onto his ass, he collapses into an ungracious heap on the floor. And he doesn't get back up because Quinn has knocked him out cold.

My mouth hits the table, and my eyes cannot believe the swiftness and speed of Quinn's attack. He's like a ninja without the whole outfit.

"Move," he snarls into my ear, reaching for my elbow and gesturing for me to get up.

I happily comply because we both need to get out of here before Varsity Jacket comes to and identifies us, drawing unwanted attention our way.

The smell of alcohol fans across my face as Quinn exhales angrily when I try to break out of his firm grip. He tightens his hold on my upper arm and guides me through the throng of people.

As we push outside, I try to jerk free, but Quinn stubbornly pulls tighter, not budging an inch. This is getting ridiculous. We've only been on the run for *two* days, and if the police or my dad and Phil don't end up killing Quinn and me first, we will do the job for them.

I protest loudly, digging in my heels and cursing for him to let me go. But it all falls on deaf ears as Quinn just quickens his step, charging toward the hotel.

The moonlight highlights the hardened set of his jaw and the incensed look in his wild eyes. I know once we get into our room, World War 3 just may erupt.

As we round the corner and approach the bottom of the

stairs to the hotel, I grab the railing and hold on for dear life. Quinn jolts forward as he ascends the first step because I won't budge and stand my ground. I'm afraid I'll be torn in two as he attempts to coax me into loosening my grip.

"Red…" he says through clenched teeth, his breath coming out heavily. "Let go, or I will throw you over my shoulder and carry you up every step, kicking and screaming."

"You wouldn't dare," I stubbornly taunt, leaning back to gain better balance.

He rotates his body, turning to look at me, and because he is a step above me, he looks all the more menacing.

"Let. Go," he spits, his hair shrouding his eyes.

"No," I reply defiantly. "I dare you to try to—"

But before I have a chance to finish my dare, his strong hands wrap around my waist and haul me off the ground, and I see the skyline of South Carolina through Quinn's legs.

"Put me down!" I yelp, kicking out crazily as he climbs up the stairs, totally ignoring the fact he has flipped me over his shoulder like a five-year-old.

His hands are strapped over my legs, just under my butt, and as I twist around, trying to crawl up his body, he slaps me on the ass—hard.

"Ouch! You motherfu—"

I don't get a chance to finish my cuss because he kicks open the door to our room, probably breaking the hinges from the force. He then tosses me onto the bed. Planting my fists into the mattress to stop myself from falling face-first onto the carpet, I glare at him something wicked.

Quinn stalks to the bed while I quickly rise and face off with him on the other side. The only thing that separates us is the mattress, which may as well be nonexistent, as Quinn is about to charge.

"You are the most impossible woman I have ever met, and that's saying a lot, seeing as I have met *a lot* of impossible women!"

"I'm sure you have!" I scream back at him. "I'm sure you've probably fucked most of them! Oh, hang on, I take that back. You only go for the easy ones."

I'm shaking in rage, eyeing him, wishing I had something pointy to throw at him.

"Easy ones? Ha! You really want to go there?" Quinn chuckles angrily, interlacing his hands on the top of his head. "If that were true, then what the hell am I doing with you?"

I take a step back because hearing him say something aloud, which I have thought over and over for the past two days, feels like a stab wound slicing through my heart.

My anger, rage, and frustration explode, and I'm afraid I won't ever stop. "No one is keeping you here! Leave!" I scream, pointing at the door. "Do us both a favor and leave! Do you think I want you here? Do you think I want you caught up in all my fucking mess? Do you?"

My body shakes from fury but also in fear that he *will* leave me because I have done nothing but make his life hell.

Quinn's hardened features soften when he sees I'm on the verge of hysteria. "Red, I didn't mean…"

But I stop him.

Storming over to where he stands, I shove him as hard as I can with both hands. "Leave!" I bellow. "Go on! Leave!" And again, I push him, but he doesn't move, his tenacious stance not budging.

Tears break free, streaming down my cheeks and burning my eyes. I can no longer see Quinn, as my vision drowns in endless tears I don't deserve to be crying. What right do I have to cry when Hank lies in a morgue somewhere, dead?

What right do I have to cry when Tristan lies in a hospital bed, healing from a wound I may as well have inflicted myself?

None.

I don't realize I'm slumped onto the floor, sobbing hysterically, until Quinn's soft lips pass over my face, hair, mouth, or whatever piece of me he can reach to calm me down.

But I don't deserve this. I don't deserve comfort. I push at him wildly, but his strong arms never let me go as they enfold me into his chest.

"No," I croak weakly, trying to shove him away, but he won't shift.

"I don't deserve this," I sob, my tears tasting salty as they slip into my parted lips. "I don't deserve *you*. I deserve to be in the hospital, not Tristan. I deserve to be dead, not Hank. And only *I* deserve to be on the run, not you."

My fears, my *guilt* pours out of me, and now, I can't stop.

"Quinn, I killed Hank." I weep uncontrollably. "I did nothing to help him! I just stood there while they shot him. I may as well have pulled the trigger!"

"Red, that's not true," Quinn says quietly, but I can hear the catch in his voice as he tries to remain calm.

"Yes, it is! All of this is *my* fault. I'm riddled with grief so deep, I don't know how to go on. How can I live with myself after all this, Quinn? How?" I pull back, my bottom lip trembling, tears clouding my view of him.

"You'll go on…" He pauses to correct, "*We'll go* on because those motherfuckers will pay for what they did to Hank, to Tristan, and to you. And I am here every step of the way, Red. Every step. I won't leave you. I promise. No matter how hard you push me away, I will push back twice as hard because I know you feel it."

He reaches for my trembling hand and places it over his heart, locking his hand over mine. "I know you feel the pain, the regret. I know every piece of anger I feel, and together, we will fight it. We will get through this because once it's over, we'll be…free."

Just the word itself sounds like my redemption, and even though I don't know Quinn's secrets, I do know he has his own cross to bear. And together, we'll get past our demons and just…live.

Plan A and B were just weak excuses to push Quinn away, hoping he would be like everyone I have ever met and disappoint me. But he hasn't. Quinn Berkeley is unlike anyone I have ever met before.

"I'm sorry. I was only trying to protect you," I explain, referring to my grade A asshole behavior over the past two days.

"Shhh," he whispers, wiping away my tears with his knuckles. "I know. It just took me a little while to figure it out. But no more, okay?"

I nod, my tears spilling over my wet lashes and onto his fingers.

"We do this together. I'm here because I *want* to be here. Because I want *you*," he says, and before I have a chance to speak, he seals his lips over mine, kissing me deeply.

My body melts as he bites my lower lip and plunges his tongue into my mouth, claiming my lips as his own. I know I belong to Quinn at this moment, and all plans of pushing him away have been rendered redundant.

So no more plans, and no more schemes. This is raw, and this is real. And this is the first time I have felt alive in two days.

Four

I wake after the most peaceful sleep I've had in two days. And I know the reason behind that is Quinn.

How is it possible I've grown to depend on him in such a short amount of time? I feel safe with him, as he seems to be my equilibrium. If we're off, then so am I. But if we're balanced, then everything is, well, steady.

"Mornin."

Rubbing the sleep from my eyes, I sit up and look around the room, which is only illuminated by the soft glow of the small TV.

"What time is it?" I ask, clearing my throat when I see Quinn sitting on the brown sofa, channel surfing with the volume muted.

"A little after four," he replies, his eyes fixated on the TV.

He's propped up his bare feet on the coffee table in front of him, and his tangled hair cascades into his intense eyes as he focuses on the TV. The hard set of his jaw reveals something is wrong.

"Come here," he says when I just sit and stare, my foggy brain playing catch-up.

It's freezing, so I reach out and snatch one of Quinn's zip-up sweaters from the end of the bed. I wrap myself into it, as it's about five sizes too big. Quinn's eyes flick up to meet mine, and a small smile tugs at the corner of his beautiful lips.

"That look suits you," he teases, opening his arm out to the side for me to cuddle into him.

"Whatcha watching?" I ask as I sit near him, tucking my legs underneath me, his sweater covering my cold legs.

He pulls me into his side, wrapping an arm protectively around my waist. "Just checking out the news."

"Anything?" I ask, gesturing toward the TV with my head.

"Nope," he says, relieved.

I know he's been checking to see if our faces have been plastered on the local news as wanted fugitives—so far, so good.

"I was thinking…what if we called the police and put in our own anonymous tip? We can say we saw two men matching my dad and Phil's description leaving Night Cats on the night…"

But I can't finish that sentence without wanting to hurl.

"We have to try something," I opt for instead. "Shake it up a bit so we're not the only ones the police want to speak to."

"It might be worth a shot," he replies, disheartened, and I realize it's a stupid idea.

"I'm—"

"Red," he says before I have a chance to finish my sentence, "I don't want your apologies. So quit giving them to me."

I give him a small smile, as it's nice to hear he doesn't hate me.

"So what do you think?" I ask, peering up at him.

"I think anything is better than nothing. Even if it falls on deaf ears, it might help take some heat off us."

"I agree."

Quinn sighs, brushing a hand down his stubbled face before he reaches into his pocket and pulls out Tabitha's phone.

"I got this earlier," he says, passing me the phone.

My eyes skim over the message.

Where are you?? Tabitha

I read it twice and panic, as the number differs from the one Abi has been texting us from.

"That's not like Tabitha to be so direct," I comment while Quinn exhales loudly.

"Yeah, I know."

Why is she being so vague? This isn't like her. Then my brain catches up, and I gasp, shaking my head.

"That's not Abi. What if…?" But I can't finish my sentence as I toss the phone to the floor, thoughts plaguing my mind.

Quinn sucks on his lip ring, deep in thought. "I thought the same thing. But if it's not her, then who is it?"

We both look at one another, not voicing what we know to be true.

"It's either the police or my dad and Phil."

Quinn nods coolly as he reaches for the phone I threw in haste. I watch with interest as he slips out the SIM and snaps it between his fingers.

"Well, that solves that problem," I say with half a smile.

Quinn shrugs, tossing the broken SIM onto the

table. "We'll just call her house from now on, and Tristan should be released soon."

"You think the police have the landlines tapped?"

Quinn shakes his head, his messy hair sliding into his eyes. "I doubt it. We're only wanted for questioning. We haven't been charged with anything."

"Not yet," I mumble, lowering my eyes.

"Hey, we'll work this out."

"Do you think Tabitha is okay?" I hope whoever texted us guessed we had her phone and hadn't confronted her about it.

Quinn nods. "Yes. Abi's family is way too well known for anything to happen to her. Your dad isn't that stupid to draw any attention to himself by hurting her."

I breathe a sigh of relief and nod because he's right. My dad and Phil will want to lay low and fly under the radar. South Boston is a small town, and people like my dad and Phil stand out.

"So what now?"

"First, you're going to stop frowning." My lips form a straight line instantly. "And second, we're going on a road trip."

"What?" I ask, taken aback. "Road trip?"

"Yup." Quinn nods, smirking at me while I gape at him like he's gone insane.

"Red, you've never been outside of LA, and South Boston doesn't count."

I frown once again.

"This is your chance to do so. And I'm still okay with just going wherever the road takes us," he says, placing his fingers on the corners of my mouth and pushing my frown into a smile.

I instantly smile at his stupidity.

"Tristan should be out of the hospital in a week or so, and until then, we'll just keep moving from state to state. Once we're able to make contact back home, we'll see what's going on and decide what to do next. And if you still want to see your mom, we'll head to Canada."

He's so organized, so efficient, and it makes me think he's done this before. I'm determined to get to the bottom of Quinn's past because he has set me free from my demons. And I intend to do the same for him.

"Okay, so it's settled. We keep moving," he says, rubbing my cheek when I hesitate.

"Okay." I nod, leaning into his hand. "But first things first…"

Quinn looks at me, waiting for me to continue.

"I need to steal us a hot-ass car."

After dropping our keys off at the reception desk, we slip into the night, hoods donned, skulking the streets to find a mode of transportation for our infamous road trip.

I huddle close to Quinn, my hands bundled into my sweater pockets with my head bowed, hair covering my face.

"You okay?" Quinn whispers, shielding my body with his from the early morning chill.

"Yeah," I reply, shivering from the cold and the situation we find ourselves in.

I've stolen heaps of cars before. My first offense was when I was eleven, and it was for grand theft auto, but doing it now, here, seems so criminal. In a town where it's clear its inhabitants work hard for a living, it feels so wrong to steal someone's car, but we're desperate.

"What's the matter, Red?" Quinn asks, tightening his hold around my waist.

"I feel guilty," I confess. "I really don't want to steal some hard-working citizen's car."

"I know." Quinn sighs, kissing my head. "But what other choice do we have?"

"Maybe we could leave them an IOU note," I suggest stupidly, as where would we leave the note?

Quinn chuckles, planting another kiss on my head. "Or we could just steal...that."

I see it as soon as he does, and we both stop dead in our tracks, eyeing the big, obnoxious black GMC 4X4 pickup truck with the license plate number **ILVVAG.**

Quinn takes my hand, and we cross the desolate road, ready to do some breaking and entering. Thankfully, the truck is parked in a darkened patch, away from prying eyes. Not that anyone is awake so early on a Sunday morning.

Quinn looks the professional, peering from left to right before approaching the vehicle while I lag close behind. As I peer over his shoulder and into the truck, I bless the irony of life as I see a varsity jacket thrown onto the back seat.

But it's not just *a* varsity jacket. It's *the* varsity jacket that belonged to the jerk in the bar. Quinn also sees it and turns to me with a wicked glint in his eyes.

"Oh, this just got a whole lot more fun." He cracks his knuckles and takes one more look around, ensuring the coast is clear.

It is.

He drops into a crouch, unthreading his bootlace, and pulls the lace out through the eyelets quickly. As he has the long lace in his hands, he adeptly ties a slipknot in the middle of it and stands, swiftly placing the string at the top, right corner of the car door. I watch in awe as he begins working the string, sliding it back and forth until the slipknot is inside the car. He uses an expert side-to-side pulling motion to loop the slipknot around the lock, pulling it tight. As he pulls up on the string, the lock pops up, and he's in.

He's done this in less than fifteen seconds.

As I peer around, keeping a lookout while Quinn proficiently hot-wires the truck in under a minute, I know he's done this before.

As the engine roars to life, I run to the passenger side. Quinn unlocks my door, and I leap into the cabin with Lucky jumping onto my lap. I hold the grab handle as Quinn puts the truck into drive and tears down the street, the black truck blending into the shadowy night.

What is it about a man who can handle a truck that I find so attractive?

However, as I look at Quinn focusing on the road, his eyes studying the scenery before him with his long hair catching in the wind, I know it's all Quinn.

"Where to now?"

"We're on the road to…" And he pauses, thinking of the right word.

But I finish it for him.

"On the road to freedom," I say with conviction.

And Quinn nods. Stepping on the gas, he speeds toward our emancipation.

I wake to "Sweet Home Alabama" blasting beside my unfortunate eardrums, which have just split into two. But it's not the tune over the radio that has awoken me in a fright. It's

Quinn, who happily butchers the chorus, his hands slapping the steering wheel in time with the beat.

I've fallen asleep with my head twisted at an awful angle into Quinn's shoulder, and after a moment of clearing the sleep from my foggy brain, I open my heavy eyes, taking a moment to adjust to where we are. Lush greenery and tall, willowy trees are before me, and I wonder how far we've driven since I crashed.

"Mornin'," Quinn happily says while I stifle a yawn behind my palm.

"How long have I been asleep?" I ask, lifting my head and running a hand through my hair.

Quinn shrugs, eyes still glued to the highway while toying with the barbell in his mouth. I can't help myself as I watch with interest in the way he twirls the end of his tongue, the silver piercing catching off the radiant sunbeams.

"A while." He yawns, interrupting my ogling, and I stretch my arms above my head.

"You should have woken me up," I say, feeling terrible for falling asleep on him.

"No way. I'd miss out on you telling me how much you love my piercings," he says seriously, indicating to make a right-hand turn.

"What?" I ask, turning around so quickly, I whip myself in the face with my loose ponytail.

Quinn laughs deeply and meets my eyes, sucking on his lip ring.

"Oh yeah, you went into great detail. You're one dirty girl, Red," he teases while giving me a quick wink before returning his gaze to the road.

Feeling my cheeks blush a beet red, I cover my face with both hands, mortified, as I turn away from him.

"Red, I'm kidding. Although, now I wish I wasn't."

I quickly reach out and slap him on the arm, his biceps feeling like muscled heaven under my hand. "You jerk!" I cry but can't contain my laughter as it feels nice to laugh after three days of sadness.

Quinn chuckles and indicates to park in a lone strip of parking spaces. "I'm starving," he says, cutting the engine. "I was thinking, instead of calling Abi's house, how about we call the diner? What do you think?"

"That's a great idea. But it's Sunday today, and I'm pretty sure she's not scheduled, but she is tomorrow."

Quinn nods. "Well, there isn't much we can do today other than have fun."

I raise my eyebrow suspiciously. "Why am I afraid of your idea of fun?"

Quinn chuckles. "Go on, Red. Live a little."

This isn't the first time he's said this to me.

"Fine," I reply smugly, crossing my arms over my chest. "Bring on the fun."

After Quinn and I devoured our burgers, we both decided we're in desperate need of some new clothes and supplies.

Thankfully, a small town in Alabama has a department store big enough to cater for all we need. We stock our cart with personal hygiene items because the complimentary motel shampoos are quickly turning my hair into straw.

Quinn tosses a razor and a can of shaving cream into the cart, as he has quite a heavy growth, but I like it. It gives him a harder edge, and with his long hair, which he is almost able to tie back, he looks like a total badass.

He sees me eyeballing his items. "You like the caveman look, do you?"

"Makes no difference to me," I reply, attempting to appear nonchalant as I grab us a couple of toothbrushes and a tube of toothpaste.

"Oh, you just want me any way you can get me." I playfully roll my eyes, but little does he know the truth behind his words.

We may have worked out what's going on while we wait to make contact back home. But we haven't worked out what's going on between *us*.

Before this all happened, we were seeing each other, but we were taking it slow. Tabitha was the only one who knew, and Quinn was going to tell Tristan the night everything turned to shit.

But now, it feels different. Quinn left his home and put his life in danger to protect me. That has to mean something, right?

"Whatcha thinking?" he asks, steering the cart into the clothes section of the store as I blindly follow.

"Nothing. I'm going to grab a few things. Want to meet me here in, like, twenty minutes?" I say, not wanting Quinn to follow me while I shop for underwear.

"Cool," he replies with a mischievous smile before he zips off into the menswear.

Once he's gone, I finger the racks of lacy bras and matching underwear. I know Tabitha would have me buying the whole rack, which I won't do. But I must admit, I do feel good in them. And after the shitty few days I've had, I wouldn't mind feeling good again.

So, on that note, I snatch a few styles off the rack and grab some essential cotton briefs and T-shirt bras. I see some cute jeans on sale and take two pairs, one black, the other blue, and reach for a few T-shirts and sweaters. It's getting quite cold now that we're nearly into December.

Ultimately, I try on about ten garments and buy them all. As I exit the change room, I see a bulk pack of socks on sale and add them to my pile of goods.

I find Quinn and dump my armful of clothes into the shopping cart. I notice Quinn has grabbed similar items— two pairs of jeans, a pair of black skater shorts, a few T-shirts, and a zip-up hoodie.

I can't help but notice no underwear, and Quinn sees me looking confused.

"Like something you see?" he asks, rearranging my stuff as I just dumped it all into the cart.

Or don't see, I ad-lib. But I don't reply, as I would be mortified if he knew what I was thinking.

We throw in a few snacks, food, and a leash for Lucky, and we're done.

While waiting in line, I notice the checkout chick checking Quinn out. Not that I can blame her, as he is the hottest man I have ever seen. And the way he holds himself so arrogantly and confidently just adds to his appeal.

Whichever room Quinn is in, he owns it.

"You're doing that thing with your lip again," Quinn whispers into my ear, wisps of his hair brushing over my cheeks.

"Am I?" I reply, knowing all too well that I'm gnawing it off.

"Yes," he replies, releasing it with his thumb, it slipping free.

Turning to meet his eyes, which are inches away from my face, I suddenly forget how to breathe.

"Next!" a snappy voice calls out.

Shaking my head and fumbling with the items in the cart, I place them on the counter. As my hands pass over my royal-blue bra and matching underwear set, I blush and hide them under my sweater. I know Quinn has seen them, but being the gentleman that he occasionally is, he doesn't say a word.

As the lady brings up the total and accepts the cash from Quinn, she makes it more than obvious that she's openly staring at him. Her eyes drop down to his broad chest, and they linger there as she licks her glossy lips.

I'm just about to clear my throat when she thankfully raises her eyes, snapping up to meet Quinn's amused ones. No doubt he's seen the jealousy radiating from me, and by his stupid smile, he likes it.

"You like The Doors?" she asks, her eyes dropping to Quinn's chest once again, eyeing his T-shirt of Jim Morrison.

"Yeah," he replies nonchalantly, accepting the change, and I notice she makes an effort to touch him when placing the money into his outstretched palm.

I roll my eyes.

"Well, a tribute band is playing tonight at Captain Frank's. You should come."

Quinn takes hold of my hand.

"Whatcha think, Red?" he asks, pulling me into his side and kissing my cheek softly.

The checkout chick frowns as she watches Quinn nuzzle my cheek with his nose. I try not to gloat, but find it near impossible not to, as I have this amazing man making it clear he only has eyes for me.

"Could be…fun," I reply on a breath.

"Might see you there then," he replies, his lips still fanning over my cheek.

But then he's gone, casually placing the rest of our things into the shopping cart, oblivious to the fact he just sent my pulse racing.

The fresh air helps cool me down, and as we begin placing our bags into the back, I look down at the bumper, cringing.

"We gotta ditch these plates," I say with repulsion when my eyes pass over the disgusting words.

Quinn nods, and a dimpled smirk suddenly makes a sinful appearance. "You're right. They are definitely too distinguishable. And besides, I'm an ass man."

I know he's joking, but I still can't help my blush, which is ridiculous. Quinn has seen me naked, well, my bottom half, but it was dim, and sadly, it was only *once*.

Quinn has given me two amazing orgasms, but I'm greedy and want more. With Quinn, I'm consumed by him, and I've never experienced what he does to my body before. And now, I'm addicted.

"I wish I was in your head right now."

I spin around quickly, totally unaware I'm standing vacantly, one lone shopping bag hanging limply by my side.

"Huh?" I ask, staring at Quinn's mouth. He's tugging on his hoop, which doesn't help my train of thought.

"Never mind." He chuckles, reaching for the shopping bag I'm still holding and placing it alongside the others.

"Do you want to find a place to crash?" he asks, jumping into the truck while I follow, as my feet can finally move.

"Sure. Let's find someplace to park the car out of sight."

"Good thinking, Red. If I didn't know any better, I'd say you've done this before," he says, reversing the truck.

I give him a small smile because sadly, it's true.

After finding a motel with a parking lot in the back, Quinn checks us in while I wait outside. I'm not sure if I'll ever be able to enter a motel office again without having a panic attack.

There are just too many memories, and with those memories comes my rolling wave of regret, something that will eat at me for an eternity.

"All set," Quinn says, snapping me out of my slump while jingling the room keys.

I nod, trying to fake a smile, but Quinn sees right through my bullshit.

"You okay?" he asks, wrapping an arm around my waist and drawing me into his side.

"Yeah, I will be," I reply honestly, giving him a small smile. "I just miss him."

Quinn nods, kissing my temple. "I do too."

We're still for a few moments, both lost in memories of Hank.

"C'mon," he says, latching onto my hand. "I know exactly what you need."

Lucky follows us, wagging his tail, and I'm glad he can stay inside with us.

As I look at the run-down motel, I can't help but compare it to Night Cats. Before all this shit happened, Quinn, Tristan, Tabitha, and I were working day and night to restore Night Cats, hoping to transform it into the immaculate condition it once was. And it was getting there. Hank was getting busier and busier, and day by day, he was digging his way out of his financial troubles. Now, I can't help but wonder what's happened to it.

My eyes well with tears, but I sniff them away as Quinn reaches our room and opens the door with the rusty key. He reaches behind the door and places the DO NOT DISTURB sign on the handle before ushering me inside.

He drops our bags onto the dirty red carpet, then kicks off his boots.

"I'll be right back," he announces before heading into the bathroom and shutting the door behind him.

I look down at Lucky for answers. But he only looks up at me, just as baffled as I am.

I switch on the tiny TV for background noise because I'm extremely tempted to press my ear against the bathroom door. But instead, I go through my shopping bags, looking at the new garments I purchased. As my fingers pass over the blue silk of my bra, my heart races at the thought of Quinn seeing me in it.

Stop being an idiot, I berate myself. You have more important things to deal with than underwear.

Fifteen minutes later, Quinn is still in the bathroom, and I wonder what he's doing. Judging by the size of this room, I can't imagine the bathroom being any bigger than a shoebox.

It remains unspoken between Quinn and me that we're to stay at derelict hotels. I can't justify unnecessary spending, especially when we crash for a few hours at a time and are out before the sun rises.

I slump onto the end of the bed, toeing off my boots, and sit cross-legged, facing the bathroom, waiting for Quinn to emerge.

"C'mon," he says, poking his head round the bathroom door, then disappearing again.

I hesitate, wondering what I'm about to walk into. But I

trust him, so I know it'll only be good.

I walk over to the bathroom, which is only a few feet away, and as I step inside, my mouth drops open. I see that the small but comfy pink bathtub overflows with bubbles, some floating over the tub. A single candle, which I'm pretty certain is a citronella candle, burns brightly on the cracked sink, but it does the job.

"Quinn," I gasp, looking at him quickly. "What's all this?"

He shrugs, scratching his scruffy jaw as he leans awkwardly against the white wall. "I thought you could use a bath."

Looking at the bath and then back at Quinn, who looks to be gauging my response, I slowly walk to the tub and sit on the edge, skimming the tips of my fingers through the boiling water.

"Are you saying I stink?" I tease, giving him a small smile.

He returns my smile, and the only sound permeating the air is the water swishing back and forth through my fingers.

"You know you smell unbelievable," he replies after a moment of silence.

But I don't say anything because I'm speechless, and Quinn mistakes my silence for something else.

"I just thought a bath might be relaxing or something. It was a dumb idea." He reaches forward quickly, attempting to pull out the plug.

"No!" I yell, latching onto his arm to stop him. "This is amazing. I'm sorry if I sounded ungrateful. What I should have said was…thank you. This is the sweetest thing anyone has ever done for me."

I do something that feels natural.

I yank on his collar and smash his lips to mine, kissing him passionately. And as I deepen the kiss, because his mouth feels too amazing not to, I grip the bathtub's edge, afraid of slipping off. But Quinn supports my nape softly, his large palm angling my head to give him better access to my lips. And we kiss this way until I'm breathless.

When he pulls away softly, his eyes are almost black as he teases, "I'd offer to wash your back, but I don't think that's a good idea."

"I won't be long," I whisper, trying to catch my breath after making out with him so fervently.

"Take as long as you like. I'm not going anywhere," he replies, kissing my lips gently before he closes the door behind him.

Looking at the bath with a smile, I eagerly strip off and lower myself into the boiling water that feels like heaven. I reach for the towel sitting on the sink and roll it up, using it as a pillow behind my head.

The water smells like sandalwood, and I instantly submerge myself, falling into oblivion.

When a nameless amount of time has passed, I wake, feeling like a floppy doll. I don't want to rouse, but I know I'm not alone.

"Hey," I croak, slowly opening my eyes and adjusting to the soft lighting.

Quinn sits on the floor, his broad back flush against the wall with his bare feet pressed against the bathtub and a sketchpad resting in his lap.

"Hey," he replies, his fingers working across the piece of paper, sketching madly.

With his head bowed, his hair shrouds his eyes, but I can see them move over the paper in deep concentration. His mouth is pressed into a thin line, and he nibbles on his hoop every so often, which drives me insane.

"Whatcha doing?" I ask, making sure I stay submerged since the bubbles cover my nakedness.

"Sketching," he replies, his fingers dancing over the paper.

"Sketching what?" I ask, craning my neck in an attempt to see what he's drawing.

"You," he replies, his head finally lifting to meet my wide eyes.

"Oh," I say on a breath, suddenly dipping farther into the water.

"Yeah. I hope that doesn't creep you out." He sits up, placing his pencil down. "I came in here to make sure you hadn't drowned. And you'd fallen asleep looking like...well, a Siren."

I can tell he's a little embarrassed by his confession.

"A Siren? Didn't they lure sailors to their deaths?"

Quinn smiles, brushing back his hair. "Yes. But those sailors happily went to their watery graves, having heard and seen the beautiful water goddesses. You see, they looked innocent and sounded angelic, but underneath all that beauty lay a powerful, misunderstood woman—like you. And if I were to die...I would be just like those sailors," he whispers, his mind in a faraway place.

I gasp, and my heart pounds against my rib cage.

"Do you believe in life after death?" I ask, not wanting to scrutinize his comment because it's just too much.

"I'd like to think there is more to life than this."

"Me too," I confess softly.

There has to be more. For Hank's sake—there just has to be.

"Can I see?" I ask, straining my neck to see his handiwork,

hoping to break the sudden silence.

"It's not done," he replies, holding the pad to his chest with a smile.

"How will you finish it? Don't you need me to pose or something?" I say shyly. There is no way I'd be able to sit still, knowing Quinn's eyes rake over every inch of my body.

Quinn chuckles as he stands and taps his temple. "It's all up here. Trust me, it's a sight I won't forget anytime soon."

My body heats under his piercing gaze, and I shift my legs nervously. After a moment of silence, he clears his throat.

"I'll give you some privacy while you change. I grabbed your stuff but didn't know what you wanted to wear, so I brought everything in," he says, pointing at my backpack and the three shopping bags sitting near the door.

"Thank you, Quinn." I smile, touched by his kindness.

He gives me one final heated look, and only when he closes the door behind him do I begin to breathe again.

Five

Quinn is always hungry.

But looking at his burly frame and trying not to drool, I guess he needs to fuel all that muscle.

I'm stuffed after our massive Southern dinner, which was amazing. But Quinn is looking for something else to eat as we're walking the streets, in no real hurry.

The night is chilly, so I'm dressed in my jeans, boots, and a fleecy sweater. I'm so thankful we stopped to get some heavier clothes; otherwise, I would be freezing my butt off now.

"Hey, there's that bar the chick who was eye fucking you was talking about," I say, looking up at the sign ahead, which flashes in fluorescent green.

"Eye fucking me?" he questions, raising his brow.

"Oh please, don't play dumb. You saw her falling all over herself to get your attention," I reply, attempting to keep the annoyance out of my voice.

Quinn laughs confidently. "I saw nothing of the sort. You're just seeing things."

"Oh yeah. I just love seeing other girls thankful they have on their best underwear in hopes of getting you naked the moment you enter a room." I scoff but shut my mouth, quickly realizing what I just said.

Quinn, however, latches onto my wrist as I blindly walk ahead, desperate to escape this awkward conversation. As I spin around to face him, he slips his hands under my tight tank and encircles my waist.

I instantly shiver with the skin-to-skin contact as he begins brushing his thumbs over my flesh. "I don't care what other girls do," he says, leaning forward to nuzzle my neck.

"Why?" I manage to reply without choking as his hands and lips caress me softly.

"Because it's only you and your underwear I'm interested in. Any time you want to drop them…feel free." He sucks on my neck with a long, wet pull.

I almost forget to breathe when he bites just under my chin. But then…he's gone.

Jerk.

Taking a moment to compose myself, I try to appear unaffected as I toss my hair over my shoulder and stroll past Quinn, walking up the three steps to Captain Frank's. He follows closely, and I can hear him chuckling, relishing in the fact he's made me all hot.

He wants to play dirty? So can I.

Quinn offers to pay for the door charge, but I wave him off and pay my eight dollars. I confidently march in while he lags behind, attempting to keep up with me as he puts the change into his back pocket.

When I push through the doors, a hundred sets of eyes fall on me, and I smile. This will be a lot easier than I thought. I slip off my sweater since I only have a black tank on underneath, and the eyes of every male in the room follow the movement.

Back in LA, I had to learn how to flirt my way out of some sticky situations, and I got pretty good at it. Men usually only think with one head. And it's not the one on their shoulders.

This time is no exception.

"Put your sweater back on," Quinn whispers into my ear, protectively wrapping an arm around my shoulders.

But I shrug him off and saunter toward the bar. "Put *your* sweater back on."

The venue is a quaint little spot with a simple layout. The bar is to the right, and the toilets are behind the stage, which sits at the back of the room with a dance floor nearby. Red leather couches are scattered around randomly, and a few tables and barstools are placed around the dance floor. The red contrasted with the black walls gives the place a sleazy vibe. And the leery guy next to me, who just looked down my top, just adds to the vibe.

"Can I get you a drink?" he murmurs, leaning in so close that I almost smash foreheads with him.

Just as I'm about to tell him to save his money and buy himself some breath mints, Quinn fills in the tiny space between us, his huge frame dwarfing my tiny one.

"She doesn't want a drink. Now move," he says with confidence, gesturing with his head for the guy to give up his seat.

The guy stands quickly because Quinn has made it crystal clear that he can either leave voluntarily or Quinn will remove him. And I'm sure there will be nothing voluntary if that happens.

"You've proven your point," Quinn says, straddling the seat near me while I flag down the male bartender.

"What point?" I ask sweetly.

The bartender, an attractive guy with a blue Mohawk and a face full of piercings, looks my way and flashes me a dazzling smile. "What can I get ya, pretty lady?"

The annoyance radiating from Quinn is almost suffocating, and I can't help but chuckle. "I'll have a…" I rear up to look over his huge Mohawk at the drink's menu board. "Slippery Nipple." I smirk, holding back my laugh when I hear Quinn huff near me.

"Red, I'm not playing," he cautions.

"Who's playing?" I reply, brushing my hair over one shoulder.

He edges closer to me, and I take a deep breath. "You know what you're doing."

"And what would that be?"

"Driving me crazy," he confesses, nipping my earlobe sharply.

I jolt at the sensation, and the bartender returns, sliding my drink toward me.

"That'll be ten dollars, please," Mohawk says, watching Quinn and me curiously.

As I reach for my money, Quinn smacks a twenty on the bar.

"Here's a tip," Quinn coolly states, and the bartender reaches for it happily.

But Quinn slaps his hand over the bill. "You get one of the other bartenders to serve her from now on." He removes his hand.

Mohawk nods uneasily, realizing Quinn's tip was not in

the form of money, and he scampers off, serving a patron at the other end of the bar.

"Real smooth," I say, raising the rim of the glass to my lips and tossing it back quickly.

"I wasn't trying to be smooth."

As I lick my sticky fingers because the liquor has trickled over the sides of the shot glass, Quinn grabs my seat and spins it to face him. I have about a second to register what he's doing before he smashes his lips to mine, kissing me with such intensity I nearly slip off my seat.

His mouth is hot and wet, and I can't get enough. I grip his hair and pull—hard. He bites my bottom lip, following the sting with his tongue.

"Now, that's smooth," he says, pulling away with a smirk.

He looks calm and collected while I'm all but combusting in my seat. Damn him for beating me at my own game.

The lights suddenly dim, and the crowd cheers as the first member of Wild Child takes his position behind the drums. The guitarist and keyboardist follow not long after, and I'm surprised because they are clones of the original band members. I can't help but wonder what the sexy Jim Morrison will look like.

But I don't have to wait too long because the girls go wild as soon as Jim comes out.

The guy, no older than twenty-one, takes his spot behind the microphone, wearing the infamous leather pants, boots, and white shirt, which falls open, revealing a nicely defined chest. His long hair is tousled.

The girls in the venue rush to the front, pushing and shoving to get a prime spot for a performance, which will no doubt get a lot of men in here laid.

Now I get why there are so many men here.

Jim starts with "Alabama Song," and the girls bop away, hands above their heads, dancing to the catchy tune of the keyboard. This happens for the majority of the show, and I must admit, I'm a little starstruck, as he is really good. His voice, stage moves, everything is down to a T to the real Jim Morrison, who I have a little crush on.

"LA Woman" ends, and Jim laughs when a thong gets thrown onto the stage. "We're going to slow it down a bit," he says, seductively running his fingers up and down the microphone stand.

"The Crystal Ship" begins, and as Jim's smooth voice lulls me into a hypotonic state, I close my eyes and get lost in the music.

"Dance with me," Quinn whispers into my ear.

My eyes snap open, and I turn to look at him, stunned. No one has ever asked me to dance before. And because of that, I don't know how.

"I don't…I…" I stutter, lowering my eyes.

Quinn reaches for my hand, leading me to the dance floor, where many bodies slowly sway.

As we reach a small spot, I look from side to side, attempting to subtly watch others and replicate their movements. But Quinn encircles my waist, drawing me into him, and I instantly relax.

"Wrap your arms around my neck," he says into my ear hoarsely, and the heat of his hands on my waist scorches my skin raw.

Nervously, I raise my arms, enclosing his neck in a tight grip. Biting my lip, I feel beyond stupid just standing there, not knowing what to do. But as Quinn leisurely begins swaying, his eyes focused on mine, I mimic his movements, shuffling from foot to foot, and thankfully, I don't feel too uncoordinated.

I lower my eyes to ensure I'm not stepping on his feet, but Quinn dips his face to meet mine.

"I'll lead you. Just trust me."

I know his words have nothing to do with what we're doing on the dance floor but rather with where we're headed. And I don't question it.

I give him a small smile and rest my head against his chest, listening to the hypnotic voice of Jim Morrison.

But what's more hypnotic is the steady rhythm of Quinn's heart, which beats wildly and in sync with mine.

The following morning during breakfast, Quinn suggests we call Tabitha at the diner, but I'm not really listening to him.

All I can think about is the way we danced last night through the rest of Wild Child's set. Being in his arms that way, snuggling into him as he sang softly into my ear, is something I will never forget.

Just thinking about it still gives me goose bumps.

Who knew I liked to dance. Although, I have a feeling I only really enjoyed it because I was wrapped up in Quinn's embrace, feeling safe.

"Red? Do you want me to do it?" he asks as he stands outside the phone box I'm squished into.

Who knew pay phones still existed? But here we are.

"Huh? Do what?" I ask, totally oblivious to what's going on.

"Call Tabitha," he explains with a smirk.

"Oh right. No, I'm good." I slip my hood over my head, wanting to hide from reality.

Slipping a few quarters in, I dial Bobby Joe's and hold my breath. On the third ring, Tabitha answers, and hearing her voice immediately causes my eyes to water.

"Abi, it's me," I stupidly whisper, seeing as no one is around.

"Mia?" she gasps softly.

"Yeah, it's me. How are you? How's Tristan?"

"What happened to your phone? I've been trying to call you," she whispers, and I can hear the background noise fade as she takes the cordless phone out back.

"We had to get rid of it. Someone claiming to be you sent us a message asking where we were."

"It wasn't me."

"I know, Abi. How's Tristan?" I ask again, looking at Quinn, who sucks on his lip ring, listening closely.

"He's better. He's still in the hospital. He'll be there for another week for observation. Mia, the police have been around here, asking questions."

"I'm sorry you're involved in all my mess."

"It's okay. I've got my dad working on your case."

"What?" I question loudly, which has Quinn stepping forward, raising an inquisitive brow.

But I shake my head at him and continue to listen to Abi.

"My dad isn't like my mom. That's why they divorced. He's kind, unlike her, and I trust him. He's a powerful man with connections, and he's trying his best to pull some strings to get the police off your tail."

"How's he doing that?"

"Don't be mad, but I told him about you, and he's hired a private investigator to look into everything."

"What does that mean?" I ask, looking at Quinn anxiously.

"It means he's trying to clear your name and hold your

dad and Phil accountable for their actions."

"You know about my dad. Phil. Me?" I add, my stomach dropping.

"I know everything, Mia," she confesses softly.

She now knows what I did. And she now also knows who I really am.

When Quinn and I took off, Tabitha only knew a sliver of my past. But now…now she knows it all.

"And you still want to help me?" I ask incredulously, tears stinging my eyes.

"More than ever," she replies, and a tear slips down my cheek.

Quinn looks like he's about ready to explode and takes a step toward me. But I raise my hand, indicating I'm okay.

"But Phil covered his tracks," she says, brushing off the fact she knows about my tainted past.

"I know."

"My dad has hired the best, and they're working around the clock to put a case together to prove to the police that you're innocent. When that happens, hopefully the police will listen, and you guys won't be wanted for murder."

"So they're blaming the murder on Quinn and me?" I ask, making eye contact with Quinn, as this proves we are *actually* wanted for murder.

We both believed in the slim chance we were only wanted for questioning. But with Brad's dad on the case, there is no such thing as innocent until proven guilty.

"Yes. Sheriff Davidson won't let it go. He comes here almost every day, looking for you. Tristan is under watch at the hospital too."

"What? Why?" I shout, instantly feeling a wave of protection at the mere mention of Tristan's name.

"Because they think Quinn will contact him."

"Fuck."

Quinn has had enough and tries to squeeze into the booth, but I put my arm up, needing some space before I suffocate.

"The sheriff has a personal vendetta against you. What happened?"

I don't want to tell Abi what happened, but she's sticking her neck out for me, so she needs to know the truth.

"I had a fight with Brad on the night he drugged you. I went after him, pulled a knife, and threatened him. Things got ugly, and he tried to..." I look at Quinn, whose jaw is clenching as if reliving the memory.

"He attacked me, and Quinn saved me. But not before Quinn beat him to near death."

There is silence on the other end, and if not for the clanging of pots and pans, I'd say Abi has hung up.

"Abi? Are you still there?"

"Yeah," she finally croaks. "You did that for me? You put yourself in jeopardy for me."

"Of course, I did. You're my best friend."

"Oh God...this is my fault."

"No! None of this is your fault. Don't you ever say that, okay?"

"Okay," she sniffs. "Thank you, Mia. What you did for me..."

"Abi, don't mention it. I better go. I'm not sure if this line is tapped."

"Okay." She sniffles again. "Just keep running, okay? Just until my dad comes up with a plan. Don't go to the police. Sheriff Davidson has an APB on you and Quinn and issued it through most counties."

Shit, that just made things a whole lot harder.

"Okay, Abi. I'll check in with you tomorrow."

"Um…"

"What's the matter?" I ask, hearing her apprehension.

"I'm not in tomorrow."

"But it's Tuesday. You always work Tuesdays."

"Um," she says with a pause yet again.

After a few seconds, she whispers, "It's Hank's funeral."

I can feel the color drain from my face, and my knees suddenly go weak, threatening to buckle underneath me.

"Mia?" Abi says, panicking when I don't say anything.

But I can't reply because all I can hear on repeat is… funeral.

"Mia, put Quinn on the phone."

Like a zombie, I hand the phone over to Quinn as I step out of the booth and blindly sit on the curb, tears stinging my eyes.

Hank's funeral? Oh my God, I think I'm going to be sick. Staring vacantly ahead, I will not allow myself to cry because I have no right.

I vaguely hear Quinn in the background, trying to get a word in.

"Okay, Abi, I…" He stops abruptly. "They haven't been *that* bad."

I wonder what she's grilling him over.

"Okay…yes…"

More pauses.

I turn to look at him, and he gives me a small, crooked smile.

"Okay, yes, I got it. Talk to you in a couple of days." He hangs up, blowing his hair out of his eyes.

"Everything okay?" I ask softly as he sits near me, his long legs stretching out in front of him.

"Yeah. I now understand what they mean about redheads having a temper. You all right?" he asks, lightly bumping me with his shoulder when I remain silent.

I shrug. "Not really. The good news is Abi's dad is helping to clear our name. But the bad news is the police are keeping an eye on Tristan, like some fugitive. And thanks to Brad's dad, who has a hard-on for us, I might add, we are wanted in every county in a thousand-mile radius. And to make matters worse…"

But suddenly, Quinn has poised his finger over my lips, stopping me from continuing.

"Red, stop talking," he says and dips his head to look me in the eyes. "We're going to New Orleans."

"What? Are you insane? Did you not hear what I just said?" I ask, widening my eyes to emphasize my point.

"I heard you."

"And?"

"And what?"

"And…I…" I falter because I don't really know what to say.

"You got someplace better to be?"

"No."

"C'mon then." He stands, extending his hand down to me. Looking at his hand, I shake my head. "Quinn, this is crazy."

I know what he's doing. He's trying to distract me from falling apart.

He waves his hand, coaxing me to take it. "Red, nothing about this *isn't* crazy. So what's a little extra crazy gonna do?"

"But Hank," I say solemnly as I finally accept his hand.

"Hank would want you to stop frowning and be happy," he says, pulling me up and wrapping his arms tightly around me.

And it's exactly what I need to feel and hear.

It should take us roughly seven hours to get to New Orleans, but with Quinn's driving, it takes five and a half.

Quinn and I have been deep in thought the whole car ride, occasionally speaking or humming along to a tune on the radio. But overall, what's happening back home hits us both, and we're happy to travel in silence.

It's about three o'clock, and Quinn's stomach rumbles while I'm gaping at the terrain of New Orleans. I've heard stories about the beauty of this place, but actually seeing it before my eyes is like nothing I ever imagined.

As Quinn's stomach gripes yet again, I tear my eyes from the magnificence before me and chuckle.

"You can't possibly be hungry again?"

"I'm a growing boy," he replies, returning my smile. "There is no sincerer love than the love of food. My mom always used to say that to Tristan and me when we were kids. I never really got it till I had my first bite of her infamous chocolate marble sheet cake."

I see him flinch at the slip of his mom, something he has never done before. He doesn't speak about his mom or dad, or his past, and I don't push because I know how it feels to want to forget your history.

"Your mom sounds like a smart woman," I say cautiously, hopeful not to upset him.

He only nods uncomfortably and pulls into a desolate gas station, which I'm pretty sure closed down in 1984.

"Um…" I say, looking at the building, which has half a

roof. "Just a hunch, but I don't think you'll find any food in there…or anything at all for that matter."

Quinn smirks, killing the engine, and reaches over his head, slipping his sweater off.

"What are you doing?" I ask, watching him curiously as he begins wiping down the steering wheel and dash.

"It's time that we part ways with this eyesore. It was fun while it lasted, but I want something bigger and badder."

"And less offensive," I add, slipping off my sweater and mimicking Quinn. I meticulously wipe down the truck from top to bottom.

By the time we're done, the cab is wiped clean of our fingerprints. Searching under the seats to ensure we haven't left anything behind, I give Quinn a nod when I've checked the truck thoroughly.

"Where to now?" I ask, looping Lucky's lead through my hand.

"Somewhere where there is food," he replies as his stomach rumbles loudly in agreement.

"Lead the way," I say with a smile, following him as we begin our trek down the highway.

Quinn shoulders both our bags and smirks. "Follow me."

The worst thing about new shoes is blisters. And judging by the pain I'm feeling in my feet, it's safe to say I have a few—a few dozen.

I'm hobbling behind Quinn, trying not to expose how much pain I'm currently in. Quinn stops and casts a grin over his shoulder as he waits for me to catch up.

I'm a few feet away when he slips our backpacks off his

shoulder, dumping them onto the grass. "Jump on."

"Excuse me?"

"Jump on," he repeats. "I'll piggyback you."

Surely, he's joking.

"C'mon, Red," he persists, wiggling his shoulder at me, trying to tempt me.

My unhappy feet celebrate the possibility of not having to take another step. "Okay, but only for a bit," I say, collecting our bags and slipping them onto my shoulder.

I hesitantly approach Quinn because I don't know how to climb up his colossal back without a ladder.

"Just jump on like you would a horse." He laughs, sensing my dilemma.

"I've never ridden a horse."

"Well, now's your chance," Quinn says, shooting me a quick wink over his shoulder.

He crouches down low, allowing me to climb on without falling flat on my face. I stand on my tippy-toes and reach up, placing my hands around his thick shoulders. As I boost myself up, I yelp because suddenly Quinn grabs behind my knees and shuffles me up his body so he has a firm grip around my legs. Once he's got a tight hold around me, he slowly stands. I firmly latch on, clutching his neck with a death grip, afraid I'm about to fall.

"Don't drop me," I squeak. "It's a long way down."

"I'll try, but if you keep choking me, I can't guarantee I'll get very far without passing out."

"Oh shit! Sorry!" I loosen my grip on his neck while he chuckles.

"Thank you," I whisper, his hair tickling my cheeks as I lean forward against him.

"Thank you?"

"Yeah, thank you. For this. For everything. There isn't anyone else I would rather be a fugitive with," I say, trying to poke fun at our situation without getting too heavy.

Quinn takes a breath before replying, "Ditto, Red. Life's what you make of it. And you make it unforgettable."

I blush at his admission and don't know how to respond, so I don't. I simply enjoy the ambience of the magical buildings and the divine-smelling foods while perched on the back of someone who changes everything.

After endless minutes of me demanding Quinn to put me down, which, of course, falls on deaf ears, we roll into the French Quarter.

And I thought the scenery was amazing twenty minutes ago.

I've heard stories about this place, but seeing it before me is beyond description. The old, historic feel mixed with a slight modern touch makes me feel like I'm in another world. The narrow streets are filled with people with no real hurry to their steps. Tourists and locals alike seem to want to absorb this soulful beauty for as long as possible.

I continue gawking, and I have the best seat in the house, perched on Quinn's back.

"Put me down." I giggle when Quinn stops in front of a street band consisting of five members and a dog.

He chuckles and bends, setting me to my feet, which wobble slightly. Reaching forward quickly, Quinn places his hand around my middle to steady me, and the response is natural to us both. It's scary how comfortable we're becoming with one another.

We stand and watch the musicians for a few minutes before Quinn throws a ten-dollar bill into their open guitar case and takes my hand, leading me down the busy street.

I take in the brilliance before me, and I've decided I love New Orleans. From the romantic, long-standing architecture to the laid-back nature of its inhabitants, it feels like magic exists here.

"You like it here?" Quinn says, catching me admiring a local French-inspired bakery, which smells divine.

I nod, unable to wipe the smile off my face. "It's beautiful. Thank you for bringing me here."

"We're not done yet."

"What do you mean?"

"We're going to stay here for a couple of days."

"Yeah?" I ask, unable to contain the excitement in my voice.

"Yeah," he replies, returning my smile, but looking a lot more mischievous than I.

"What are you up to?" I ask, narrowing my eyes at him with a smile.

"What makes you think I'm up to something?"

"That shit-eating grin is a dead giveaway," I reply, shaking my head and elbowing him in the ribs.

He clutches his side dramatically, laughing. "Vicious, Red. You need to come with a warning."

I laugh because it's kind of ironic, as that's exactly how I feel about him.

Quinn stops in front of a huge building while I continue walking on in my own little world. However, when he doesn't follow and his hand snags in mine, I turn at the waist to look at him.

"Whatcha doing?" I ask, watching him tip his head to the side as if examining the mammoth white hotel in front of him.

"Just checking out our hotel," he replies, not looking at me as he lets go of my hand and crosses his arms over his broad chest.

"What?" I ask, stunned, mimicking him and gazing up at the beautiful building before us. "We're staying *here*?"

"Yes, we are."

"But we can't stay here," I say, looking at the snobbish people pulling up to the sidewalk in their expensive cars.

"Why not?"

Pondering his question, I know the answer lies in Hank being placed into the ground tomorrow. A hole six feet under that could not provide him warmth or comfort like our ritzy hotel. So why do *I* deserve something as extravagant as this?

I don't.

"I don't des—" I begin, but Quinn cuts me off by placing his finger over my lips.

"Do I need to gag you? Or carry you over my shoulder again?"

I know he's not kidding as I vividly recall the memory of being carried, kicking and screaming, over his shoulder in South Carolina. However, I open my mouth, but Quinn shakes his head, his finger still poised on my lips, warning me not to speak.

"You're so bossy," I muffle from under his finger, and he cocks an eyebrow.

"Oh, you have no idea."

Flushing a bright scarlet at his admission, I feel he is speaking about something entirely different.

"C'mon, Red." I take his outstretched hand, realizing my nickname has just taken on another meaning.

As we stroll up the covered walkway to the foyer, we get the worst sideway looks from patrons walking toward us. One lady with a peacock feather in her big floppy hat curls her lip up at me in disgust, leaning into her husband's arm to prevent any accidental touching.

I look down at my tattered blue jeans, which have a small hole in the knee, and my sloppy striped sweater, which hangs off one shoulder, and suddenly, I feel inadequate.

"Don't change who you are for people who don't even know who they are. You're beautiful, inside and out."

"You know, you can be really sweet when you want to be." I was touched, looking over at him as the kind concierge holds the glass door open for us.

As we step into the amazing foyer, which looks like the ballroom out of *Beauty and the Beast*, Quinn turns to me and whispers out of the side of his mouth. "No man wants to hear he's sweet, Red. Reckless and dangerous, yes. But sweet?" He pulls a face, shaking his head.

"Well, you're all those things…and sweet," I add with a mischievous smile.

We approach the front desk, and my good mood dies when I see the pretentious older woman behind the counter.

"How can I help you?" she says curtly, looking down her nose at Quinn and me while tightening her aqua scarf.

"A room please," Quinn replies, purposely leaning onto the counter to invade her personal space.

As she nervously fiddles with her name tag, I notice her name is Janet. "There are no *standard* rooms available," she replies, leaning away from Quinn, repulsed by the way he nibbles on his hoop.

"Any room is fine," he replies with a sickly sweet smile.

She huffs but decides to humor us as she taps her French-manicured fingernails on the keyboard under the wooden desk. I take in my surroundings as I hear the keys whining under her punishing fingers.

It's really beautiful in here, and I love it because it's not obnoxious like some of the other snobby hotels I've seen in LA. It's historical, and I'm pretty sure the huge spiral staircase in the center of the room, leading to who knows where, is an original article from when this place was built.

"The only suite we have is the Empire Wing," Janet says, ruining my moment of serenity.

"That'll do," Quinn says quickly, reaching into his back pocket for his wallet.

Janet cackles. "I mean no disrespect, but that room is one thousand dollars...a night."

Quinn grins, loving that Janet is about to have a coronary. "Well, in that case, we'll stay for a few nights."

My eyes widen, and I shake my head, as that's just too much money to spend on a room. But he ignores me and slaps a wad of cash onto the counter with a loud thud.

Janet's eyes broaden wider than mine, and she clears her throat, her face changing instantly as she probably thinks we're two spoiled rich kids splurging on our daddy's money.

"Wonderful." She claps. "Please forgive me if I came across as—"

I roll my eyes, refraining from filling in the blanks.

"A Negative Nancy," she continues, while reaching for the money greedily. "Okay, so you're paid up for two nights," she says happily after counting the mountain of cash. "I just need some ID or a credit card. It's hotel policy. I know it's silly."

I begin to panic as we're supposed to keep a low profile and not leave any tracks. Presenting any form of ID is just as good as broadcasting to the police where we are.

My heart begins to quicken.

Quinn senses my instant terror, and suddenly, his whole demeanor changes.

"Is this your daughter?" he asks, gesturing with his chin

to a photo in a silver frame, sitting on the desk.

The photograph is of Janet and a young girl, aged no older than five. There is no way she is her mother, and I bite the inside of my cheek, suddenly catching on to Quinn's ingenious plan. Even though I cannot stand the idea of him flirting with her, I know this is a pretty good plan to help dodge the whole ID situation.

Janet giggles as she places her hand over her mouth, which I preferred when it was scowling at me.

"Oh no," she says, her Cajun accent coming through, which makes me think her aristocratic accent is staged.

"She's my grandbaby."

"No way!" Quinn says, mocking surprise. "You're way too young to be a grandma, sweetheart." And he throws her a killer grin.

Both Janet and I are stunned by his comment, our mouths dropping to the floor. I'm just about to stomp on his foot and tell him to chill it with the compliments, but Janet begins giggling again and playfully slaps Quinn on the arm, making sure to feel his muscled biceps, defined through his tight blue T-shirt.

My eyes narrow on her fingers, and I tell myself to calm down, as he's only doing this for me. But I hate seeing it. It makes me sick to my stomach. I don't think I can hold my tongue.

"So how about we forget about the ID?" he says, subtly slipping her a hundred-dollar bill.

She quickly extends her fingers forward, and her hand overlaps Quinn's. "I really shouldn't, but it'll be our secret."

She has five seconds to get her hand off Quinn before I rip her fingernails out, one by one.

"Thanks, darlin'," Quinn says, cleverly sliding his hand out from under her claws.

She reaches under the counter, producing a key card *and* a business card. "If I can do *anything*"—she emphasizes the word *anything*—"you don't hesitate to call. That there is my direct line. You call me any time. Day *or* night."

That's the final straw. I turn around and walk away before I vomit.

My boots thump onto the marbled tiles as I walk toward the elevator, trying not to gag.

Quinn approaches me casually. "Ready to go?"

"You're sick," I utter, stabbing the call button for the elevator.

"What?" Quinn says innocently when I roll my eyes.

Crossing my arms over my chest and ignoring his chuckling, I occupy myself with the elevator's progress, watching for its arrival.

"It worked, didn't it?" he says, stepping in front of me and unfolding my arms.

I struggle but don't stand a chance against his strong hands. He may have succeeded in uncrossing my arms, but that doesn't mean I have to look at him. Thankfully, our elevator arrives, and I walk in, leaning back against the silver railing as Quinn casually strolls in, swiping the card and pushing our floor number.

Some cocky businessman shouts at us to hold the door, but Quinn presses the button, making the elevator slide shut. He gives the disgruntled man a sarcastic wave through the closing doors. Normally, I would find his defiant behavior comical, but now, I'm in no mood to laugh. And that's because, who knew, I'm a jealous person.

I hate that most women would happily fuck him, no questions asked. I know the reason behind it was for our benefit, but it still pisses me off. I don't like this feeling of uncertainty, and I certainly don't like this feeling of raging jealousy I experience every time someone loses their shit over Quinn—which is *all* the time.

I don't realize I'm grinding down on my jaw until the cart stops with a jerk, and I fall forward.

Snapping out of my daze, I meet Quinn's stare. "W-what happened?"

"I stopped the elevator," he replies coolly, crossing his arms over his chest and leaning up against the mirrored wall.

"Why?"

"Because we're not going anywhere until you tell me what's wrong."

"Nothing's wrong." I lunge for the control panel to start the elevator. But Quinn slaps my hand away.

"Bullshit. Tell me," he demands, taking a step toward me while I step back.

"Nothing," I stubbornly huff, my back hitting the wall, and I'm trapped as he advances.

"You think I *liked* her?"

"No," I mumble, looking away. I can't meet his baffled eyes because I'm being so irrational.

"Then what is it?" he says, leaning his body into mine, our chests inches apart.

"I…"

"You what, Red?" He places his finger under my chin, forcing me to look at him.

I see nothing but concern reflected in his deep eyes and feel horrible for getting angry with him. He's doing all of this for us.

For me.

"I'm jealous," I finally confess with a blush.

"Of the clerk?" he asks in disbelief, pulling a repulsed face.

"No. Yes. I don't know. Start the elevator," I say, attempting to push him aside, but he won't budge.

"Tell me what you're thinking."

I know he won't let this go, and I owe him the truth. "I'm jealous of every girl looking at you, all right. Happy?" I snap, narrowing my eyes at him.

Quinn nibbles on his hoop, head poised to the side. But he's obviously not happy with my response. "Why? Why are you jealous?"

He wants me to say it. He wants me to tell him that…he's mine. So I will.

"Because you're m—" I yell but am interrupted by a nasal voice through the intercom.

"Excuse me. This is reception. Is everything okay in there?"

No! I scream within but settle for, "Yes."

"Your car seems to have stopped. We're getting maintenance to have a look. Sit tight."

Looking at Quinn from under my lashes, I slowly reach around him to push the emergency button. The elevator resumes its journey like nothing happened.

But it did.

And now I have to deal with the consequences.

I can see why they call this suite the Empire Suite. This room could easily house a large family and their pets.

Speaking of which. Lucky has his own room, equipped with a heated doggy bed. I wouldn't believe a hotel such as this would allow pets, but thankfully, they do.

What I also can't believe is the extravagant size of the bed.

I'm nervously eyeing it while leaning on the kitchen's marbled counter, sipping a beer. Draped in gold and maroon linen and a million and one throw cushions, this bed was made for rolling around on without fear of falling off.

The conversation in the elevator has played on repeat in my mind. What would Quinn have said if I admitted I see him as being mine? Would we be making use of that inviting bed right now? That thought scares me.

And it's not because I don't want to.

Quite the contrary, and *that's* what scares me.

I lose all control when Quinn is involved, and it's a feeling I'm not used to. After relying on no one other than myself for such a long time, letting someone in like Quinn changes everything. But am I ready for that change? I have a feeling there will be no turning back once I embrace it.

"Starting early?" Quinn says from behind me, startling me.

As I turn, I see him running his hands through his damp hair, which does not help the perverted images that plague my brain involving that huge bed.

His white T-shirt hugs every hardened inch of his chiseled torso, and I try to close my gaping mouth, but it's a struggle when I see the top button of his blue jeans is undone.

"I'm going downstairs," I blurt out while pushing off the counter, as I want some time to clear my head.

"Give me a sec, and I'll come down with you," he says, looking for his shoes.

"No, it's okay. I wouldn't mind checking the place out."

Quinn understands I mean alone.

"I don't think that's such a good idea."

"I won't be long," I say over my shoulder. I'm out the door

before he can follow or argue with me.

My boots thump against the carpeted floor as I walk down the hallway and into the elevator, deep in thought.

I've never been in lust or *love* before.

Before meeting my friends in South Boston, I didn't even know what love felt like—how could I? My mom split, my dad had no qualms about using me for his gain, and the people I associated with were only in love with the junk they injected or snorted.

But this, with Quinn, is this something like love? This all-consuming, overpowering urge to be near someone. Is that what love is?

I need a drink. Thankfully, I don't have to look too far.

I see the hotel bar up ahead as the elevator doors slide open. Not watching where I'm going, I bump into a little old man in gray suspenders and trousers. My heart freezes when I see the silver-rimmed glasses perched on his narrow nose.

"Are you okay, child?" he asks, his kind hands bracing my upper arms to support me from falling.

My eyes descend on his hands, mesmerized by each wrinkle, each crease representing a chapter in his life. And the feeling of guilt I've managed to push down into the pit of my stomach comes gurgling up, threatening to spill free from my body in a wave of terror.

Remorse.

Shame.

Anger.

But most of all, utter guilt overwhelms me when I realize that Hank's wrinkled hands will no longer add another crease or chapter to his life because he's dead.

"Child?" he asks again when I remain catatonic.

Child...

Tears burn behind my lids, and vomit slowly rises up my throat. But I mentally slap myself, forcing my mouth to speak and my feet to move.

"I'm fine. S-sorry."

I'm running out the front door before my brain can catch up to where I'm going.

Many hours and many shots later, I'm in some bar, wearing colorful beads and feathers in my hair.

I don't know where I am, or how I got here. But what I do know is that I've buried the pain by drowning my guilt in every spirit known to humankind.

Lucky for me, New Orleans doesn't have strict policies on checking IDs.

I'm sitting in a corner on my own, watching humans interact with one another like it doesn't hurt to exist. I wish I knew how to do that because, at the moment, it hurts to breathe.

My run-in with the Hank look-alike has sent me into a funk that I don't think I'll be able to pull myself out of anytime soon. The only way to deal with this is to get drunk. Really, *really* drunk—which goes against everything I believe in. But I can't face my life right now.

Two girls sitting at a table off to my right are laughing happily and whispering their deepest, darkest secrets, and I envy them. I envy them because I want to be them. I was them. For a moment in my life, I was normal.

But now. Now I'm reminded that I'm anything *but* normal. I never will be.

"Hey, you look like you could use another. Let me buy

you a drink."

As I look up and meet the eyes of a stranger who looks insipidly normal, I suddenly crave that normalcy. I need it to get through today.

"Sure," I reply, meeting his big blue eyes. "Why not?"

He takes a seat, eyeing my arrangement of empty glasses in front of me with a smile.

"I'd ask what you're drinking, but it looks like you're not fussy."

He raises his hand, and a server in a tight white shirt and black jeans saunters over, holding a tray.

"Is a rum and Coke okay?" he asks, looking at me politely.

"Sure."

The server bounces off, and the man turns to me, cocking his groomed dark eyebrow.

"So rough day?"

I laugh and then cringe because it sounds homicidal.

"You don't wanna know," I reply, sipping the rest of my beer.

He nods, respecting my reply. "What's your name?"

It's out before I can stop myself.

"Paige."

He can never know the real me because the real me is someone no one wants to know.

"Well, Paige, I'm Sean. Nice to meet you." He extends his hand over my mound of glasses.

As my hand slips into his, there are no fireworks, no static—just nothing. Unlike Quinn, who can set me alight with a look alone.

"Likewise. So what brings you to…" I look around, trying to work out where we are. "Wherever the hell we are."

We make small talk, and Sean proves to be quite a

distraction, which is surprising. We've been sitting and drinking for a while, and I haven't wanted to bail or claw my eyeballs out in boredom.

"What time is it?" I ask, knocking back a shot and making a pained face when the booze hits my empty stomach.

Sean holds up his watch and closes an eye to focus. "A little after midnight."

"Oh fuck," I mutter, grabbing his arm to look at his watch myself because he's surely mistaken.

But he's not.

I've been drinking with Sean for…I'm not sure how many hours, but it's been a long, long time.

"You got someplace to be?" Sean asks with a smile, twirling his shot glass.

A niggling voice screams at me to say thank you and good night to Sean, but that would mean I would have to deal with the wrath of Quinn.

"Nope." I shake my head, my hair slipping free from my bun. "The next round is on me."

The next ten rounds are on me, and I know I'll regret this in the morning.

But I'll deal with it then because right now, I can't even remember my name, let alone the bullshit mess I'm in. But I know that has nothing to do with the booze and everything to do with my brain needing a night off from overthinking.

"Where're you staying?" Sean asks when we get kicked out of the bar because it's closing time.

"Hmm, Château Rousse." I trip over a step as I hit the sidewalk.

Sean whistles as I straighten up. "That's a long way away."

"It is?" I ask, blowing my hair out of my face as the wind has picked up.

"Yeah, like maybe an hour away," he replies, snuggling into his leather jacket.

"Great."

How did I get here? My alcohol-soaked brain begins churning through the events that led to the now, and I groan. I remember sprinting out of the hotel, haunted by the face of the kind old man who reminded me way too much of Hank. And then I remember the desperate need to run. To keep running until my lungs protested with every step that I took.

After that, I don't remember much else.

This stands against everything I believe in. I see alcohol as a weak excuse to escape reality, just like drugs. And I'm in a strange city, miles away from my knife and Quinn.

He's going to kill me. But I still wish he was here because I miss him.

Looks like my plans of going out to clear my head have fallen flat on their ass. But who was I kidding? Quinn is embedded into my entire being, and the sooner I accept it, the sooner I can stop behaving like this.

I clumsily stumble over a lone beer bottle and smash into Sean, headbutting him. "Shit! I'm so sorry. Are you okay?"

Sean chuckles, taking a step back. "Holy shit! You've got a hard head."

"Oh, you wouldn't believe the half of it," says an irritated voice from behind me.

I shiver, and it's not because it's beginning to rain. No, I shiver in desire for the man behind me. No matter how drunk or lost I am, I will always recognize his voice.

I turn around and see Quinn. His jaw is clenched, his hair

97

is mussed, his eyes are pure black—which all point to the fact that he is pissed.

But his mouth gives away just how mad he is. The way he turns his lip ring between his teeth looks painful, but I'm transfixed by it. And I want it in my mouth.

"Who is this guy?" Sean slurs, grabbing my hand and tugging me lightly toward him.

But I remain fixed on the concrete, unable to move.

Quinn waits to hear my reply, narrowing his dark eyes at me, and I say what I should have said the moment we met.

"He's mine."

Sean begins to protest, but I ignore him and throw myself into Quinn's arms, smashing my cold lips to his. He isn't expecting my actions, as they are sudden and out of the blue, but as soon as I nudge my tongue into his mouth, he opens up and devours me whole.

I whimper as he angrily bites my lip, but he sucks away the pain quickly, and I lose track of space, time, everything. Nothing else matters other than this moment of being consumed by the man I will want with my very last breath.

He grabs the back of my nape, angling my head at a slant, which leaves me vulnerable to the driving force of his unyielding tongue, and I love it. I love the feel of his tongue ring, which strokes me brutally, and I love the way my knees weaken whenever I kiss him.

However, as my knees nearly buckle, I realize it's not only the head rush of Quinn's kisses that have me wobbly-kneed, it's all the booze I've ingested catching up with me.

I pull away breathlessly, my body feeling heated all over, and my eyes droop to half mast. Admiring Quinn's muscular, strong frame, which radiates pure masculinity, I can't stop my mouth from going on a tangent.

"You're so fucking sexy," I say with a hiccup as I wrap my hands around his neck for support.

Quinn's mouth twitches, and he reaches behind him, squeezing my fingers softly.

"You're obviously very drunk," he says, his mouth sloping into a smile. "And I'm going to remind you all about it tomorrow when you're sober."

"I may be drunk, but you're still fucking hot," I say. Unwrapping my hands from around his neck and pointing my finger at him, I suddenly realize there are two of him.

Quinn laughs. "Okay, let's get you inside because there's a storm coming."

"Yeah, there is," I say in a singsong voice, and almost fall flat on my ass.

Quinn smirks while shaking his head, but as the rain begins to get heavier, he grabs my arm and drags me across the street.

"Hey, where are we going?" I slur as the world suddenly tilts on its axis. "Bye, Shane."

"It's Sean."

But the truth is, I don't care what his name is.

"Quinn, where are we going?" I ask again as he continues dragging me down the street.

"Inside," he replies, pulling me into a brightly lit fluorescent foyer that burns my retinas.

Covering my eyes with my forearm, I groan. I guess those last ten or twenty shots were a bad, *bad* idea.

"Can I book a room please?"

I hear muffled voices, but they all sound like gibberish, and all I really want to do is sleep. My eyes droop shut, and I'm pretty certain I have fallen asleep standing up. But as my arm is jerked on and my feet begin moving, my eyes snap open, and my dreams of sleeping have just been shattered.

"Quinn, slow down," I say groggily. I try to slow him down by dragging my feet, but he doesn't listen. "You're a big, bossy meanie."

I can see from one eye, which is the only open eye, that Quinn shakes his head at me, but thankfully, he's smiling. Before I know what's going on, I'm being lifted off the ground and into the arms of my Superman.

My weary arms wrap around his neck inadvertently, and I cradle myself into his warm chest. As I bury my nose into his damp T-shirt, I can't stop myself as I inhale his scent deeply.

"Oh fuck, even your smell is sexy."

Quinn's chest vibrates, and I know he's chuckling at my embarrassing confessions. I need to shut up, but my mouth has a mind of its own.

"You're so warm," I say with a yawn, snuggling into his body and closing my eyes. "I'm just gonna nap. Wake me when we get there."

I have no idea where "there" is, but I trust Quinn with my life.

I hear keys jingle, and then the click of a key turning into a lock.

"Red, I'm going to put you down, okay?" Quinn says after a few seconds of him shuffling through a room.

I nod against his chest, my eyes still shut, my breathing even.

The soft mattress dips when Quinn places me onto the bed, but the contents of my stomach threaten to spill forth if I don't sit up. My eyes snap open as I bolt upright and kick off the bed, wobbly standing in a strange room.

"Where are we?" I ask, trying to focus on where we are.

"Some hotel, far, far away from where we should be," he

replies with a hint of exasperation.

I feel horrible. He's been looking for me this entire time. Why didn't I just wait for him instead of freaking out and running?

I seem to be doing that a lot lately.

And not to mention, we just paid a lot of money for a room we won't even be staying in. Just the thought of the room reminds me of Janet, the overly helpful clerk.

She was one of the reasons I bolted. Not because of her, per se, but because my feelings for Quinn keep getting stronger and stronger, and I don't know how to deal with them.

So again, I ran.

But the biggest reason was of course, Hank.

My pain cannot be summarized into words, and that's because simply no words can describe how I feel. When I picture the light leaving his warm, tender eyes, the feelings from that night come crashing over me, and each time, it's getting harder to swim to the surface.

I'm a damn mess, and I'm seriously questioning my mental stability as each day passes. I'm also angry. And I'm sick of it because the person I'm most angry with is myself.

Suddenly, I feel hot, as these clothes are swiftly suffocating me. I rip off my sweater, nearly falling on my ass while trying to get my arms out, but I manage to do so staying upright.

Unthinkingly, I reach for the hem of my T-shirt and pull it over my head, it snagging on my tragus.

"Ouch!" I muffle, but thankfully it slips free without ripping my ear off.

"Red, what are you doing?" Quinn's voice is muffled because my head is still tangled under my shirt.

"Getting undressed, Captain Obvious," I reply, finally tearing the shirt off and discarding it onto the floor.

As my eyes focus, I see him slowly scan down my body. And as I watch him tug at his lip ring, I wonder what the hell is wrong with him. He's seen me in my bra before, given this is a little more forward, as I'm usually slipping a T-shirt over my head and him catching me getting dressed, as opposed to being undressed.

But he's looking at me like he's about to attack.

I look down, wondering what the fuss is all about, and realize I'm wearing the new bra I purchased a few days ago. My *very* transparent lacy bra. And because it's cold, my nipples are pretty much on display, as the lacy material does nothing to cover them.

I should be wrapping my arms around myself, shielding my nudity, but I don't. I like the way Quinn's chest dips on each deep inhalation and expands with each exhalation. It shows me he's as affected by me as I am by him.

"Red," he says, and the hitch in his voice has me stepping toward him.

I want so desperately for him to touch me, and if it's the alcohol giving me courage with each step I take, I don't care. All I know is that I want his hands on me because I feel most alive when they are.

"Touch me," I whisper within a few steps of him.

Quinn clenches his fists and exhales through his nostrils, his breath coming out unevenly.

"Please put your top back on," he says, walking away from me.

"No," I reply defiantly. "Touch me. Please."

Hesitantly reaching for his clenched fist, I slowly move it toward my chest. But he tears it away, turning his back to me. His shoulders are rising and falling quickly, his breaths leaving him in labored pants.

Is he angry with me?

"Quinn...I..."

"Red, please," he says and does something I never expected him to do.

He walks out the door, slamming it shut behind him.

What the fuck?

A tsunami of emotion drowns me, and I feel vulnerable and exposed. So I reach down and slip on my T-shirt with shaky hands.

What just happened? I practically threw myself at Quinn, and he shot me down. He knew how hard that was for me, yet he still turned me down.

Suddenly, a horrible thought hits me. Doesn't he want me that way anymore? Doesn't he want *me*? Has he finally realized how bad I am for him?

How bad of a person I am.

That thought has me running to the bathroom, heaving up the entire contents of my stomach until nothing remains. But it's still not enough.

However, sadly, I just feel the emptiness taking over until all that is left is pain.

Six

I wake the following morning, hurting everywhere. My whole body aches—inside and out.

After purging my guts out, the pain was still there, so I decided to sleep it off, but sleeping without Quinn's warmth was near impossible. But I must have slept some because it's now morning.

It's the day of Hank's funeral.

The slice of sunlight that pokes its happy head out through the blinds does nothing to transfer any warmth into my life.

I'm dead inside.

I know Quinn's reason for coming here was to sidetrack me, an attempt to distract me from the reality that by the end of today, Hank will be buried in a small hole in the ground. And I have a sneaking suspicion that's what Tabitha grilled Quinn about on the phone.

Everyone worries about me like usual—and all I have done is cause them pain.

My stomach roils with nausea, and the burn is welcomed.

I need to feel.

I deserve it.

I look to my left and wonder where Quinn is, as the bed beside me hasn't been slept in.

My problem with being drunk is that I remember almost everything—no luxury of blackouts or memory loss. I remember every damn embarrassing moment, wishing I didn't. I'm beyond mortified I threw myself at him, calling him mine when he clearly isn't interested in me. If I were him, I would be running the hell away from me too.

Groaning and throwing my arm over my eyes, I wish I could singe the repulsed look in Quinn's eyes from my mind. But sadly, I can't.

I kick off the covers, then head to the bathroom for a hot shower. After standing under the hot water until I shrivel into a prune, I get out and brush my wet hair, then use the complimentary toiletries.

Twenty minutes later, I look human. Well, half human. The other half is a robot, functioning on autopilot.

Quinn is still nowhere in sight, and I have to face the fact that he may never return. He may be on his way back to South Boston right now about to turn me in. I know he would never do that, though I wouldn't blame him if he did.

I slip on my boots, grab my sweater, which smells of Quinn, and softly shut the door behind me.

Sean said I was about an hour from my hotel. Well, that gives me a lot of time to plan what the fuck to do now.

I slip the cab driver an extra twenty since he remained quiet the whole cab ride back to our hotel, obviously picking up on my need for silence. I don't have the energy for idle chitchat.

I walk the streets of New Orleans with no real direction in mind. I walk and walk, unable to stay in one spot for too long as my thoughts catch up to me, and I can't deal with them. I spend hours wandering the French Quarter, going into shops I've never seen before and probably will never come across ever again.

As I pass a strip of stores, the food smells delicious, so I decide to grab a spicy Cajun dish. But after two mouthfuls, I have to throw most of it out when my stomach gurgles in protest.

It's dark and cold, and I'm shivering, but I keep walking because I know when I stop, I'll have to face what I've been trying to avoid all day.

Hank is gone.

He's really gone.

He's buried in a plot someplace with a little grave marker, the only article telling the world who he was. What he was. And that grave marker, I know, cannot contain all the words to do Hank justice because there aren't any words. There will never be enough words to do him justice.

My eyes take in the bright lights around me, but I'm only drawn to one thing. Something I've *never* been drawn to before. Something I never gave much thought to until I met Hank.

I ascend the bluestone steps, gazing up at a place that

has never appealed to me in the past, but now, it's screaming out my name, drawing me in. Pushing open the heavy doors, them creaking in protest, I try to muffle the sounds of my boots on the polished wooden floors as it's so quiet and calm.

Taking a seat in the back and looking from side to side, I really don't know what to do next. A middle-aged woman sits two rows across from me, so I watch her. I watch her lips move silently, and as she closes her eyes, a look of serenity and peace colors her cheeks.

Is that what's supposed to happen? At the end of it all, are we supposed to experience peace?

Taking a deep breath, I slowly drop to my knees and interlace my hands, and…I pray.

"Hi, God. It's Mia. Long time no speak. I'll keep it short because I don't deserve more than a minute of your time. I accept my life for what it is. But I can't accept the fact that Hank is dead. I don't understand, and I'm trying really hard to. But I'm angry, and I'm pissed off. Why wasn't it me? Why did you take *him* instead of me?" I pause, my lip trembling. "It was his funeral today. And I didn't even get to say goodbye."

Tears fall from my weary eyes, but I silently continue.

"Hank believed in you. But I didn't. I still don't. But then I question myself. You must exist to have created someone as beautiful and as kind as Hank. So I'd like to think that wherever he is, he's happy and with Betty."

My tears run into my lips and down my chin, but I don't wipe them away. "If heaven really does exist, then I know he would be there. So please tell him I miss him, and that I… love him."

A sob escapes me, and I whisper, "Goodbye, Grandpa."

I don't know how long I sit, staring at the stained glass window in front of me, but it must be a while. Leaving the church, I feel I've made peace with…something. But it's still not enough. Only when I'm standing over my father's and Phil's dead bodies will it be enough.

The cold air hits me as soon as I step outside. I keep walking, my feet protesting with each step I take, but I keep going until I finally arrive at my hotel.

But the truth is, I don't know if Quinn is here.

I'm literally on autopilot as I enter the elevator, pushing the button to my floor. The sappy love song playing softly over the speakers hurts my brain, and once the elevator arrives on my floor, I get out, walking like a robot to my room.

I don't have a key, so I gingerly knock on the door, hoping that Quinn is inside and not someone else.

"There you are!"

I open my mouth but am robbed of air when Quinn wraps his arms around me and hugs me tight.

Instantly, the worry plaguing me floats away because being in Quinn's arms makes everything all right.

"Red, where have you been? I have been looking everywhere for you!"

"I went for a walk," I muffle against his shoulder.

"Where did you walk to? Australia? You've been gone for over twelve hours!"

"I have?" I ask in a daze, pulling out of his arms.

"Yeah. Are you okay?" Quinn questions as I stare vacantly at him.

I shake my head, but, "Yes," slips past my lips.

I'm so not okay, but I don't want to talk about it, especially after he bailed on me last night.

"How do you know how long I've been gone for?" I reply, confused. "You were gone when I left. I just assumed you…"

"I, what? Split?"

I nod, lowering my eyes. "I wouldn't blame you if you had."

A loud exhale leaves him before he grips my wrist and pulls me inside.

"What's that supposed to mean?"

I don't want to have this conversation, so I walk backward, hoping to hide in the bathroom. But Quinn stops me.

"Answer me."

He wants to talk to me *now* after he all but ran out on me last night, making me feel like an utter fool.

I meet his eyes, which are filled with concern and confusion as he waits for an explanation.

"Because you all but ran away from me last night. I don't know how to be sexy or flirty like other girls, but I was honest, something I've never been with anyone, not even myself. And to have you throw that back in my face…fucking hurts."

"Red—" But I cut him off.

"I bared myself to you, and you just shrugged it off like it wasn't a big deal. I know for you it probably wasn't, but for me, it was. I've never done that with anyone before. I've never been vulnerable with another person. And to have you reject me that way, to not want me, hurts. I may not be your typical girl, but underneath all this baggage and bad attitude, I'm still just a girl!"

And now, I take a breath.

"Is that what you think? That I don't want you?"

"Well, isn't it?"

Nothing makes sense. Not that it ever did. But now, everything is a big fucking mess.

Quinn closes his eyes, and I know once he opens them, he'll reveal a big secret that'll change everything.

"No, it's not," he says, opening his eyes. "It's so far from the truth it's not even funny. I fucking *want* you. And I have never wanted anything, needed anyone, as much as I do you."

"Then why did you leave last night? I needed you. As pathetic as that makes me, I needed you to make me forget." He doesn't need me to clarify what I needed to forget. "Why do you always stop me when I try to touch you? You won't let me in, and that's unfair because you know everything there is to know about me."

"Because," he says, storming toward me. "Because, Red…I don't want you to stop looking at me the way that you do."

This conversation is a familiar one, as it's one we had not so long ago when the tables were turned.

"How do I look at you?" I ask softly.

"Like I'm *worth* looking at. Like I'm worth *something*," he replies.

"You don't realize how much you're worth," I whisper.

"I'm not a good person," he says, and I suddenly realize Quinn has lived my past in his own way.

He has a soul-crushing secret that consumes him just like I did. But I have to make it better for him, just as he did for me.

"Yes, you are. You wouldn't have left your home for me if you weren't. And you wouldn't put yourself in danger for me, time and time again."

He takes a deep breath, his beautiful features contorting with his confession. "Last night when you said I was yours, you don't realize how badly I wanted that to be true."

I gasp at his confession, but he continues.

"Then to see you open up to me, asking me to touch you, goddamn, I'm an asshole because that's all I wanted to do. That's *all* I ever want to do. I have to stop myself from touching you every goddamn second of the fucking day."

"Why?" I ask, confused and stunned by his admission.

"Because I don't deserve you. I don't deserve to be happy, and with you, Red, that's what I am—happy. And the guilt I feel knowing that eats away at me. I don't deserve any happiness because…"

But he doesn't continue and lowers his eyes.

"Why don't you deserve to be happy?"

When he meets my eyes, I can see the pain behind his, and I know that Quinn lives with whatever he did every second of his life.

"You're not the only one who has a past. But like I told you, you didn't have a choice…but I did."

"What did you do?"

But it doesn't matter what he did because it would never change how I feel about him.

He only shakes his head, his hair shadowing his torn eyes. "I can't tell you."

"You're fucking kidding me. After everything, you still won't tell me? After everything we've been through?"

He firmly shakes his head once again, chewing on his lip ring. "No."

His curt reply hurts, and I feel like I've been slapped with his distrust. "Fuck you, Quinn Berkeley."

I turn on my heel, not sure where I'm going because I just got back.

"Where do you think you're going?"

"I'm not sure, but anywhere is better than here."

I'm trying to be understanding because I have firsthand experience with how Quinn feels. I've lived it. But back then, I didn't know him. I didn't know I could trust him with my secret like he knows he can with me.

Or does he?

"You're not going anywhere." He steps in front of the door, arms crossed.

"Oh please, what are you going to do? Gag me? Tie me to the bed? Throw me over your shoulder? You're all talk. Now move," I demand, my voice never wavering as I stand my ground.

The air sizzles with an unseen static, and as we stare at one another, our chests rising and falling steadily, I know something big is about to happen.

I just don't anticipate what.

Quinn is on me before I have time to back away, but who am I kidding? I lunge for him at the same moment he lunges for me. He pushes me up against the wall, his warm body entrapping mine. Our mouths collide, and it feels like an atomic bomb exploded, causing a ripple effect throughout my entire being.

I can't get close enough to him, fast enough. I'm in desperate need to consume him whole, but it's still not enough. I claw my fingernails down his back as I reach underneath his T-shirt.

And I can't stop.

Neither can Quinn, as his hands and mouth seek out every part of me. His hoop bites into my lip, and I moan, loving the pain. His hand braces the back of my head, controlling the intensity of the kiss, and I happily comply because there is nothing I want more than this.

His other hand slips under my shirt, and I gasp at the skin-to-skin contact. As his fingers trail up my torso, stopping at my right breast, he matches the rhythm of his mouth to complement the feverish way his fingers begin rubbing over my nipple.

I'm squirming under his hand, wishing to feel his touch

against my bare skin. He reads my needs and slips a finger into my mouth while we kiss before pushing my bra cup aside and circling my nipple with his finger.

The sensation has a gasp leaving me and a yearning steadily throbs between my legs as he places long, wet kisses down my throat, sucking over my pounding pulse. I'm hot and needy, and I want, no, I *need* a release.

I need it before I explode.

"Don't worry, I'll get you off," he promises against my throat.

His huge hard-on presses against me, and I want him all over me. I slip my hand between us and rub over his dick.

Quinn's fingers still, and he groans, leaning his head forward, his long hair brushing my cheeks.

"That feels amazing," he commends hoarsely.

His words spur me on.

I want more than anything to do to him what he does to me when he places his hands on me. But I don't know how.

"Show me."

He bites his lip ring as I begin to stroke him faster.

"I will. But you first," he says, slipping out of my hold and removing his fingers from the inside of my bra.

I whimper, but that turns into a groan as he grips my hip with one hand while the other flicks open the top button of my jeans and slips into the front of my pants. His hand stills when he feels I have no underwear on.

He cocks an eyebrow at me. "Oh, Red...you're a bad, bad girl."

I moan louder as he sinks a finger inside me, sliding in with no difficulty.

With my tight-fitting jeans, Quinn has limited space to work with, but that makes it hotter. I'm shamefully riding his hand as he stretches me wide with another finger, his thumb rubbing over my clit, and I scream, about to come.

I brace my hand on his shoulder, unable to hold myself up.

"Not yet," he commands, slowing the tempo of his fingers, his thumb lessening the pressure, knowing how close I am.

I whimper, wanting nothing more than to come, but Quinn has other ideas. I can see it in the way his mouth tips into a slanted smirk.

"I want you in my mouth when you do."

I'm too far gone to blush or shy away because I want it too. I want it so bad my fingers overlap his, about to finish the job myself. However, he removes my hand.

I moan as I'm desperate to get my pants off before I burst into flames.

"Take your jeans and T-shirt off."

I reach down to untie my boots, but Quinn shakes his head slowly.

"Leave the boots. Just the jeans and T-shirt."

My eyes widen, unsure why he's requesting this, but by the heated look in his eyes, I know I'll like whatever he has planned.

Shyly fumbling with the hem of my T-shirt, I quickly yank it off over my head, only standing in my bra and jeans, which sit dangerously low on my hips.

My hands awkwardly hang by my sides, anxious to cover my sudden bareness. But I don't because as Quinn's eyes heat hotter than the pits of hell, I know his response is elicited because of me. And I like it.

So I stand bravely, my deep breathing the only betrayal of my nervousness.

Quinn's tongue darts out to wet his lower lip, and my

breath hitches, knowing what that tongue can do to my body.

"Jeans," he says, pointing at my legs.

Why is he just standing there and staring? This would be a lot easier if he did it himself. And if there wasn't so much light.

Quinn can see me mull over his request and slowly reaches to his left. He flips off the light, shrouding the room in partial darkness, and it's simply beautiful.

My clumsy fingers fumble as I slowly glide my jeans down my legs, and I ensure my eyes never leave Quinn's as they reach the floor. They are tight fitting, but I manage to get them past my boots without taking them off.

I kick them onto the floor and shyly stand to full height, totally bared to Quinn's heated stare. I feel nervous, but I also feel excited. However, I'm grateful the lights have been switched off because I can sense Quinn's hunger even in the darkness.

I shift my legs, attempting to conceal myself, but Quinn stops me by stepping toward me. "You're the most beautiful thing I have ever seen."

But all sentiment is pushed aside when he orders, "Hands against the wall."

I don't know why he's asking me to do this, but I nervously obey, my heart pounding with each movement.

"Spread your legs," Quinn whispers as he drops to his knees behind me.

"W-what are you doing?" I stumble over my words as my tongue sticks to the roof of my mouth.

"Worshipping a Siren."

My breath hitches, and as the cool air brushes over my drenched core when I slowly spread my legs wider, I shiver in absolute desire, knowing he means every word.

Quinn runs his lips along the back of my left thigh, and I automatically attempt to shut my legs, embarrassed.

"Nuh-uh," he scolds lightly, catching his hands on my inner thighs to stop them from moving an inch.

He glides his hands up my legs and cups my ass. My insides involuntarily clench as he squeezes, and my stomach ripples in excitement.

"Arch your back," he gently commands.

I do as he says, aware that I'm spread wide open to him. I anticipate what comes next, and I know Quinn prolongs his next move to torment me further.

He places a hand on the back of my thigh while he grips my waist with the other and coaxes me onto his face. A blush spreads from head to toe, but I forget all coyness when Quinn tongues my sex in one long, agonizing lick.

A shudder rocks me so hard, but Quinn doesn't give my shaky legs a minute to steady as he thrusts me even farther back, granting him deeper access to his hot tongue. A moan leaves my parted lips as my head droops forward and my eyes slip shut.

His skillful tongue works deep inside me, thoroughly exploring every part of me. I moan, as Quinn owns my body without apology, and I love it.

He bites over my clit, and I buckle, suddenly aware of why Quinn told me to stand here. I'm able to hold myself up when pleasure overcomes me, and my legs are about to give out at any moment when he flicks his tongue back and forth over my center.

I never thought I could feel sexy standing in just a bra and boots, but I do. I feel like a total goddess.

"Holy fuck," I gasp as Quinn buries his face deeper into my sex and thrusts his tongue in and out.

He encourages me to rock on his face as he eats me out without shame. His rough stubble brushes over my ripened flesh, and I bite my lip, tasting blood. He holds me prisoner—his hands, mouth, and tongue—and I never want to be set free.

His hands on my hips coax me to buck faster and harder, and it's like he knows my body better than me because it's exactly what I need to chase my release.

My hands are splayed against the wall, but when Quinn grips an ass cheek and spreads me wide so he can devour me from front to back, I slam my fist against it, moaning in utter bliss.

"More," I shamefully demand, pumping my hips and fucking his face.

And more he gives as he moves his face back and forth, back and forth, his tongue penetrating me deep.

I lose myself to the rhythm. My body is wound so tight, and each stroke of Quinn's tongue makes me so desperate to come. But I don't want to give up this feeling—not yet. So I resist temptation and hold back my release as I focus on the present.

I focus on Quinn's wicked tongue. The way it strokes me in all the right ways. His tongue ring only adds to the delicious torture as he works me into a breathless mess. I'm so full, and when he circles my clit before sucking hard, I come undone loudly, my body convulsing and almost collapsing, my spaghetti arms only just holding me up.

But Quinn doesn't give me a reprieve.

He spins me around and begins tonguing me again, my hypersensitive skin on fire.

I scream, gripping his long hair.

Quinn pulls his mouth away, replacing his tongue with

two long fingers.

"Fuck," I whimper, looking down and watching how he plays with me wickedly.

He wraps his hand around my waist to steady me. But his other hand never misses a beat. He fingers me relentlessly, and before long, my body greedily demands another release.

He senses my fatigue and removes his fingers from deep within.

I protest with a sigh, and he chuckles.

"Don't worry, I'll take care of you, baby."

I don't question why and simply do it, and watch in awe as Quinn buries his head between my legs.

He's on his knees, dominating and submitting all in the same breath. I tug on the long strands of hair and shamelessly ride his face.

I cry out louder than before as my body is sore, but the pain is beyond pleasurable because it's more heightened this time. As he buries his face deeper between my thighs, I hook one leg over his shoulder, opening the angle, and Quinn takes full advantage of it.

He uses his mouth and fingers—fucking me with both.

I can't take my eyes off him and the way he eats me out. He is pure sin. And he's all mine.

"You're…mine," I manage to push out on a breath.

Quinn pulls off my sex, but his fingers never still. "Say it again."

Our eyes are locked, a silent promise that this means more to us than simply getting off. This is forever.

"You're mine. And—"

"And?" he coaxes, running his tongue along his bottom lip.

The visual is so fucking hot that I can't contain my

whimper.

"And I'm…yours."

Quinn closes his eyes for a split second and inhales deeply. He inhales in victory.

"Yes, Red," he says, opening his eyes. "You are."

He lowers his mouth to my sex, gripping my thighs and coaxing me to spread them wider. The heel of my boot digs into Quinn's back, and when I press down harder, he groans, enjoying the pain.

It seems we both do.

I'm so close to coming again.

Quinn slows the tempo and pulls away but is still inches away from my sex. "I want nothing more," he whispers, his warm breath fanning over my flesh, "than to bury myself inside you. But when that happens, and it *will* happen, Red, I want you squirming underneath me, *begging* me to fuck you."

I convulse, nearly coming at his sinful promise, and I know that's his intention.

"So, for now, I'll have you begging me for something else." He spreads me wide and buries his tongue deep, but he's dancing over where I want him to be.

I now understand what he means by having me beg. He's in no real hurry as he languidly fucks me with his mouth, waiting for my pleas.

I whimper as the ache between my legs heightens with each stroke, and I can't take it a second longer.

"Please," I beg softly.

"Please what?"

"Please…make me—"

"Make you what?" he asks, peering up at me.

I'm so needy and don't waver as I command, "Please make me come."

Quinn growls, pulling on his lip ring before planting his head firmly between my legs and eating me out with an intensity so fierce that I cry out loud.

But I can't stop.

My moans get louder and louder, and suddenly, tears of pleasure burn my eyes.

"Okay, baby," he huskily states. "I'll make you come."

He sucks over my clit while fucking me with his tongue and mouth. I don't stand a chance.

A wave of pure ecstasy tackles me hard, and if not for Quinn wrapping his hands around my waist, I would have fallen to the floor. But I happily ride this feeling because for the first time in my life...I feel free.

Finally, after what seems like hours, my body calms, but every so often, a shudder rocks me, still coming down from a drug that isn't manufactured—it's pure.

It's pure Quinn.

My whole body feels numb and floppy, and when Quinn stands and kisses me, I realize I'm a selfish lover. I'm sure Quinn needs a release too.

I reach down between us, stroking his hard-on.

But he stops me as he bends low, scooping me up and cradling me to his chest.

"What are you doing?"

"Putting you to bed," he replies as he strolls toward it.

"But what about you?"

"That was more for me than for you."

"I seriously doubt it."

Quinn chuckles as he pulls the blanket back and lays me on the white sheets. I then remember I still have my boots on and make a move to take them off. But Quinn is there first, placing one on his lap as he unties my laces.

"I can do that," I say, flopping back onto the soft pillow and closing my eyes.

"I don't mind." He slips off one boot and then goes to work on the next.

"Thank you."

"It's okay. I like taking care of you," he whispers, bending forward and kissing my ankle softly.

"I like it too."

Seven

I'm so comfy, wrapped up like a burrito, but as I feel a pair of lips brush over my cheek, my eyes slip open, wanting to see the man before me.

"Do you ever sleep?" I mumble as his lips flutter over mine.

Quinn chuckles, kissing my chin. "I sleep enough. And besides, it's hard getting a decent night's sleep with you being all over the bed."

I blush, as this isn't the first time he's told me this. It's hard to share, especially when I've never had to before.

Quinn leans on his side, head propped up on his palm, looking down at me. "So I was thinking…" He pauses, mulling over what to say next. "Will you go out with me?"

I choke on air, my bodily functions refusing to operate until I clarify what he means.

"Go…out with you?" I ask slowly, raising my eyebrows.

Quinn clears his throat. If I didn't know better, I'd say he's nervous. Well, there *is* a first for everything.

"Yeah, like a date," he says, making a pained face. "I sound like such an idiot."

I place my hand against his cheek. "No, you don't. You sound sweet."

"Red, I think we've had the whole 'sweet is not cool' talk." He smirks, leaning into my palm.

"I'd love to go out on a date with you, Quinn Berkeley," I say with a smile, the words rolling off my tongue naturally.

"Really?"

"Without a doubt." I feel like a giddy teenager because this is my first ever date. And I wouldn't want to experience it with anyone other than Quinn.

"I just thought, after everything we've done…" My cheeks heat as the memories of last night come floating back. "That we skipped a step."

"What do you mean?"

"I thought you said you didn't do flowers and romance," I reply, referring to our conversation that seems like a lifetime ago.

"I don't. But you're the exception to that rule."

I can't keep the smile off my face.

"And besides, my mom would have given me an earful for not taking a nice girl like you out first before I…" He tugs on his silver hoop.

"You know you can tell me anything," I whisper, searching his face.

He nods as he reaches for a strand of my hair, placing it above my lip to give me an instant mustache. I smile, fully aware that he is attempting to steer me off the topic of his

123

mom. But I won't budge on this and cock my head to the side in all seriousness.

"Whatever it is, I will never judge you. I mean, I'm certainly not one to point fingers," I say, trying to brush his finger off my lip.

"I know," he replies, tickling my nose with my lock of hair, distracted by his memories.

I want to know everything there is about Quinn. Good *and* bad. It won't change my feelings for him, feelings I've never felt for another.

"But not now." He smiles, tapping the end of my nose with his finger and letting my hair go. "Because you have to get ready."

"Where are we going?" I ask, watching him hungrily as he gets off the bed, his bare, ripped chest facing me.

I still haven't asked him about his tattoo, but I can see intricate script writing rising out of his pants and hugging his ribs.

"First, breakfast. And then, wherever you want to go."

I bite my lip, feeling like a nervous schoolgirl. "I've always wanted to go for a boat ride down the Mississippi River. If you wanted to, of course."

Quinn kneels by the bed, leaning into me. "Then we'll ride down the Mississippi till we get kicked off the boat."

"And what if that never happens?" I reply with a smile.

"Then we'll ride it all night until you're ready to leave."

"That sounds amazing."

Quinn places a quick kiss on my lips, then stands to his full height. "It sure does. So hurry that sweet ass outta bed. I'll meet you downstairs."

"Downstairs?" I sit up, gripping the sheet to my chest.

"Yup," he replies with a smirk. I know he's up to something, but I don't get a chance to ask him because he's out the door in a flash, grabbing a shirt along the way.

This man is just too good to be true.

Taking one last look in the mirror, I think I look okay for my first date at age nineteen. And it doesn't matter that it's taken me nineteen years to be asked out on a date because it's with Quinn.

I'm wearing my skinny black jeans, the only pair I own without a hole in them, and a cute off-the-shoulder sweater. My hair is down. My makeup is light.

I take the elevator downstairs, and my heart begins beating like crazy, which is stupid since I just saw Quinn a little while ago. But isn't this what first dates are all about—sweaty palms, heart palpitations, and high hopes?

The elevator doors slide open, and I take a deep breath before stepping out into the foyer, but that breath is in vain because when I see Quinn, it hitches in my throat, threatening to choke me.

And that's not because his hotness takes my breath away. No, it's because Quinn stands leaning against the wall with a bouquet of white tulips in his hands.

I can't believe he bought me flowers.

"Hi," I say with a small smile as I approach him.

"Hi. You look amazing."

"Thanks."

This is awkward and feels exactly how a first date should feel. And I like it. I like that I'm experiencing all my firsts with Quinn.

"Are those for me?" I ask when Quinn continues to stare

at me.

"No," he replies with a smirk, finally meeting my eyes.

"Oh."

"Of course, they are," he says, handing them to me.

"Jerk." I smile, accepting them, and I can't help but laugh, as this is not considered normal to your average person.

But I've given up on that dream long ago because to me, this is something like normal.

"I can't believe how beautiful it is out here," I gasp, looking over the railing of our rickety paddle wheeler into the murky depths of the Mississippi River.

This date has turned out to be one of the best days of my life. And even though I wish circumstances were different, it's still nice to be able to forget, if only for just a while.

Breakfast at Mama Yolanda's was incredible.

Quinn and I had the traditional dish of sickly beignets and a fancy coffee, which was the best coffee I've ever had. Stuffed beyond belief, I suggested we take a walk to burn off our breakfast.

But it really was just an excuse to have another look at all the amazing stores New Orleans has to offer. Of course, Quinn humored me and happily walked by my side as I stopped at every store, window-shopping in awe of the merchandise inside.

After strolling hand in hand, enjoying the sights around us, we boarded the white paddle wheeler and have ridden it for most of the day, just as Quinn promised.

The sky sets with a bright orange, mixed with vibrant pinks, and everything is so fresh and untouched out here. I could stay here forever.

"Thank you for today," I say, looking at Quinn, who leans with his chin on the railing, watching the moon rise. "It's been the best day of my life."

"It's not over yet."

"It's not?" I ask, my eyes widening at the prospect of this day never ending.

Quinn shakes his head, his hair blowing in the gentle breeze. "Come here."

Shifting off the rail, I shuffle over to him. He steps back, indicating I'm to squeeze between him and the ledge, and I couldn't think of a better place to be. I slip between the small gap and sigh the moment he presses his chest to my back.

"I don't know about you, but I'm not ready to say good night just yet," he says, brushing the hair off my shoulder and kissing my neck.

I whimper, and Quinn chuckles, knowing his effect on me.

"As much as I want to eat…you again. I'm going to take you out someplace nice. You deserve better than burgers and fries."

"I don't mind."

"Well, I do."

I dare not disagree with him, fearing he'll stop kissing my neck.

"Okay. We can pretend we're a couple of ordinary kids going out for dinner."

But Quinn stills from kissing me, keeping his lips at my racing pulse. "Nothing about you is ordinary. Nothing at all."

I've had the best day, and I'm so excited there's more to come. Quinn has been secretive about what's next, making me feel like a giddy schoolgirl.

While waiting for the elevator at our hotel, Quinn latches onto my hand and draws me into his arms, kissing my forehead with care. I rest my head against his warm chest, and his familiar, comforting fragrance engulfs my senses.

"I love the way you smell," I say without thinking, realizing I just dropped the L bomb.

Freezing in his arms, afraid of his reaction, I kick myself for not putting a lid on my emotions.

After a second of silence, Quinn whispers, "I love the way you smell, too."

I bite my lip to suppress my moan.

"But I'm sure you already knew that," he says with a hint of seduction.

My cheeks instantly heat, but thankfully, the elevator arrives because I have no idea how to respond. I step in, but Quinn doesn't follow, and I raise an eyebrow, silently questioning him.

"Meet me down here in an hour," he says, giving nothing away.

The elevator doors begin to slide shut, but I hit the button, making the doors jerk open. "Where will you be?"

"I'll be down here, waiting for you," he says, a smile tugging at the corner of his sinful lips.

"I—"

But Quinn reaches into the elevator, prying my finger off the button so the doors quickly shut. As they do, I look at him, his figure becoming narrower, and he smiles, ducking his head to meet my worried eyes.

"See you in an hour."

I attempt to retort, but the doors slam shut on Quinn's smiling face while I'm doing anything but smiling.

What's he up to?

When the elevator reaches our floor, I walk to our room and burst through the door, looking from left to right, attempting to seek any clues as to what is happening. Everything looks the same, and I'm not sure if I should be relieved or frightened.

My eyes take in the pristine condition of the room, and as they fall onto the bed, a flicker of red catches my eye, resulting in my heart skipping a beat. Walking over to the bed quickly, I gasp when I see a stunning red dress draped across the gold duvet.

The long-sleeved dress has an extremely low bustline and looks to come about mid-thigh. I finger the soft material and can't stop the smile from spreading across my cheeks when I see a box of red hair dye sitting near it.

I can't wipe the smile off my face at how thoughtful and how…sweet Quinn is. He's taken this whole first date thing and set the bar pretty high for our second one.

Well, I hope we have a second one.

I walk into the bathroom to dye my hair and get ready. However, as I switch on the light, a laugh leaves me.

Under the towel rack sits a pair of black Doc Martens. Quinn knew I would probably break my neck, ending our fabulous date, if I wore anything other than flats.

I can't believe this; this is too much. He's gone to so much effort, and now I realize what he was up to when he went downstairs this morning.

With no time to waste, it's time for this Cinderella to

prepare for the ball.

I use the hour to get ready, and with two minutes to spare, I look at myself in the wall of mirrors and can't believe the reflection staring back at me.

My newly dyed hair looks fresh and sits curled around my face. My blue eyes are coated in a gray shimmer, and my lashes look insanely long as I've applied ten coats of mascara. I haven't put on a lot of foundation, only a light dusting, and a sheer red gloss coats my lips.

The dress is a little short, but Quinn thankfully supplied a pair of black opaque tights, which look amazing under the tight red dress and with the black Docs. The neckline was a little low, so I've slipped on a black tank to feel more comfortable.

My diamond nose stud and earrings are the only pieces of jewelry I'm wearing, which is fine, as I feel dressed up without any on.

The wall clock reads 6:59 p.m.—time to meet Prince Charming.

I grab my jacket, loving how my freshly painted black nails sparkle in the light.

As I approach the elevator, my heart does that unhealthy thumping thing it does whenever I'm about to see Quinn. But it's a good feeling, like a thousand butterflies fluttering around in my stomach, ready to take flight when I see him.

The elevator ride is way too fast, and before I know it, I'm approaching the ground floor. I give my reflection one final look in the mirrors, ensuring I don't have lip gloss on my teeth.

The doors ding, indicating I've reached my destination, and I step out slowly, not knowing where to look. But I don't have to look far, as the most gorgeous man I have ever seen stands off to the left, patiently waiting for me.

I almost don't recognize Quinn because he looks, if this is possible, hotter than I have ever seen him before. I almost forget to swallow as he stands before me in black jeans tucked into black combat boots, a black-and-white-checkered shirt with the sleeves rolled up to the elbows, and a black tie hanging loosely around his neck.

His slicked-back hair is tied back, exposing his chiseled face.

I cannot stop staring at him. He is *epic*—in every sense of the word.

I want him naked, in my bed, and I want him now.

He's on me in about two seconds, smashing his lips to mine, and the way we both paw at one another, the feeling of trying to keep one's clothes on looks to be mutual.

We break apart only when we hear a throat clearing since we're standing in the middle of the foyer, blocking the elevator call button.

Quinn's eyes are hooded, and he seems to find us getting caught by a group of Girl Scouts hilarious. On the other hand, I apologize profusely as I grab Quinn by the arm and tug him out of the way.

"You look beautiful," he says, nuzzling my neck as we walk toward the front door.

"Thank you for my clothes," I say, leaning into his warm embrace.

I can feel Quinn's mouth dip into a smile against my throat. "Thank you for looking so hot in them."

"I kind of feel like Julia Roberts in *Pretty Woman*."

As Quinn pulls back, tweaking an eyebrow at me with a smirk on his face, I suddenly realize how that could be interpreted.

"Without the whole prostitute thing, of course," I add quickly, which earns me a soft chuckle from him.

The concierge opens the glass door for us, and I notice him give Quinn a happy smile like one would give a friend, and I wonder what that's all about. But I disregard it, as I'm too excited about what Quinn has planned.

"Where are we going?"

"You'll see," he says as we walk among fellow couples, leisurely strolling on the sidewalk.

My senses cannot absorb the sights, sounds, and smells quickly enough, and I feel like a kid in a candy store as I take in the bright lights, delicious Cajun smells, and vibrant atmosphere around me.

At this moment, everything is how it's supposed to be.

We walk a few blocks, hand in hand, taking in the magical surroundings with a smile. Regardless of the circumstances as to why we're here, I'm happy. I know I don't deserve to be after everything I've done, but I am. And for once, I won't shy away from it but embrace it and not let go.

"What's got you so happy?"

"You."

"Oh?" Quinn questions with a smirk. "What about me?"

"Nothing specific. Just you in general."

"Well, in that case, thank you," he says, smiling. I'm still mesmerized by his striking features, with his hair tied back this way.

"I like your hair like that," I say, my eyes glued to his handsome face.

"I like your hair like that too," he replies, giving me a once-over. "But I just like…you."

I don't know how to respond to him as my throat is about to close over by his compliment, so I don't.

Thankfully, after a couple of minutes of walking in silence, we arrive at our destination.

"We're here," Quinn says, leading me into a lush green garden.

"Here?" I ask, looking around at the beautiful park lit up with streetlamps.

"Yup. Close your eyes." Stepping behind me, he places his hands lightly on my shoulders.

"Close my eyes?" I ask as I turn my head to look at him over my shoulder.

"Yes, it'll only be for a minute."

"Okay," I reply, feeling a bundle of nerves somersault in my stomach as I turn around to face the long, cemented walkway in front of me. "They're closed."

"No peeking," he says, turning me back around. "No matter what, keep them shut."

"I'm a little nervous."

"Don't be."

My senses are on high alert, hoping to figure out what this surprise involves. I don't have to wait long because my ears pick up on the unmistakable sound of horse hooves trotting on the pavement, steadily approaching us and getting louder with each step.

I step back, afraid I'm about to get trampled, but Quinn is behind me, drawing my body into his, and I instantly relax.

Once the trotting comes to a halt, Quinn whispers, "Okay, you can open your eyes."

Slowly opening them, I gasp when I'm faced with a pair of warm brown eyes staring as inquisitively at me as I am at it.

Quinn leans over my shoulder, kissing my cheek. "Do you like him?"

"I love him!" I gasp, my eyes never leaving the huge brown

horse before me. "Can I pet him?"

"Of course," the man sitting in the carriage says.

I hesitantly reach forward, my fingers twitching to pat the wild beast in front of me. As I stroke his nose softly, he nuzzles into me, no doubt checking to see if I have any food.

I laugh, rubbing him on his head, his bristly hair tickling my fingers. "I think he likes me."

The horse neighs, and both Quinn and I laugh.

"Of course, he does," Quinn replies, reaching around me to pat his white nose. "You ready to go for a ride?"

I spin around quickly, eyes wide. "Yes. Hell yes."

Quinn climbs into the back of the carriage and offers me his hand, which I accept. He drags me across the seat the moment I'm in so I'm nestled into his side. "I'm glad you're happy. I thought with your horse tattoo that horses meant something special to you?"

"Yes, I wish I was free like they are."

"One day, baby, you will be."

As we walk into the foyer of our hotel, I can't help but feel a little sad since this will probably be our last night here. I could almost pretend that, for a moment, I was just a normal girl on her first date with someone who has changed everything.

"You don't want to leave?" Quinn asks as we wait for the elevator.

"No. But I know we have to."

"We'll come back. I promise." I don't correct him since I will be in jail or dead at the end of this.

I don't want to spoil the moment, so I simply remain quiet as we get into the elevator.

I can't believe Quinn went to so much effort, and now that we're back, I want to do something for him. I psyche myself up for what I have in mind, blowing out a small breath before the elevator doors open.

Quinn reaches for my hand, and we silently stroll down the hallway toward our room. As he unlocks the door, my heart begins thumping so loudly that I'm surprised he can't hear it.

Slipping off my jacket, I toss it onto the chair.

"Do you want a drink?"

"A water, thanks." I sit on the sofa and curl my legs underneath me.

He returns with a tall glass of water for me and a beer for himself.

"Are we staying here tonight?" I ask as I accept the glass from his outstretched hand.

Quinn nods, most of his hair slipping loose around his face, and as he sits near me, his scent smacks me in the guts with its delectable fragrance.

"Yes, I paid for another night."

"Cool," I reply softly, and then, there is silence.

A static crackles between us, and I know what I want and need to do. But how am I supposed to do this? I've seduced men in the past, but that was all make-believe. But this, right here, is real. And that's what makes it feel like it's the first time. And in a way, it is.

I watch Quinn's throat as he sips his beer, mesmerized by the way his Adam's apple bobs with the movement. There is no part of him I don't find attractive or don't want.

"Thank you for today, Quinn," I whisper and make my move.

"It's okay, Red," he replies, looking at me in surprise as I shift slowly to straddle his lap.

"It was the best day of my life. And as far as first dates go, I dare say it is up there as being the best first date in history."

Quinn smirks, tilting his head back against the sofa. He peers up at me, his eyes sparkling. "You're very welcome."

He appears calm, but I can feel his heart race as I place my palm over his chest.

"But it doesn't matter what we do. As long as I'm with you, everything else will fall into place around us."

I lean forward, kissing him softly.

Nothing around us exists when our lips connect, and it's just us against the world. I wouldn't have it any other way.

Being on top of Quinn, I'm able to control the kiss, and he allows me to. I deepen our connection, opening up to him, my mouth never leaving his lips as my hand trails down his chest. I can feel his nipple ring under my fingertips, and I want to toy with it with my tongue more than anything. But now, I'm on a mission to toy with something else with my tongue.

My fingers pass over each bump in his abs, and he exhales loudly as I pause at the waistband of his jeans, brushing over his belt buckle to make my intentions clear.

"You don't have to," he says, his heated eyes searching my face, fully understanding what I wish to do.

"I want to," I reply quickly, because I do. "But I don't know how. I'm sorry."

I'm embarrassed at my lack of experience.

Quinn shakes his head. "Don't ever apologize for something like that. You've shared your body with me, and you wanting to touch me makes me the luckiest son of a bitch in the world."

His belt buckle comes freely undone as I flick it open, and my shaky fingers thankfully unbutton his jeans easily enough. My eyes drop to his lap, and I can't help but admire the impressive bulge.

Now the hard part.

I watch Quinn's eyes darken as I slowly slide his zipper down halfway and gently slip inside with hesitant fingers. When my fingertips pass over him, I gasp and pull my hand away because he's not wearing any underwear. But I should have figured as much, seeing as he didn't purchase any from the store.

Wetting my lips, I tell myself to woman up because I want this. Biting my lip, I place my hand back into his pants. I gasp because he feels unlike anything I've ever felt before. He's soft and smooth, as well as being hard and firm all at the same time.

Quinn's eyes never leave my face as I explore him more confidently, enjoying the hot silk feel of him gliding under my fingertips. I lower my eyes, witnessing my hand moving gently within his jeans and seeing his coarse dark hair peeking out from his open zipper. That, combined with his hardened V muscle, which tenses as I stroke him a little firmer, leaves me wet.

"You're soft," I whisper, meeting his eyes.

Quinn smirks, tugging on his lip ring, his eyes drooping to half mast as I rub over the slit of his dick.

"Red," he gasps, trying to remain still. "No man wants to hear they're soft when his girl has her hands down his pants."

A tiny laugh escapes me, but I don't fail to notice that he just called me his girl.

"Am I?" I ask, stroking him softly, my small hands trying to hold all of him but not even coming close.

"Are you what?" he pants, his mouth parted, the light catching off the barbell on his tongue.

"Am I your girl?" I ask, which also comes out breathy. Watching Quinn come undone because of what I'm doing to him is a bigger turn-on than him doing it to me.

"Red, you were my girl from the moment I saw you. That'll never change, I promise you. I'm yours for as long as you want me."

I bite my cheek to stop myself from saying forever.

I seem to be getting a good rhythm, stroking him from base to tip, and before long, I'm working him harder, feeling his body shudder underneath my hands. But it's not enough.

I want to see it.

I want to taste him.

My hand slows as I glide out of his pants and bend forward, kissing him on his parted mouth softly before sliding down his body until my knees hit the carpeted floor.

"Red, you don't—"

But I cut him off, shaking my head. "I want to. Tell me how."

"Whatever you do will feel amazing."

Looking up at him, I slowly reach for his zipper and pull it down the rest of the way. His rock-hard dick springs free, and I can't hide my surprise at how big he is. My mouth waters, and I'm shocked by how badly I want to take him into my mouth.

I slide his jeans down his legs and pull them out of his boots. My eyes fall between his legs, as I can't look anywhere *but* there. Thankfully, I somehow get his jeans off over his shoes, and the sight before me of Quinn in boots, a shirt, and a tie is a memory I will revisit often.

And another memory I will never forget is when I bend forward and take him into my mouth, sucking lightly. Quinn jerks off the seat, his hands clenching the cushions underneath him while hissing. I look up at him, with him in my mouth, and witness his eyes turn desperate and frenzied. So I take him in farther, slipping my tongue out to lick the underside.

"Holy fuck."

He tastes how he smells—delicious. And I want more.

My hands slide up his legs and rest on his knees, and I use them as leverage to lean further into his lap. This allows me to take more of him into my mouth, and I don't realize how far down he is until he hits the back of my throat, and I gag.

Pulling back, I don't let him go because I like the feel of him so deep. But I soon appreciate that I don't even have half of him inside my mouth. Wrapping my hand around his thick base, I begin stroking him to match the motion of my mouth.

Quinn moans, and I can feel him flex underneath me. And the harder I suck and stroke, the harder he tenses.

Circling the head of his dick with my tongue, I taste a salty liquid seep out of him, and as soon as his flavor hits my taste buds, a whimper escapes me. I do it again, and Quinn groans, throwing his head back and closing his eyes.

"Red, you gotta stop," he pants, his body quivering beneath me. "I'm going to come in your mouth if you don't."

But I don't want to stop. Like he's said to me, I want him to be in my mouth when he does.

Slowly licking him from base to tip, I don't know if I'm doing this right, but I'm using his curses as a guide. And judging by the profanity passing through his clenched lips, I must be doing okay.

I love the way he felt at the back of my throat, so I relax and slide my lips over his length, taking him back down until he hits my throat. He shudders and tries to pull back, but I don't let him go, loving the power I have over his body as he crumbles beneath me.

His taste, sight, smell, and feel turn me on. The pressure building in my sex makes me ache as he murmurs how good it feels, and I need a release.

Wickedly, I slip my hand under my tights and begin touching myself over my underwear with Quinn still in my mouth. My moan comes out muffled as he slowly thrusts his hips forward, his hands resting in my hair, guiding how fast and deep he wants me to go.

I pull back to catch my breath, meaning I can only suck a quarter of him. So I begin jerking him off, watching him come undone.

Lost in a wave of pleasure, his eyes shut tight and wisps of fallen hair shrouding his face, he parts his full lips, gasping for air. The look of unrestrained yearning contorts his entire being, and when he draws his lip ring into his mouth, my body shudders in heated desire.

Quinn's eyes snap open as he hears me moaning, rubbing myself while pleasuring him.

"Holy fucking hell. Are you touching yourself?" he asks, his eyes widening as he sees my fingers working quickly between my legs.

Whimpering as I rub over my swollen clit, I examine the way he watches me pleasuring myself while pleasuring him. As my fingers quicken, matching the rhythm of my mouth, Quinn groans loudly, and he tenses underneath me.

"Oh fuck," he gasps, trying to pull out of my mouth, but I latch on, my cheeks hollowing with the suction.

The first spurt jets down my throat, with more to follow in quick succession, and I nearly gag, but I swallow everything he gives, wanting him inside me. As his body jerks and spasms under my mouth, my hand quickens, desperate to bring myself to release. And I'm not far off because watching

Quinn come with a thunderous scream because of me is the hottest thing I've ever seen.

Before the last tremor rocks his body, he's on me, pushing me backward and shoving the coffee table out of the way so he can throw me onto the carpet.

I'm taken off guard and confused. But everything becomes crystal clear when he reaches between us, frantically yanking my dress up and my tights and underwear down.

He lowers his head and buries his face between my legs, his mouth devouring my sex. I cry out because I'm already so close, and it doesn't take long before I'm screaming out my release in long, labored pants.

This is the most erotic experience of my life, and the thought of what I did, combined with what Quinn is doing to me now, has me riding this pleasure for as long as I can. And Quinn doesn't stop until I beg him to, certain I will die if I come apart again.

I'm spent. I'm sticky. And I'm shaking.

But would I trade this feeling for anything in the world?

Hell to the fuck no.

Eight

'm the first to wake this time, although I wish I wasn't because I'm curled around Quinn's body. I wish we could stay this way forever.

However, that quickly changes as I hear a distinct banging on the door, followed by a loud voice shouting, "Open up! It's the police!"

I spring upright, my heart about to burst through my chest. I brush back my hair, my ears needing to confirm if what I heard is real.

As the thumping pounds louder against our door, I jump out of bed and frantically shake Quinn to wake him up because this shit *is* real. Lucky growls low in his throat, but I softly shush him, and thankfully, he seems to understand the dire situation we're faced with and remains quiet.

When Quinn doesn't stir, I shake him once again.

"What?" he moans, his eyes slipping open.

But I place my finger over his lips as the banging continues.

The moment I widen my eyes and mouth, "Police," Quinn bolts upright, his eyes wild as he jumps out of bed, slipping on his jeans and sweater in record time.

I follow suit, balancing on one foot as I slide my boot on, not bothering to tie my laces as I slip my knife snugly inside.

Quinn grabs his wallet and backpack, motioning with his head toward the window. I nod, reaching for my backpack, but sadly, I don't have enough time to gather anything else as the banging continues to get louder and louder.

Quinn softly unlatches the lock and steps out onto the balcony, holding the bifold door open for Lucky and me.

"What are we going to do now?" I ask, looking for an escape route but not seeing anything unless I fancy plummeting eighteen stories to my death.

Quinn sucks on his lip ring, his eyes frantically searching for an escape. As he looks to his right and peers up, he sees it.

"Up, Red. We gotta climb up."

I see where he's looking and cringe, but there is no other option.

"What about Lucky? We can't leave him here," I say on the verge of tears.

"I'll carry him," Quinn says, giving me a quick kiss to the forehead.

He carefully steps over the low balcony rail and settles onto the narrow ledge, testing its strength. His back rests against the railing, his hands braced behind him, holding on tight.

His hair whips violently in the wind, and he turns his neck to look at me.

"I'm going to scale across, okay? When I'm about halfway,

close to the platform on the other side, you follow."

Looking at the rusty old platform about twenty steps away, I can't believe how a five-star hotel can have such a dangerous fire escape and not be shut down. It looks like it hasn't been operational since 1901, and I can see some missing steps. But it's the only escape route we have.

"You can do this," he affirms, in tune with the fact that I'm nearly having a mental breakdown.

Quinn extends his hand, indicating he's ready for Lucky.

Nodding, I pick Lucky up and carefully pass him to Quinn, who tucks him securely under one arm. Lucky whines, and Quinn coos him as he takes his first small sidestep, scaling across the thin ledge to the platform with a rickety old fire escape leading to the roof. My heart hammers against my chest as I watch him holding the rail with one hand and Lucky in the other. I can't watch, but I also can't turn away until I know my two boys are safe.

This is the stuff you see in movies, where trained stuntmen and safety cables are involved. Sadly, we have neither.

Only when Quinn is close to the platform do I take a deep breath and step over the rail, just like Quinn instructed. Everything inside me shrinks in fear. I'm not a fan of heights, especially death-inducing heights. I don't know why, but I feel safer doing this with my eyes closed, which is certainly not recommended by anyone, I'm sure. But I can't do this with my eyes open because the less I see, the better.

I mentally count each step, and counting to twenty has never taken so long. My hands have a death grip on the rail, and I try my best to step as quickly as possible without slipping, trying to think of anything other than the fact I'm eighteen stories up in the air.

Mercifully, Quinn's hand grabs my wrist, and I open my

eyes as he helps me over the rail and onto the platform, which shakes violently in the cruel wind.

"Watch your step," he says, looking up. "I'll be behind you, Red. I won't let you fall."

I know he means that in every possible way, and I nod, taking a deep breath as I hold the banister and take my first step.

True to his words, Quinn is only one step behind me, and when I step through a stair, nearly falling straight through, Quinn grabs me from behind to steady me. Thankfully, the rest of the climb is less eventful, and we make it up in one piece.

Quinn grabs my hand the moment we make it to the roof, about twenty-two stories up, and pulls me toward the door. I let out a breath as it opens, and we bolt down the stairs, two at a time.

The only sound is our feet pounding frantically on the steps and our labored breaths bouncing off the concrete walls. As I see the numbers on the walls decreasing as we descend, floor by floor, I tell my burning muscles it's only a little farther, and then this will all be over.

Finally, we get to the ground floor in a matter of minutes, both panting and puffing, but running on pure adrenaline.

Quinn opens the door cautiously, looking out through a sliver, and after a few seconds, he motions with his head that the coast is clear. We both walk out quickly, not wanting to draw too much attention to ourselves, as patrons already look at us strangely, probably appalled by our disheveled state.

Both our boots pound on the marbled floor, and as the front door slips into view, I breathe out a premature sigh of relief because a policeman steps out of nowhere and blocks the exit while talking into his walkie-talkie. Quinn reaches for me and pulls me behind a wall, shielding me with his body.

"What are we going to do now?" I ask into his chest, panting loudly as his heart pounds against my cheek.

Quinn doesn't reply. He only peeks out from behind the wall, spying on the officer. He pulls back in, cursing under his breath.

"This is my fault. I'm so sorry. I didn't think the police would be onto us so soon."

Pulling out of his embrace, I raise my eyebrow. "What do you mean?"

But he only shakes his head and peeks back out to see if our exit is still blocked.

My heart races, and my stomach churns. This is it. This is really it. But I'll be damned if Quinn goes down with me. I try to shrug out of his hold, but his arms tighten around me.

"Don't even think about it," he snarls, understanding my plan to give myself up.

"It's the only—"

But Quinn pulls me out into the foyer before I have a chance to finish my sentence.

We head toward the door that is no longer manned, and I shrink into my hair as I can see two police officers by reception, talking to Janet, who has her hand pressed to her chest. A look of pure horror is plastered all over her painted face, no doubt realizing that she was flirting with a fugitive.

We're almost at the exit when the concierge steps forward, opening the door for us, his back toward the police, blocking us from their view.

"Go to 300 Labouri Street. Tell Jason I sent you and that you're Quinn."

Quinn sighs, touching the concierge on the arm. "Thanks, Rodney."

Rodney? How does Quinn know his name? Before I have time to question him, I'm getting yanked outside, and we're running down the street, our boots thumping on the pavement.

I'm gripping Quinn's hand like it is my lifeline because I'm afraid to let it go. But I'm not afraid for me. I'm afraid for him. What if he gets hurt because of me? My stomach roils with the thought, and I think I'm going to be sick.

"We're nearly there, just a couple of more blocks," Quinn says reassuringly, mistaking my apprehension as fatigue.

We reach the address minutes later, which is a two-story house with a big garage attached around the back. Quinn lets go of my hand, jogging to the side of the house, calling out to Jason. I follow close, my steps slower than Quinn's, as I feel like my legs are about to collapse from under me.

A young man comes out from the garage, rubbing his greasy hands on a dirty blue cloth.

"Can I help you?" he asks, eyeing us suspiciously.

"Hi, I'm Quinn. Rodney sent us."

The young man nods, looking behind us before replying, "Follow me."

Quinn and I follow quickly and are led to the adjoining garage.

"Wait here," Jason says, walking into the side door.

"Quinn, is this safe?" I whisper, keeping my eyes peeled on the door.

"It'll be fine," he says, drawing me into his arms and kissing my brow.

We stay this way until we hear keys jingling and the garage door motor groaning as it winds up, revealing the inside of a workshop. As I look inside, I see endless cars and workers modifying them. I don't want to know what goes on here. I have a feeling the less I know, the better.

"Okay, she's all yours," says Jason, tossing Quinn a set of keys and opening the door of a late seventies black Chevy truck.

My eyes widen because I'm seriously in the dark about what is going on. But now is not the time to question it because we need to get the hell out of Dodge.

Quinn opens my door, all but lifting me into the cab and reaching over, buckling my seat belt for me.

"Sorry, Red," he says, kissing me quickly on the lips before racing over to the driver's side. Lucky jumps in before him.

"Thanks for what you did for my dad," says Jason, and Quinn gives him a quick smile before starting the engine with a roar.

"Don't mention it," he replies, throwing the car into drive and fishtailing it out of the garage.

Quinn pulls onto the road with skill and speeds away from our near capture in a matter of seconds. The road blurs before me, and I grasp the door handle for support. And it's not because of Quinn's erratic driving. Now that the adrenaline has worn off, my body threatens to give out.

"What did you mean by sorry? And who is Rodney?" I ask breathlessly, looking at Quinn who is concentrating on the road.

Quinn blows out a frustrated breath before he replies, "It's my fault the police are here."

"What are you talking about?"

He clenches his jaw, and I know he's furious at himself for whatever he did.

"I used my credit card to pay for your things. I wasn't thinking, and it was too late to take it back without making a scene. I didn't think the police would catch up to us so quickly. I knew we were leaving today, so I thought by the time the police got around to checking out if it really was me who used the card, we'd be long gone. I'm so sorry, Red, this is all my fault."

But I'm not really listening because all I can focus on is the fact that Quinn paid for everything. I just assumed he'd used Tabitha's money.

"Did you pay for everything?"

Quinn nods, confused. "Yeah, of course, why?"

"I just…I just assumed you'd use Tabitha's money."

Quinn opens his mouth in understanding and turns to face me as we stop at a red light. "I wanted it to be a real date, and using Tabitha's money didn't sit right with me. Call it pride or whatever, but I wanted to do it right." He pauses, fisting his hair into an angry peak as he sighs. "But now I've gone and fucked everything up." He steps on the gas as the light changes to green.

His notion of paying for everything is old-fashioned and totally unnecessary, but it's also so incredibly…sweet. He did this, all of this…for me.

Before I can stop myself, I slide across the bench seat, nearly squashing Lucky in the process, and throw myself into Quinn's lap, straddling him.

"Red!" he shrieks with a chuckle as the car swerves slightly.

I crouch down low and nestle into him, wrapping my arms around his neck, toying with the hair at his nape. I don't care he nearly got us caught, and I don't care that the police are probably a hair's breadth away from finding us.

All I care about is holding on to him and never letting go.

"Thank you," I mumble against his chest.

"Thank you? You're thanking me for nearly getting us

caught?" he questions, pulling the car over when I make my intentions clear that I'm not moving.

"I don't care about that. All I care about…" I pause, afraid of my honesty.

But as I hear the steady beating of his big heart, a heart that has been so kind and cared for me since the very beginning, I'm sick of being afraid.

"Is you," I whisper.

Quinn wraps his arms around my back, pulling me tighter into him.

After a minute of silence, Quinn says against my head, "All I care about is you too, Red."

Melting into his arms, I sigh when I bury my nose into his neck, relishing in his familiar, comforting smell.

"Good. Now shut up with the apologies."

And that earns me a chuckle.

"How do you know Rodney? I mean, we've been here for less than seventy-two hours, and you're making friends with someone who just saved our ass. What's the deal?"

"I helped him out," he replies vaguely.

"How?"

"Those pretentious jackasses at his work were accusing him of stealing."

"How do you know he wasn't?" I ask, snuggling closer into him.

"I just knew. Rodney's not a bad guy. Some other asshole was stealing, and because Rodney was 'just' a concierge, of course he had to have done it. In those people's eyes, he was nothing but an underprivileged, uneducated doorman."

"So…" I say, encouraging him to continue.

He chuckles, resting his lips on my head as he speaks. "So I bribed them."

"Bribed who?"

"Rodney's manager. I told him if he cleared Rodney's name, I'd make it worth his while. And this time around, I did use Abi's money. But I didn't think she'd mind since I know she would have done the same."

I pull back to meet his eyes.

"But Rodney *could* have been thieving. I mean, you saw what was going on at the address he sent us to. I don't think his son, Jason, is a qualified mechanic, if you know what I mean."

Quinn laughs, kissing the tip of my nose. "Think of Rodney as Rodney Hood."

"Huh?" I ask, scrunching up my face, frightened Quinn has lost his mind.

"Rodney steals cars from the rich, who can have a newer, better model delivered to their doorstep within the hour, to feed his family of eight, plus three dogs."

"This is not really helping Rodney's case," I say with a small smile.

Quinn smirks, toying with his lip ring. "They accused him of stealing personal items from guests."

"What would a man like Rodney want with that stuff?" I ask. Even though I don't know Rodney, his humbled appearance was a dead giveaway he wasn't like everyone else in that place.

"Exactly."

"So you bribed his boss? With money?" I ask, needing to clarify that Quinn didn't use his fists but money to seal the deal.

"Yes, Red. Money is the universal language, sad but true."

"So you vouched for a total stranger? Why?" I ask, not that I'm unhappy he did so, more that I need to know why.

"Because everyone, regardless of what they have done, deserves a chance," he replies softly, and I have a feeling we're no longer talking about Rodney.

I let it go because I can feel Quinn tense up underneath me, not wanting to discuss this further.

I can't help but marvel at the fact that Quinn did something incredibly kind to help out a stranger. And even though I'm pretty certain Rodney helped Quinn set up our date because they most likely became friends the day I went missing, what Quinn did for him was something not many others would have done. But whatever the reason Quinn decided to help Rodney, I'm glad because Rodney came through for us when Quinn needed him the most.

After a few moments of silence and me snuggling back into Quinn's chest, clinging onto him like a koala, I ask, "So what are we going to do now?"

"I think we should take the back roads and keep driving. No stopping till we're far enough to get the cops off our tails. And it'll give us some time to figure out what the hell to do next."

I nod. "We'll take turns driving, then, and drive through the night, okay?"

"As long as you're okay with that. It'll probably mean using gas stations as our bathrooms and supermarkets for the next couple of days, but it'll give us some breathing room to figure out what to do next."

"Sounds good to me. What's a road trip without excessive amounts of artificial sugar and frozen burritos?"

"Any place special you wanna go?"

"No, anywhere with you is special."

And I mean every single word.

We drive through Louisiana, taking remote back roads that look to be used only by the locals and hopefully not patrolled by the police. Thankfully, the dirt, lonesome roads link back up to the highways, so we know which direction we're traveling in.

We drive nonstop, only stopping for gas and the occasional bathroom break, but Quinn is right. We need to give ourselves a big head start now that the police are onto where we are.

Quinn has driven all of the way, but after nearly running us off the road because he fell asleep at the wheel, I demanded he pull over. He's driven for way too many hours without a break. He insisted he was fine, but when I told him this wasn't negotiable, he agreed and was out like a light.

So now it's just me and the open road, as Lucky has also crashed, snuggled into Quinn, who is using the window as a pillow. He'll be sore when he wakes, but I don't have the heart to wake him up.

I'm not sure of the exact time, but judging by the coyotes and raccoons and whatever other wildlife wants to jump out in front of me, scaring the bejesus outta me, I'd say it's well after midnight.

We're headed for Arkansas, and I'm aching for a bed and shower and to eat something that isn't defrosted in the microwave. But I'd never tell Quinn since he feels bad enough.

Even though we almost got caught, I'm not freaking out because I'm with Quinn. If I were doing this on my own, or with someone other than him, I doubt I would be this composed or sane. But with Quinn, I feel like I can pull through anything.

Lost in my thoughts, I fail to hear a small whimper until it becomes a steady, panicked moan. I look over, believing that it is Lucky. But the distraught whimpers come from Quinn and are becoming increasingly worse.

I try to reach out to comfort him, but he's too far away, and even with one hand on the steering wheel, the other reaching for him, I can't touch him.

My eyes dart between the road and Quinn, wanting nothing more than anything to comfort him, especially when his whimpers turn into spoken, hushed words.

"Mom…I'm sorry. I'm so sorry," Quinn cries, whipping his head from side to side. "I'm sorry I made you choose. I didn't know…and it's too late."

What's too late?

Oh God, I feel like I should wake Quinn as his face contorts in pain. And I also feel as if I'm intruding in on a private memory, one Quinn wishes to keep to himself.

"Don't tell Tristan. Please don't tell him. If he ever found out, he'd never forgive me." And a guttural sob robs him of air, jerking me with its intensity.

I can't stand to hear him in such pain, so I quickly pull over at a rest stop off the highway and am by Quinn's side in seconds.

"Quinn," I whisper while he mumbles incoherent words under his breath.

But he doesn't rouse.

"Quinn," I say a little louder, shaking him lightly on the arm.

Nothing.

"Quinn! Wake up! You're dreaming," I shout while shoving him harder.

I hate to be so rough, but if I were dreaming as he is now,

then I would want someone to wake me. I know this from experience, as I often wished someone would wake me from the horror of my dreams.

Luckily, it works, and Quinn jumps up, startled, eyes wide, trying to place where he is and if the dream was real.

I know that feeling all too well.

"Red?" he croaks, still half asleep, his eyes landing on me.

"Yes, it's me. I just woke you up, you were dreaming," I say softly, brushing his hair off his damp brow.

"I was?"

"Yes. Can you remember what you were dreaming about?"

By the way his cheeks turn a ghastly white, I know he does, but I won't push. He meets my worried eyes and slowly nods.

"Do you want to talk about it?" I softly invite, my hand resting on his stubbled cheek.

Quinn shakes his head slowly, and I let it go.

"Okay, but if you ever change your mind, I'm here. Nothing you ever tell me will change anything between us."

"I know. Thank you," and he leans forward, kissing me softly.

It's meant to be an innocent kiss, but we both seem to need the intimacy.

The moment our lips touch, I crawl onto his lap, wanting to close any physical space between us. Quinn moans in the back of his throat as I run my tongue over his lower lip, sucking his piercing into my eager, hungry mouth.

I claw at his shirt, desperate to get underneath to feel his warm, bare skin. And when I do, we both groan at the contact. Whether it's our dire circumstances, or the fact I always want Quinn, I'm so turned on that I'm whimpering in need.

As I begin rubbing up on Quinn's lap, my jeans don't

provide much of a buffer, and I can feel him deliciously hard under me. I can't help but remember how he felt in mouth, against my tongue, and the way he tasted.

And I want it again.

Quinn pulls his lips away, and thumbs my pouty bottom lip.

"You fucking drive me crazy." He unsnaps my button and slips a hand inside my jeans.

I moan the moment he bypasses my underwear and goes straight in for the kill, sinking a finger inside me. In this small space with nowhere to go, I lean backward, my hips arching into his touch.

I cry out his name, my knees quivering on either side of his thighs as I'm half straddling, half sitting on him. But he makes it work by wrapping an arm around my waist to steady me, and his other hand stretches me further by adding another finger. I use the dash as extra leverage to pump my hips into his torturous fingers.

Tasting my approaching climax as I push harder into his fingers, my hips drive forward forcefully. Quinn is relentless, never breaking his punishing rhythm.

As I gaze into his beautiful green eyes, watching him nibble on his hoop, the arousal evident on his flushed cheeks, I don't stand a chance and detonate around his fingers. My scream tears from my throat, which Quinn catches between his lips as he smashes his mouth to mine, kissing me fiercely.

Moaning against his mouth, I feel the convulsions rock my body long after I have exploded. Our eyes never lose connection, and watching him watch me come apart was why I set off so quickly.

His fingers are still in my pants, and I mewl in satisfaction as each orgasm keeps improving.

Quinn slides his fingers out of me, and I miss him being inside. But as he places his fingers inside his mouth, the same two that were inside me, I whimper and turn a bright shade of pink.

"Mine. Every part of you is mine."

I'm stunned by his confession and do the only thing I can do. I throw my arms around his neck and promise never to let go.

Nine

My back aches because something sharp digs into my spine, causing me to contort at an angle that cannot possibly be good for me. But I don't care because I'm wrapped up in the arms of Quinn Berkeley.

I must have fallen asleep in his arms as it's now daylight, and I don't remember much after I clung to him like a spider monkey, never letting go.

I look at him closely as we are pretty much nose to nose, lying along the bench seat, arms and legs entwined, and wonder, how on earth do I tell him that I think I'm falling in love with him?

Just the thought of telling him has my heart pounding against my chest, but not because I'm afraid of him knowing. No. I'm afraid if I tell him, the feelings won't be reciprocated. I know he cares for me, but love is a whole different ball game.

"Mornin'," Quinn says huskily, his green eyes slipping open, stunning me with their vibrancy. "What time is it?"

I shrug, in awe of how someone can look this hot when they first wake up. "I'm not sure. Sometime after dawn."

Quinn smirks and runs a hand through my hair. "You sleep okay?"

I nod.

"We should get moving," he says, and he's right because last night's stop was an impromptu one.

"Sure. I gotta use the bathroom before we go," I say, thankful I saw restrooms when I pulled in last night.

Quinn nods, letting out another yawn. "I'll come with you."

I'm about to protest, but he adds, "Don't know what kind of country bugs are out here, hiding under the seats."

I blanch and nod quickly, not eager to face these country bugs on my own. I fucking hate bugs.

"C'mon, boy," I call out to Lucky, who lies on the floor, looking up at us, also desperate to make a pit stop.

The cold breeze slaps me in the face. It's been quite cold in the South this winter. Being from LA, where we don't get cold winters, I understand why people go nuts and celebrate the whole white Christmas thing. Playing in the snow and waking up to a real pine tree and eggnog on Christmas morning would be magical.

"Whatcha thinking about?" Quinn asks as we walk toward the restrooms, hand in hand.

"About Christmas," I confess, turning to look at him shyly.

"Oh shit, it's December already," he says, stunned that Christmas is just around the corner. We've had other pressing issues to deal with—like not dying.

"Yeah. I was thinking about how I get the whole white

Christmas thing. It would be nice sitting around an open fire, the smell of fresh pine needles engulfing the house while opening presents with loved ones," I reply, lost in a fantasy.

"You're big on Christmas, then?" Quinn asks, ducking so he doesn't walk into a branch.

Tucking a lock of hair behind my ear, I shyly confess, "I've never really celebrated it."

"Really?"

"Yeah. I was too busy playing Santa on Christmas morning, dealing a different kind of snow to crackheads to worry about anything else."

Quinn nods, biting his lip. "I'm sorry."

"Don't be. It's fine. You can't miss what you've never had, right?"

Quinn squeezes my hand softly, and we walk to the restrooms in silence.

Once we reach the bricked bathroom wall, Quinn smiles as he watches me chew my lip, thinking of all the bugs hiding inside. "I'll take Lucky. Be back in five."

I nod and watch him leave.

The bathroom is horrible, and I think a raccoon family lives under the sink. So I'm in and out in under a minute. I splash some water on my cheeks and think about my conversation with Quinn.

Will we still be on the run at Christmas? New Year's? Independence Day? When will this end? We really need to get in contact with Abi because we need a plan of attack ASAP.

Throwing the paper towel into the trash, I run my fingers through my messy hair, pulling out a bobby pin from my backpack and pinning back a lock. But I suddenly pause.

"Hey, you're Mia's friend."

My ears prick up when I hear the muted male voice just

outside, obviously addressing Quinn.

"Yup, and you're Justin," Quinn replies calmly.

Justin? As in Justin Miller? What is *he* doing out here?

"Yeah, good memory, bro. What brings you guys out here?"

I know this won't end well, so I quickly bolt out of the bathroom, and as I turn to go outside, I fall into a casual step.

"Fancy seeing you here," I say with a rigid smile as I approach them.

Quinn has his arms crossed while Justin smiles. "This must be my lucky week." And he gives me a big hug.

I awkwardly hug him back, looking at an extremely unimpressed Quinn.

I pull away, trying not to offend him, but this is not good timing, and it's also not safe for him. He's in danger of being caught up in all my bullshit and being beaten to a pulp by Quinn.

"So…what are you guys doing here?"

"Just a road trip," I reply vaguely.

Silence.

Quinn and Justin are sizing one another up, and I don't like the look on both their faces as they're not exactly hiding the fact they both dislike one another—a lot.

"What are you doing here?" Quinn questions, his head cocked to the side.

Justin looks at Quinn, his eyes narrowing. "Just stopping to use the restroom, pure coincidence bumping into you."

Quinn scoffs, unbelieving of a single word.

I've got to stop this macho bullshit before they whip out their dicks and measure whose is bigger.

"We better hit the road, Quinn," I suggest, grabbing his arm, which remains solidly crossed.

Okay, moving him is going to be an issue. "Quinn?"

He slowly takes his eyes off Justin, looking down at me. I give him big eyes, hoping he can read my facial charades, but he only smirks.

"Yeah, sure, you're right," he thankfully replies while reaching for my hand.

"Catch ya later, Justin. It was nice seeing you again," I say while trying to drag Quinn away.

"You too, Mia. Hey, what's your ride?" he asks randomly.

That has me stopping in my tracks as I look at Quinn, wondering why Justin would ask such a strange question.

But he clarifies. "The reason I ask is because there are a couple of cops checking out a black Chevy parked near the highway."

I feel my face ashen as I squeeze Quinn's hand in dread.

"Just wondering if it was yours, that's all," Justin says innocently.

Shit, we shouldn't have stopped.

Justin looks at me, and a big smile passes over his amused face. "Are you causing trouble again, Mia Lee?"

Shrugging as casually as I can, considering our predicament, I give him a small smile and reply, "What can I say, Justin? Trouble seems to follow wherever I go."

Quinn looks calm, while I'm borderline having a full-blown panic attack.

"If you guys like, I can give you a ride? I'm headed for Canada. I'm not sure where you're headed, but I'd love the company," Justin says, and I wonder what the hell he is doing in the South if he's on his way to Canada.

This doesn't make sense.

I look at Quinn, who shakes his head, his long hair slipping into one narrowed eye. "No, we're good."

My eyes widen. What's he doing? We need wheels…

"Okay, well, I'm just going to use the restroom. The offer stands if you change your mind. Catch you around, Mia," he says, stepping forward to give me another hug.

Quinn still has my hand and is not letting go, so I awkwardly give him a one-handed hug.

"See you, Justin."

And he gives me a warm smile before taking off.

As soon as he's out of hearing range, I shake my hand out of Quinn's, spinning around to face him.

"Quinn, we have to go with him."

"Over my dead body."

"What about the police?" I whisper. "We can't steal another car because they are onto us, and are no doubt just waiting for us to fuck up and hot-wire another so they can track us. Hitching a ride with Justin makes sense. We can evade the police by riding with him.

"Just until we're far enough away from here, then we'll part ways. It's the only option we have right now," I say, pleading with him to see reason on this.

Quinn's jaw clenches, his livid eyes meeting mine. "If we ride with him, I may quite possibly kill him."

Raising an eyebrow, I stupidly question, "What's your problem with Justin?"

Quinn laughs, but in no way is it a happy sound. "I don't even know where to start, but let's just say, if he so much as looks at you like he's fantasizing about you naked, I will happily gouge out his eyeballs."

My mouth falls open into an O.

He's jealous.

"Quinn, listen to me." I take a step toward him and place a palm on his cheek. "I'm yours."

My brutal honesty is needed because we're running out of time.

"So push aside that huge ego because we're doing this."

I'm not sure if it's my determination or honesty, but Quinn finally nods.

"Fine. But I meant what I said."

I smile up at him. "I know."

I'm second-guessing if this idea was such a good one.

Justin's truck is a mammoth Dodge, but it may as well be a mini, as the tension fills any remaining space in the cab.

What also fills the cab is the constant dinging of Justin's cell, alerting him to an awaiting text. I'm not sure who's texting him, but after the twentieth message, he switches it off.

I didn't want to be rude, so I sat up front, which was a huge mistake, as I can feel the tension radiating from Quinn every time Justin talks to me, or looks at me, or breathes the same air as me.

But what choice did we have?

As we drove out of the rest stop, three cops were checking out our vehicle, no doubt discovering it was stolen.

"I have to stop just outside of Arkansas. Is that okay with you guys?" Justin asks, looking over at me, his warm chocolate eyes revealing nothing but kindness.

"That's fine. Thanks again for doing this."

"No worries, Mia, anything for you."

I hear Quinn snarl in the back seat, and I sigh.

We ride the rest of the way in almost silence, and finally, as we pull up at a hotel, Justin suggests we stay the night. He mentions he has some business to take care of, so we may need to stay for a couple of days. I don't think that's wise, and we should keep moving, but I won't say anything until I speak to Quinn.

I'm not sure what our plans are, but I could use a shower and some decent food. And I also want to check in with Abi.

Justin parks his truck in front of the hotel.

"Did you want to stay with me?" Justin asks, killing the engine.

I whistle, looking up at the fancy building through the windshield.

"Perks of my job," he replies vaguely. He still hasn't clarified what he does for work.

It would help, seeing as the police are probably looking for us at every cheap, hidden-away motel along the highway. The odds of them looking for us here are slim. We lived large in New Orleans, so they probably think we've blown all our cash.

I look at Quinn over my shoulder, and he shakes his head, clearly opposed to the idea.

"Thanks, Justin, that would be awesome," I say, ignoring Quinn's snarl.

Justin nods and places his hand on my arm. It's an innocent gesture, but I'm certain Justin has roughly two seconds to remove his hand before losing it to Quinn.

Justin gets the hint, and thankfully, he lets go. He tells us to wait out here while he checks in. As soon as the door shuts behind him, Quinn reaches for my arm from the back seat, yanking me toward him.

"Jesus Christ, Quinn!" I cry, shrugging out of his grip. "Do you think you could quit it with the homicidal tendencies?"

"I meant what I said. He's lucky he still has any fingers left."

I roll my eyes but secretly love this possessive streak in him.

"He's doing us a favor. The police won't look for us here. They're probably guessing we'd be slumming it in some shithole," I explain, and Quinn sighs, knowing I'm right.

"I get that, but it doesn't mean I have to like it. He's obviously still in love with you."

"What?" I gasp, repulsed. "Ew. He is not."

"Trust me on this, Red. That torch is burning so brightly, it's shining outta his ass."

"You're being ridiculous," I scoff, hoping he is.

"I'm not. That guy has a permanent hard-on for you."

"Oh my God!" I say, mouth agape, as I turn to look at him. "That's not true, and you've just put visuals in my head that I wish I could burn out with acid, so thanks for that."

Quinn leans forward, inches away from my face. "Good. The only visual I want in your head is me."

I gasp, and Quinn gives me that damn lopsided smile before slumping back into his seat.

The car door opens, which startles me, and I yelp, jumping about five inches off my seat, nearly hitting my head on the truck roof.

"Okay, all set," Justin says, tossing the key card onto the dash as he takes a seat behind the wheel.

He looks over at me and smiles.

"Everything okay, Mia? You look flustered. Is it hot in here?" Justin asks, turning on the A/C.

Giving Justin a polite smile, I don't reply.

He parks his truck, and we exit. Quinn and I look around. The hotel is perfect.

Not only does it have an underground parking lot for easy escape but the pretentious clienteles' heads are so far up their own asses, they won't want anything to do with us.

Looks like Quinn and I should be fine—for now.

As we enter the two-bedroom apartment, Justin tosses his bag onto the carpet in the living area.

"I can crash out here if you two want to take a room each," Justin suggests, sinking into the huge brown sofa and crossing his legs onto the coffee table in front of him.

"No need," Quinn says, which are the first two words he's spoken to Justin in hours.

I cringe when I hear the bitterness behind his tone. It's probably better he doesn't speak to him again.

Justin looks over at me, raising his pierced eyebrow, and suddenly, I feel embarrassed for some stupid reason, so I avert my eyes, finding the corner lamp the most interesting thing in the world.

"Oh, right," Justin says, clearing his throat uncomfortably as he stands. "Okay, well, I'm just going to make a call."

And he awkwardly reaches for his bag, entering the room to his left. Thankfully, ours is across the hall from his.

When his door shuts, I look up at Quinn and raise an eyebrow at him.

"What?" he says, faking ignorance with a dimpled smile.

I roll my eyes and decide to take a shower before I make contact back home.

After a scorching shower I only stepped out of because I didn't want to hog all the hot water, I'm sitting on the edge of our king-sized bed, waiting for Quinn to finish up in the bathroom so we can call Abi. She's working the late shift at the diner, and I can't help but think about Bobby Joe's.

I miss it.

I miss the simplicity of going to work, doing my job, and coming home to Hank.

After visiting the church in New Orleans, I feel like I've made peace with myself over Hank's death. I will never forgive myself for what happened to him and will forever be at fault, but I have to try to move on because Hank would have wanted that. The selfless person he was, he would tell me to go on because I'm alive, and he would want me to live my life without this awful sense of regret.

However, deep down, I know the only way for me to ever really move on will be when the people responsible for his death pay for what they did to him. And by pay, I mean them being dead.

"Whatcha thinking?" Quinn asks as the bathroom door opens, and when he steps out, I forget to swallow.

He's dressed in snug black jeans and nothing else.

His hair is wet from the shower and slicked back off his perfect face. The light catches off his nipple ring as he searches his backpack for a T-shirt. I'm staring at him, but I can't help it.

"Um, just about Hank," I confess, snapping me from openly gaping.

Quinn freezes from searching through his bag, his hands stilling from their rummaging.

"Are you okay?" he asks apprehensively, no doubt fearing I'll take off or break down like I have in the past.

Looking up at him from the edge of the bed where I'm sitting cross-legged, I meet his concerned eyes.

"Yeah, I think I am," I reply, fiddling with my sleeves and pulling them down over my fingers.

"I'm proud of you, Red."

"You are?"

He nods, wisps of wet hair slipping into his eyes. "Yes. What you've gone through, not just the past few days, but your entire life, is something not a lot of people live through and stay sane."

"Sometimes I question just how sane I really am," I reply softly, lowering my eyes.

"Hey, look at me," he says, walking over to the bed and crouching down.

I meet his concerned stare.

"I've never met anyone like you. You are the strongest person I know."

I give him a disbelieving look, but he shakes his head. "I mean every single word. You have every right to be barely holding on after everything you've seen in your lifetime. And you could be a cruel, bitter, cynical bitch, but you're not. You care about others and put them before yourself. If that isn't strong, then I don't know what is."

I don't know how to respond to him. He is the kindest man I have ever met, and I'm...falling desperately in love with him.

"Thank you," I whisper, reaching for him and wrapping my arms around his warm neck.

Quinn kisses my temple and asks, "What for?"

"For believing in me," I reply, leaning into his lips.

Quinn sighs as I toy with the wet locks at his nape. "And one day, you'll believe in yourself."

I hope he's right.

Looking at the clock on the dresser, I know it's now about four o'clock in South Boston, so the diner should be a little less chaotic for Abi to chat.

I don't need to say a word as Quinn and I make our way downstairs. We find a pay phone and decide to make the call quick, just in case the line at the diner is tapped. I know we're probably overreacting, but it's better to be safe than...dead.

Thankfully, Abi answers on the fifth ring.

"Hi Abi, it's me," I say softly.

I hear her gasp, and then her footsteps quicken. I know she's walking out back for some privacy.

"Hi, Mia, how are you? I was so worried about you two," she says on a rushed breath.

"We're okay. Sorry to worry you. We had some shit go down," I say, referring to nearly being caught by the police—twice.

"I'm glad you called because my dad told me you and Quinn need to head to Canada until he can clear your name. It's taking longer than expected, and with the town pressuring Sheriff Davidson for your arrest, the police are more persistent than ever."

I look at Quinn and sigh. Out of all places to run, why does it have to be Canada? Is this the universe's way of looking down at me and laughing at the irony of where I'm running to?

Quinn lifts an eyebrow to ensure I'm okay, and I nod.

"Okay, Canada it is, then."

Quinn's eyebrow shoots up into his hairline.

"Are you going to stay with your mom?" Abi asks.

Looks like her dad *has* been busy checking me out.

"I'm not sure."

"My dad just thought it would be safer if you stayed with her," Abi says cautiously while I feel like I'm about to be sick.

Safer with my mom? I hate that I can't give Abi a definite answer that staying with my mother would indeed be the safer option, as opposed to running.

"My dad said his guys have tracked down your dad, Mia. He's always a step behind you. How does he know?" Abi asks when I remain mute about the whole mom topic.

I close my eyes, as hearing Abi confirm what I've known to be true just sucks. I know my dad and Phil will eventually catch up to me. And when they do, I'll be ready.

"Because he's my father. He knows how I think," I confess, wishing I could change that fact.

I see Quinn out of the corner of my eye shift forward at the mention of my dad.

"Well, change that. If your gut tells you to go left, then go right. Shake it up so you throw him off."

"You're right, Abi. Thank you," I say, wanting this conversation about my dad to end as my throat feels dry. "How's Tristan?"

"He's okay. He's just been released from the hospital. I think they were sick of him being such a pain in the ass."

"He's been released already? Isn't that too early? I thought you said he'd be in there for a week or so?"

Quinn looks at me with a small smile on his face. He obviously knows his brother is as stubborn as he is.

"He was determined to get out and help you guys. He knows everything and wants to do anything he can to help," Abi replies, and I can hear the strain in her voice.

No doubt she's been trying to convince him otherwise, seeing as he's still probably in a lot of pain, and in no condition to be helping anyone out, other than himself.

"He knows everything?" I ask with a catch in my throat.

"Yes. I told him. Oh God, I hope that's okay?"

"Yes, of course. I'm just—" *Embarrassed. Mortified.* "I just hate that you both are involved in my mess. You're really sticking your necks out for me."

"We're doing this because we love you and want you to come home."

"I want to come home too," I reply, close to tears. "I better go. I'm not sure about this phone line."

"Okay."

"Abi, can you do me a favor?"

"Anything," she replies without delay.

"Can you get Tristan there tomorrow, around four, your time?"

"Yes, of course."

There is a big elephant in the room, and I really want to address it, but I don't know how.

"How was the…" *Funeral*, I silently add, but am unable to voice it aloud.

But Abi gets it. "It was beautiful."

A tear slides down my cheek, and Quinn is instantly at my side, wrapping a hand around my waist.

"Be safe," Abi whispers, and I can hear she, too, is crying.

"I will."

"Tell Quinn I say hello, and he better have done what I told him to," she says, half laughing, half sniffling.

I laugh, which comes out muffled as I'm still crying.

I know she's referring to him taking me out in New Orleans, and I wish I could tell her all about it.

"He did."

Abi claps her hands happily. "Based on that response, it's safe to say you had fun?"

"You wouldn't believe how much," I reply, smirking at Quinn, as he so knows we're talking about him.

"I can't wait to hear all about it. I miss you so much."

"I miss you too. I better go," I say unhappily, hating to cut it short.

"Okay, I'll talk to you tomorrow. Bye, Mia."

"Bye, Abi." I hang up, wishing I could talk for hours.

"Everything okay?" Quinn asks when I remain in the

phone booth, my hand resting on the receiver, wishing I never had to let go.

Shrugging, I let go and step out into the cool breeze.

"Well, the good news is, Tristan is out of the hospital. I think he was being a pain in the ass, so they discharged him early."

The relief is clear as it passes over Quinn's features, and he fists his long hair. "That's my boy," he says with a smirk. "So what's the bad news?"

I bite my lip. "Abi said my dad is always a step behind us."

"Fuck. How does he know where we're going?"

"Because he knows me, Quinn. No matter what, I'm his daughter, and he knows I'll eventually end up in Canada to find my mom."

And that fact depresses me. He knew before I did where my heart would lead me. And that is to my mom.

"So we won't go to Canada. We'll go to Mexico instead. It'll buy us some time."

"No, we've got to go to Canada. Abi's dad told us to go there until he figures out what to do," I reply, and suddenly, I'm so tired all I want to do is sleep.

Quinn clenches his jaw. "I hate that he's so close to you."

"Me too. But now that we've got some direction on where we're headed, we can play it smart."

"What do you mean?" Quinn asks softly, raising my downcast chin with two fingers to meet his questioning gaze.

Giving him a small smile, I reply, "Tabitha said not to listen to my gut to throw my dad off. If I feel like I want to go left, then I should go right."

Quinn nods, sucking on his piercing in thought. "That's pretty good advice."

However, as his face contorts and his chest heaves, I know

what he is thinking.

"What about Justin…the jockstrap?" He smirks at his clever pet name.

Biting my lip, I attempt to contain my smile. "Quinn, that's not nice."

"I never said I was trying to be nice," he rebukes, pulling me toward him by my belt loops and kissing the tip of my nose.

"Well, he did say he's going to Canada," I reply, biting my lip, afraid of Quinn's response.

Quinn shakes his head in sheer defiance, and by the repulsed look in his eye, I'm certain that will not happen.

"There is no way I'm driving all the way to Canada…with *him*."

"I know, but with my dad and the police breathing down our necks, any stolen car or suspicious sightings will draw attention our way," I plead, hoping to appeal to his rational side, as his irrational side is being a total ass.

"Red…I *will* kill him," Quinn plainly says, and I believe him.

"What other choice do we have?" I ask, knowing if I had to ride with someone who I felt threatened by, I would probably be behaving the same way as Quinn. "But if you really don't want to do this, then I understand. We can do it your way."

Quinn looks as if I've just told him unicorns are real. "Did I just hear you correctly?"

I slap him on the arm lightly. "Stop being such a smart-ass. If riding with Justin makes you that uncomfortable, then we won't do it. Simple."

Quinn smirks sweetly. "He's the one who will be uncomfortable when I stick my foot so far up his ass he can't sit down."

"Quinn."

"Red," he parrots with a grin.

"I mean it. If we're not going to ride with Justin, then we need to come up with another plan," I reply, hoping to God we don't need to think of something else because I'm fresh out of ideas.

Quinn sighs, finally seeing reason. "You're right. But that doesn't mean I have to like it."

Leaning forward, I wrap my arms around his waist and bury my head into his welcoming chest.

"It's only till we get to Canada."

"Well, Canada can't get here soon enough."

And I couldn't agree more.

Ten

Day two of our road trip is no better than day one.

Quinn has decided the only person he wants to speak to today is Lucky. He seemed to be angry with me the moment we packed our bags and hit the road early this morning, as Justin said he didn't have to stay in town after all.

I'm not sure what I've done, but I'm hoping once we stop, he'll tell me what the hell crawled up his ass and died. Justin was thrilled to have us accompany him to Canada. Sadly, Quinn was not.

We've been on the road since first light and headed to a town just outside of Missouri to stay for a couple of days because Justin needs to stop over for work. I'd rather not stay in a place for longer than a few hours.

But what other choice do we have?

We travel in silence for many hours, only stopping for gas

and food, but thankfully, once we finally pull up at our hotel, I'm grateful for two reasons. The first is my butt is asleep, and second, I need to separate Quinn and Justin, who are seconds away from killing each other.

The silence in the truck has been deafening, and if I hear Quinn huff one more time, I'm going to gag him.

Justin has caught on to the fact that he gets under Quinn's skin whenever he touches me or his eyes linger on me for too long. And previously, those actions were innocent, but now he seems to be doing it to piss Quinn off.

But I could just be reading into things.

Justin turns to address me and only me. "Just going to check us in, Mia Mouse," he says with a grin. "Remember I used to call you that in high school?"

Giving him a strained smile, I try not to cringe at the nickname. "Yeah, I sure do."

Unfastening his seat belt, he turns to me, raising his pierced brow. "You never asked why I called you that. Weren't you ever curious why?"

Not really, no. Justin's nickname for me was the least of my concerns, but I play along.

"Sure, I was," I lamely say. "I was just…"

"Too busy for a geek like me?" he offers with a smile.

That's so far from the truth, but I see no point in correcting him as this is just trivial, nostalgic bullshit.

"Well, just in case you're curious now, I called you that because you were as quiet and as small as a mouse, but you had the whole school terrified of you. You could get a classroom full of jocks and cheerleaders running in the opposite direction with your presence alone."

"Thanks…I think." I chuckle, as the nickname is kind of cute, in a creepy, rodent kind of way.

"Anytime, my little mouse." Justin smirks, placing his hand on my knee, which is poking through a hole in my jeans.

My face heats as Quinn listens to our conversation, no doubt ready to explode.

"How about you fu—" Quinn snarls, but I don't allow him to finish as I subtly remove my knee and unbuckle my seat belt, as it's suffocating me.

"Food. How about Quinn and I find some food, and you check us in?"

Justin smirks, and I know we have about three seconds to exit the truck before Quinn checks Justin into a hospital.

"Great idea. Bring me back something juicy." Justin eyes me but thankfully exits the car without another word.

The truck's walls are closing in on me, and I too jump out, desperate for some fresh air. The door slams shut, and I tell myself to woman up and face the inevitable.

Risking a glance at Quinn, who looks like he's about to break anything in sight with the way his fists are clenching by his sides, I say lightheartedly, "C'mon, sugar, lead the way."

Quinn breaks his evil stare-off with Justin, and all I get is a grunt in response.

"Hey, why does he get a nickname? Where's mine?" Justin says, stalling from unloading the bags from the tray.

I take a deep breath, hoping this comment doesn't bite me in the ass, and I reply, "That's because he's my boy…"

I want to say boyfriend, but after everything we've been through, Quinn is much more to me than that.

I watch Justin's face drop, as this is the first time I have really clarified what Quinn is to me. I don't feel comfortable labeling it, but I need to clarify that Quinn and I are more than just friends.

However, I instantly feel horrible as Justin nods and clears his throat before saying, "I'll just go and check us in." And he walks off, unable to get away from me fast enough.

I close my eyes and sigh, feeling beyond awful for saying something that obviously upset Justin, especially when he's helping us out. Rethinking my ingenious decision, I feel Quinn wrap his arms around my middle, his front pressing to my back.

"I'm your boy, hey?" he whispers, his warm breath tickling my earlobe.

At least he's talking to me now.

I nod in response, leaning back into his embrace as I missed his warmth during the car ride over here.

"I would have preferred man or handsome fucker, but boy will do," he says comically, biting my neck softly.

The mewl that passes through my lips is involuntary, and Quinn chuckles his confident laugh, knowing I'm melting under his touch. Before I know what is happening as my eyes are still shut, Quinn presses me against the passenger door, his hard contours molding to my back.

"Red, I meant what I said," he says, his arms tightening around my middle while he kisses under my jaw.

Interlacing my fingers through his and leaning my head back, allowing him better access to the needy flesh of my neck, I whisper, barely audibly, "What did you say?"

"I will kill him if he touches you," he replies as his lips suck my skin delicately.

"Please, Quinn, can you do this for me? And do you think you could try to be less…homicidal?" I plead on a gasp as he bites my shoulder, his sharp teeth grazing my skin.

Quinn moans softly, his hard-on digging into my back.

"Okay, but only because you begged," he says, and with one final kiss on my neck, he pulls away, leaving me panting, needy, and extremely turned on.

It takes a minute for my heart to cease from thumping like a bass drum, and I slowly turn to face my boy, or should I say, man.

I know Quinn has baggage, baggage which gives him nightmares. Baggage that he feels will change the way I feel about him if I ever find out what it contains. But what he doesn't realize is we all have baggage. Ours is just a little more fucked up than others, and that's what draws us to one another—two broken, fucked-up souls.

We are possessive, jealous, and protective over the other, but that's because I feel we have found the missing piece of the puzzle. And the missing piece of my puzzle is Quinn. And I can only hope that I'm his—in every sense of the word.

Quinn smirks at me, as I'm sure he can see me mulling over this whole fucked-up situation.

"Let's eat," he says, his eyes heated as he licks over his lip ring, and I can't help but feel he is sizing me up for his next meal.

"Let's call the diner first," I manage to get out.

Quinn reaches for my hand, and we silently cross the street to use the pay phone near the gas station.

Reaching into my bag, I pull out a handful of quarters, extending my palm to Quinn.

"Did you want to call? I'm sure Tristan will be waiting by the phone."

Quinn runs his long fingers through his hair and nods.

The strain around his deep eyes reveals that he's anxious but also excited to talk to his brother. He picks up the receiver, feeding coin after coin into the phone, and quickly dials the diner. As he chews on his lip ring, waiting for it to connect, I decide to walk away to give him some privacy.

But Quinn quickly reaches for my arm to stop me from leaving and nods. "Stay."

So I do.

"Hey, bro," Quinn says, and my tears fall the moment his face tips up into a beautiful smile.

I can faintly hear Tristan on the other end. "Quinn?"

"Yeah, it's me. How are you feeling? Did any hot nurses give you a sponge bath?"

I roll my eyes, and Quinn chuckles.

"Good to see things haven't changed." Tristan laughs. "How are you? How's Mia?"

"We're both good. Well, as good as can be, considering," Quinn replies, affectionately rubbing my cheek with his thumb.

"Yeah, I bet. I've spoken to Abi about the plan," Tristan says, and I can hear he has lowered his voice.

"Yeah? What about it?"

"I'm coming with you," Tristan says, the determination clear in his voice.

Both Quinn and I shout, "No!" at the same moment.

"Hey, I heard Mia's voice. Is she there? How's she looking?"

Quinn looks at me, eating me up from head to toe.

"Oh, she's looking unbelievable."

Again, I roll my eyes.

"Put her on," Tristan says, ignoring Quinn.

Quinn chews on his hoop, setting my skin on fire with his intense gaze.

"In a sec, we gotta talk about this idea of you coming with us. You're staying put." Quinn's humor has been replaced with a serious tone.

"No fucking way. I wanna help."

"Tris, do you need another trip to the hospital to remind

you of what happened the last time you wanted to help?"

"That's totally different. They caught me off guard."

"This isn't negotiable. Stay put until we figure out what to do after we arrive in…" But Quinn doesn't finish his sentence.

He's smart and won't mention where we are headed, just in case the police are listening in. Here's hoping they aren't, as I should have spoken in code when Tabitha told us where to go.

"No way. I'm not leaving you alone out there to deal with those two motherfuckers. I want my revenge just as much as you do yours."

Tristan is right. Not only has my father and Phil killed Hank but they forced his brother to go on the run. They also attacked him, nearly taking his life. I understand the need for vengeance, I really do. But I agree with Quinn. It's bad enough that I'm putting one Berkeley brother's life in danger. I can't do that to both.

I extend my hand, indicating to Quinn I want the phone.

"Good luck," Quinn says with a chuckle, handing me the phone.

"Luck? What the hell do I need luck for?" Tristan says as I place the receiver to my ear.

"Hi, Tristan," I say, looking at a chuckling Quinn.

"Oh, now I get it. Hi, Pai… Mia," he corrects quickly. "How are you?"

"I'm okay. More importantly, how are you?"

"I'm fine. I would be better if I could come help you."

"Quinn is right. Stay where you are. It's not safe for you," I reply, feeling like a total ass for saying that to him, seeing as I'm dragging Quinn into my bullshit.

"And it is for you?" Tristan asks softly.

"It's not safe for any of us, but it's too late for us. We have no other choice but to run. But you do," I say, hoping to talk some sense into him.

"You can't expect me to sit here while you two are in danger." I can hear the frustration in his voice.

"That's exactly what I expect. Please, Tristan, help Abi clear our names. That's more help to Quinn and me than you coming out here, okay?"

When he doesn't reply, I reiterate, "Okay, Tristan? Promise me you will stay put."

"Okay, fine. But if anything changes, I'm coming to find you."

I sigh, rubbing my forehead.

"You Berkeley brothers are so stubborn," I reply, looking at Quinn, who only shrugs, not defending his honor.

"You wouldn't believe how stubborn we are. Can you put Quinn back on?"

"Of course. Tristan—" I pause.

How do I thank him for risking his life to save me? How do I tell him I owe him my life?

But he gets my silence for what it is. "Don't mention it, Mia. You're worth it. I would do it again in a heartbeat," he whispers, his voice reflecting the sincerity behind his admission.

I don't know what to say because his kindness and honesty throws me off.

"Thank you. I…um, better go," I reply, feeling incredibly thoughtless for disregarding his confession.

Tristan sighs but replies, "Bye. I…miss you."

I don't respond, but quickly hold out the phone to Quinn, who gives me a small smile as he reaches for the receiver.

Sitting on the curb, I can no longer hear what the boys are talking about, but after Tristan's confession, I don't want to hear what he has to say, and that's because a small part of me knows he has feelings for me. But he had feelings for Paige, not Mia.

Quinn is looking at me while listening to something Tristan says. The way his eyes take me in, I know they're talking about me.

I not only have one incredible man trying to protect me and putting his life in danger for me. I now have two. But I could never live with myself if anything happened to Tristan—again.

"I've got an awesome idea," Quinn says, bumping me with his shoulder as he sits near me after he ends his call to Tristan.

"What's that?"

"Let's go find a liquor store and drink."

I laugh because, at the moment, there is nothing else I would rather do.

Once we're checked into the hotel, I feel terrible for my insensitive jab and invite Justin to join us for drinks after he's finished doing whatever he needs to do for work. Quinn hates me right now, as his stress-free night of getting drunk and forgetting our troubles has just taken a nosedive.

But I feel horrible, as Justin is helping us out without even realizing how much so.

I decide I need new clothes, seeing as I left the majority of my things in New Orleans. A thrift shop down the road is a perfect place to pick up some cheap clothing. Quinn was in the shower when I left, which was good because I need some alone time after speaking with Tristan.

Why do I have a feeling our conversation was one-sided?

Deep down, I have an awful premonition that Tristan will come find us regardless of my and Quinn's warnings.

However, trying to focus on the task at hand, I pick out some clothes for Quinn and me and figure that'll do us for now.

As I exit, I pull my newly purchased jacket lapels over my face as the cold December breeze has picked up. Jolly fat Santa decals and fairy lights are displayed in every shop front, preparing shoppers for the mad Christmas rush. I wonder where I will be spending Christmas this year.

I'm hoping it's not in a 6x8 cell.

Or dead.

Shaking those thoughts aside, I ride the elevator up to our floor and find Quinn walking around the bedroom in only a small towel. The towel barely covers anything, and if he shifts the wrong way, I'll be getting an eyeful.

I quickly turn my back, not really knowing why. I am still learning the ways of being in a relationship with someone.

"Hi?" Quinn asks my back, phrasing it as a question, as he's obviously just as puzzled by my weird behavior as I am.

"Hi."

"Whatcha doing?" he asks, laughing.

"I don't know," I reply, as I suddenly feel nervous.

We haven't spoken about what happened in the hotel room back in New Orleans, seeing as we had other important matters to deal with, like not falling to our deaths.

Quinn and I have said, in a roundabout way, that we're dating.

But he hasn't actually said, *"Red, I want you to be my girlfriend."*

Do people even do that anymore? Have that talk?

After being with Quinn, I would be a liar if I said I haven't thought about sex. I have a feeling once it happens, Quinn will own me; mind, body, and soul. I've never wanted to do that with anyone—ever. But with Quinn, it's all I can think about when he's near me, especially when he's half nude.

"Why have you gone shy all of a sudden? You certainly weren't shy back in New Orleans. Or in the truck," Quinn whispers into my ear.

He is leaning into my back, and I hope to God he has put pants on, as the thought of a pantless Quinn, pressed up against me, leaves me breathless, totally giving my thoughts away.

Thankfully as Quinn steps into view, I see he has indeed slipped into a pair of sweats, but no shirt. My eyes dip to his navel, which is perfectly covered in a fine dusting of soft, dark hair leading to his low-slung pants.

Will I ever get used to seeing him without my heart ending up in my throat?

"What's the matter?" he asks, taking a step toward me.

"I was just thinking."

"About?" Quinn prompts.

"About what happened between us back in New Orleans."

"You want to be a little more specific?" He smirks, knowing damn well what I'm talking about.

"Never mind. Anyway, I bought you some stuff," I say, hoping to evade this topic as I rifle through the plastic bags.

Quinn is about to speak, but Justin chooses that moment to enter, and thankfully put an end to this awkward conversation.

Happy's Bar and Grill is anything but happy.

Looking at my untouched burger, I internally apologize to all the starving kids in the world because there is no way I can eat my meal as I feel like I'm about to be sick. Justin is at the bar, waiting in line to get another pitcher of beer, and I wish Quinn would quit it with the death stares.

"Would you please stop looking at him like he's the Antichrist?" I sigh, pushing at my fries.

Quinn's eyes are narrowed, and he's rubbing his stubbled jaw, deep in thought.

"I don't trust him. Something is off about him. I just can't put my finger on it."

I blow out a frustrated breath. "Quinn, please. Just till we get to Canada."

"Yeah, well, Canada is over a thousand miles away. And he's about zero miles away from me ripping off his arms and beating him to death with them," he replies, tossing back his beer.

Justin returns, and we all dive for the booze, desperate to drown the evening with alcohol.

However, after one too many pitchers of beer, I decide the next girl who accidentally on purpose touches Quinn will lose a finger.

There is something about Quinn, and it's not just his phenomenal looks. His ego alone is enough to fill a room, but his presence and his confident, cocky demeanor seem to attract…everyone.

I can't help but watch him as he casually stands at the bar, surrounded by women. Justin is talking to me about something, and I know I'm being extremely rude, peering over his shoulder, watching Quinn, but I'm hoping he won't notice.

But he does.

"You really like him, huh?"

My eyes snap to his sheepishly, totally busted. "Sorry."

Justin shakes his head. "It's nice to see you smile."

I'm anything but smiling at the moment, but I guess he is referring to the times when Quinn and I don't want to throttle one another.

"It's nice *to* smile."

"You were at school, but not really there, if you know what I mean," Justin comments, fiddling with a coaster.

"I know exactly what you mean." I had more important stuff to deal with other than algebra. Like delivering drugs and being a parent to my dad.

"Don't judge me, but I had the biggest crush on you," Justin randomly says, his eyes lowered by his confession.

I blush, taken aback. "Really?"

"Yeah, you were such a badass. I think every guy had a crush on you."

I doubt that. I was the brunt of everyone's jokes, and I accepted that.

"Trust me, Mia," Justin says when he sees my reaction to being told I wasn't as invisible as I believed to be.

He reaches across the table, surprising me by taking my hand, and I don't have time to pull it back. "This is kind of pathetic, but no one has even come close to you when we kissed."

Suddenly, I feel extremely uncomfortable and want my hand back. I pull back subtly, but he won't let go.

"What are you running from, Mia?"

Again, I attempt to pull back, but his grip is strong.

"What makes you think I'm running from anything?"

"We're all running from something."

"What are *you* running from?" I ask, suddenly feeling a

chill pass over my body.

"I'm not running away from everything, Mia. You could say I'm running toward it."

"Toward what?" I question, suddenly seeing a side to Justin I never knew existed.

"Revenge," he simply replies, meeting my eyes.

I've seen that look before. It's one I see every day in the mirror. Justin has obviously lost someone he loved and is seeking retribution.

I was too wrapped up in my bullshit to remember much about Justin, other than the fact he was deemed a freak, just like me. His family life was rough, but whose wasn't? Unless you were the fucking Brady Bunch, then every family had their problems.

The two times we kissed were not earth-shattering.

The first time was under the bleachers, near the gymnasium, and I felt vulnerable and tired after my dad was on one of his three-day benders. And the second time was at some party where we were two misfits wanting to belong.

After the non-eventful kisses, I saw Justin now and then in the hallways at school, but like I said, at that stage, my dad was so far gone, I was more at home than at school, trying to fix his problems, and I failed senior year, eventually dropping out.

So safe to say, Justin was the furthest thing from my mind. But it's funny how you can make an impact on someone's life without even realizing it.

"We all good here?" Quinn asks, slamming the pitcher of beer so hard onto the table that it spills over the sides.

I pull back my hand, and thankfully, Justin lets go this time.

"Red?" Quinn questions, sitting near me when I don't

reply.

"Yup, all good," I mumble, reaching for my glass and downing my beer.

Justin smirks, seeming to enjoy the discomfort between Quinn and me.

"Excuse me, I gotta make a call," he says, standing up and heading outside.

I can feel Quinn's eyes pinning me with a heated stare, and I bravely meet his gaze.

"What?"

"What did I tell you? As long as he keeps his hands to himself, he'll be fine. But the minute my back is turned, that motherfucker has his hands all over you," he says, looking over my shoulder to where Justin went.

"He was not all over me. We were just talking about…" And I pause.

Oh shit, I need to shut up. Telling Quinn that Justin had the biggest crush on me and still fantasizes about our kisses won't help my case.

"About what?" he asks, leaning back into his seat.

"Nothing. Forget I said anything."

"No, I will not. The more I'm around this guy, the fishier he gets. I didn't like him from the get-go, but something is off about him. Him just popping up, offering to help and expecting nothing in return is damn strange. Unless…"

"Unless what?" I ask, interested to hear Quinn's thoughts.

"Unless he expects payment in the form of you," Quinn spits, and his jaw clenches.

"What?" I gasp. "That's ridiculous!"

"Is it?" Quinn questions, raising an eyebrow.

"What do you know about this guy, Red? Apart from an old crush from school?" And the word "crush" has never sounded so dirty.

"He's here on business."

"So he says. What business? And why is his goddamn phone going off every thirty seconds?"

"You're just suspicious of everyone!" I say angrily, but I don't actually know *why* he's always on his phone.

"No, I'm realistic. When a guy offers to drive a girl halfway across the country without expecting anything in return, something isn't right. The only reason I'm not breaking his nose is because you've asked me not to, and to trust you on this. And you're right; he *is* our best option at the moment, allowing us to fly under the radar. But that doesn't mean I have to like him."

"Why don't you like him?" I ask, as I really don't understand. Justin seems harmless to me.

"Because I don't like the way he looks at you when you're not looking."

I cock my eyebrow. This is news to me.

"He looks at you," Quinn explains simply. "Like he wants to fuck you...or fuck you over. I just haven't figured out which yet."

My mouth falls open, because both options are horrible.

"You're wrong."

"I hope I am."

But now that the seed of doubt is planted, I'm afraid it'll just grow.

Justin returns, slipping his cell into his jeans before sitting down.

I give him a small smile, hoping I don't look guilty, but I can't help it as Quinn's words repeat in my head.

Why would Justin want to fuck me over?

Eleven

The banging on our bedroom door has me shooting up in bed, reminiscent of the last time someone knocked on our door. And that time wasn't good because it was the police. Quinn sleeps peacefully near me, curled onto his side, his head resting on my pillow.

I can't run again. I just can't.

Thankfully, the banging ceases, and Justin's soft voice echoes outside our door. "Mia? Are you awake?"

The bedside clock reads 3:34 a.m. What does he want?

Silently slipping out of bed, not wanting to wake Quinn, I grab his hoodie off the floor and slip it on before opening the door and stepping out to face Justin.

"Everything okay?" I ask because he looks a little stressed out as he slips his cell into his back pocket.

Justin rubs the back of his neck. "Um, yeah. Sorry to wake

you," he apologizes, stalling about why he's outside my door at three o'clock.

"It's fine, what's up?" I ask, crossing my arms over my chest as the room has dropped to an arctic temperature.

"Um, plans have changed, and I no longer have to stay here. Wanna head out at first light?"

This is great news. The sooner we hit the road, the better. But I can't help but wonder what's changed. And what work is Justin involved in. We all have our secrets—God knows I have enough for us both—but I feel unsettled not knowing why exactly Justin is headed for Canada.

"That's great," I whisper, not wanting to wake Quinn. "What changed?"

Justin sniffs, looking away, and I don't like it.

"Oh, um…"

"What's going on?"

I spin around quickly, knowing this doesn't look good. Quinn meets my guilty eyes, waiting for an answer.

"Justin just wanted to let me know that we can leave at first light. He doesn't have to stay here after all," I reply on a breath.

"Peachy," Quinn replies, his arms crossed over his bare chest in defiance. "And this couldn't wait till the morning?"

Justin speaks up, and this is the first time he has addressed Quinn in hours. "Sorry, dude, my bad. I just wanted to let you guys know. I'm not much of a sleeper and forget that other people are."

Justin's attempt at a joke falls flat on its ass, and Quinn grunts in response, his eyes narrowed. "Whatever, *dude*."

I'm so sick of this bullshit between them. Quinn is not helping this situation by attacking Justin, and Justin being vague all the time makes me suspicious of his intentions.

Turning on my heel in frustration, I huff, "Well, if you two are done being little bitches, I'm going to sleep."

And I stomp into the bedroom, not caring if Quinn follows. If he and Justin need to have a fight or whatever boys do to prove who the bigger man is, then so be it. I'm sick of playing peacemaker between two opposites.

Throwing off the covers, I slip into the sheets, hoping to catch at least twenty minutes of sleep. But I know I won't because this whole fucked-up situation keeps worsening. I don't know where my dad is, and I'm constantly looking over my shoulder, afraid I'll see him or the police. I just can't seem to catch a break.

And with Justin and Quinn at each other's throats, I honestly don't know what else to do. As much as I hate it, Justin is the only way for us to remain undetected. I wish Quinn could get over whatever issue he has with Justin. I don't know what else I can do to show him I'm his.

"I'm sorry, Red."

Sighing, I roll onto my side, away from Quinn. I don't want to talk to him right now.

"Don't ignore me. I'm sorry, okay?"

The resolve in his tone tells me that he is, but I remain silent.

The bed dips, and strong arms wrap around my waist, pulling me toward a familiar chest.

"Please don't be mad at me," Quinn whispers close to my ear, his hair tickling my cheek.

"I'm not mad."

"And please don't lie to me."

Quinn is right. Maybe if I tell him how I feel, like *really* tell him how I feel, he will stop with this bullshit jealousy crap with Justin.

I shift slowly to face him. Quinn's grip on my waist slackens, allowing me to turn. He is the most handsome man I have ever seen, and he is insane if he believes I would ever want anyone other than him.

"I'm not mad," I reiterate. "I'm just tired. This whole situation we're in, the situation *I've* put you in, makes me sick. I hate that you are in this situation because of me. And I hate that you have to play nice with Justin because I know you just want to hang him up by his balls and let the wildlife have their way with him."

Quinn's mouth tips up into a small smile, but he allows me to continue.

"But I know you won't leave me, and you know that I don't want you to go," I confess. "What you've done for me, no one has ever done for me before."

"Red," Quinn says, but I place my finger over his lips, silencing him as I need to get this out.

"Quinn, you are in here." I remove my hand from his mouth, placing my palm over my chest. "No one will ever, *ever* take your place. No one. I promise you. So please, just please, can you try to tolerate Justin? I'm not asking you to like him. Hell, you don't even have to talk to him. It's probably better if you don't. But can you, for me, can we just get to Canada and…"

But this time, Quinn is the one to silence me as he places his finger over my lips.

"Okay," he replies, his warm eyes meeting mine.

"Yeah?" I ask around his finger, hoping he'll say yes.

"Yeah," he confirms with a nod, his finger slowly sashaying across my wet lips.

"Thank you."

Quinn nods, his eyes transfixed on his finger as he plays

with my lower lip.

"You're in here too," Quinn replies softly, reaching for my palm and placing it over his warm chest.

His beating heart drums steadily underneath my hand, comforting me in a way I've never felt. Knowing that his heart beats for me makes all of this bullshit worthwhile.

"Kiss me," I whisper, my palm still resting against his chest.

I can feel his heart rate speed up at my suggestion, and it's nice to know his heart beats as fast as mine.

It's now seven thirty, and we're checked out and ready to hit the road.

After our chat, I feel like Quinn and I reached an agreement, and we also made some headway with what's going on with us. There is no doubt in my mind that I'm falling for Quinn and falling hard. And for once, I'm not scared or confused by it. I feel alive.

Justin has been quiet, and I really want to ask what's up, but I have a feeling he wouldn't tell me. There is more to Justin, and Quinn *is* right. What do I really know about him? The Justin I now know has changed from the Justin I knew in high school. This Justin is guarded, and this Justin is definitely hiding something.

I just don't know what.

"Where are we headed?" I ask, jumping into the passenger seat with Lucky sitting on my lap.

"Wisconsin," Justin replies, placing his paper coffee cup in the cupholder and starting the engine.

"Cool," I say even though I have no clue what happens in

Wisconsin.

Quinn chuckles, and I love that the air has cleared somewhat. I don't expect Quinn and Justin to become best friends, but if they can tolerate one another, I will settle for that.

Justin suggests Quinn and I do some sightseeing while he checks in with work. He still hasn't elaborated on what his work involves.

Quinn and I are walking hand in hand, strolling the city streets with Lucky by my side. I know we should keep a low profile, but I'm getting a severe case of cabin fever, or should I say car fever.

It is so nice to be outdoors. I just wish the circumstances were different.

It's a shame we don't have enough time to explore the sights and sounds of such a wonderful place. There is one thing I want to do, and as soon as I see it, I yank on Quinn's hand, leading him toward where I know he wants to be.

An art gallery.

Quinn follows, chuckling at my enthusiasm, but I know he will enjoy this. That night, all those nights ago when I stumbled into Quinn's room by mistake and saw all of his drawings pinned to his wall, I remember thinking his work needs to be in a gallery somewhere, where people come from all corners of the globe to appreciate his talent.

One day, I can only hope that becomes a reality for him.

Tying Lucky to a pole just outside the building, we climb the stairs, and when we enter, I gasp at the works I see. They are like nothing I've ever seen before. The vast warehouse is painted a bright white with spotlights showcasing the paintings and photographs hanging on the walls. The carpet is light beige, and the black stools positioned in front of the artwork allow one to sit and admire it for hours.

It's so quiet here that I feel like I'm in a library, so I speak to Quinn in a whisper. "There is so much to see."

"Why are you whispering?" Quinn says, matching my low tone.

"I don't know," I reply and laugh softly.

As Quinn takes in the beauty before us, I know dragging him in here was a great decision. I'm silent and allow Quinn to lead me. I want him to discover every inch of this place and not leave till he's ready to go.

We reach the first painting, and it looks like an explosion of color. Random shapes are scattered within the dark shading, and if you look close enough, you can make out images that are subjective to the beholder.

It makes no sense to me since it looks like a bunch of chaotic squares and lines, but by the way Quinn tilts his head to the side, his intense eyes taking it all in, I know there is more than meets the eye.

Kind of like Quinn. As we move from painting to painting, they all seem a little repetitive, but I don't say a word, as I know Quinn is absorbing it all. Thankfully, the abstract art section ends, and we get to a section of charcoal sketches.

Now, this stuff, I get. This stuff reminds me of Quinn's work.

The elegant lines, which appear careless and messy, are far from unplanned. Each stroke was done with intent, making the picture whole. But when we reach a picture no bigger than a postcard, I gasp because this picture is my favorite one of all.

It's of a man and woman, both bare, entwined around one

another so tightly that their form becomes one. The painting is called *Love Blurs*.

Quinn sits in front of it, pulling me to sit on his lap. And I move effortlessly, as there is no comfier seat in the world.

"It's brilliant how they've used cross-hatching to follow the contours of their torsos. It gives the picture a different dimension," he explains, stroking over the lines in the air.

His hypnotic voice lulls me into a sleepy bubble, and I nod in response even though I have no idea what he's talking about.

"Your stuff should be hanging in here," I say with sincerity.

"My stuff is far from being ready to display in a gallery such as this."

"And why not?" I ask defensively, twisting my neck to look at him over my shoulder.

Quinn smirks, his arms tightening around my middle. "It just isn't."

"Who says?"

"I say," he replies, kissing my nose playfully.

"Well, I disagree. Your stuff is as good as these. Maybe even better. I mean, did you see that lamp?" I pull a face, shaking my head.

Quinn chuckles, and the sound warms my insides.

Turning back around and looking at the picture while Quinn cocoons my body with his, I ask, "When you were younger, what did you want to be?"

Suddenly, I want to know everything there is about Quinn. He has shared bits and pieces, but I want to know it all now.

"A paleontologist," he replies with a small chuckle.

"Huh? Did you just make that up?" I question, not able to wipe the smile off my face.

Quinn laughs, his chest rumbling with his chuckles. "Nope. It's the nerdy truth. Don't judge me."

"Sheesh, I never knew you were an overachiever," I joke while Quinn playfully nips my shoulder.

"I loved the idea of getting my hands dirty and finding the next undiscovered dinosaur," Quinn states, nuzzling my neck.

"What changed?"

"I found out the chances of that happening takes years. Or in some circumstances, never," he replies, sucking the underside of my neck, his lip piercing chilling my skin. "And I'm not that patient."

I shiver at the contact, heated by his words as I wonder if he is referring to something else. "And now?"

"Now what?"

"Now that you've grown up, what do you want to be?"

There is silence for a moment, and I can feel Quinn thinking over his answer before he replies.

"Now…now I just want to be a good man," he finally answers, and the truth behind his words hurts my heart.

"You *are* a good man, Quinn," I reply, turning around so I can meet his eyes.

"Thanks, Red. I'm glad you think so," he says in return, and his eyes focus on the drawing on the wall, not able to meet my probing stare.

I think so? What about him? What does he think he is? A bad man? That is so far from the truth, and I need him to believe that.

"Quinn—" But he silences me as he reaches for my chin, arching my head back and capturing my lips with his.

I know this is his way of ending our conversation, and it's a clever derailment because I can never say no to a kiss from Quinn. We sit, making out for a while, until I need to find the restroom.

"I have to use the bathroom," I say begrudgingly, sliding off Quinn's lap.

Quinn attempts to move, but I place my hand on his shoulder to stop him. "No, stay. I'll be right back." I know he is enjoying his time here and not ready to leave yet.

"You sure?"

"Yes," I reply, kissing him and quietly exiting through the back door.

The cool December breeze hits my cheeks, and today is one of those days where magic is in the air. It could just be all the frantic shoppers buying last-minute Christmas gifts, but whatever it is, it makes me feel fortunate to be alive.

The restroom has seen better days. I enter the middle stall and quickly do my thing since I'm not a fan of public bathrooms. As I'm about to flush the toilet, I hear a gentle whispering catch on the cool winter breeze.

It's so faint that I have to strain my hearing to confirm I'm not imagining things. But as I raise my head upward, positioning my ear under the window above the toilet, I hear it again.

I can't make out what they're saying, but the voices belong to men. I listen closely, blocking out all other noise, and focus on the hushed voices. The moment I hear the voice of one of the men, the walls close in on me, and I can't breathe.

It can't be.

It can't be *him*.

Jumping up onto the toilet lid, I'm just tall enough to peer through the window, but I don't see anyone.

Am I going crazy?

Am I imagining the voice of my...father?

Turning my head from left to right, I frantically search

for the face of the man I want dead. But it's useless. There is no place for him to hide since this window overlooks an open courtyard.

So where is the whispering coming from then?

Softly lowering my feet onto the concrete, I crouch low and reach silently into my boot for my knife. If he's out there, then I'm facing him, armed and ready for battle.

I flick open the blade but accidentally fumble, slicing across the length of my palm when I hear his voice echoing off the dirty walls.

"Mia…it's only a matter of time."

I slam my back against the door, knife in hand, ready to attack, as I alternate from looking above me from left to right. My heartbeat pounds so loudly in fear that it's almost deafening, and I only just resist the urge to cover my ears because I can't concentrate on what to do next.

Why did I have to choose the middle stall? No doubt if my father really *is* here, then Phil is not too far behind. Therefore, I have to look over *both* shoulders, as I have not only one psychopath after me, but two.

How could I have been so careless? I should have scoped out my surroundings before I entered. But, if they're coming for me, then fuck me going down in a cubical no bigger than a sardine can.

Taking three deep breaths, I slowly peek through the sliver of a gap through the door to see if anyone is out there. I can't see anything, nor can I hear the whispering any longer.

Giving myself a pep talk and internally counting to five, I slowly unhinge the lock and push open the door with my boot, on guard with my knife poised in front of me. Ducking my head from left to right, I see that the coast is clear, but I still won't breathe easy till I'm out in the open.

As I wedge my body through the door, my entire frame shakes from pure adrenaline and fear. Taking my first step toward freedom is not freedom at all, as something squishes under my boot.

Looking down, I gasp, and the color drains from my face in a second.

A blue dog collar with a silver tag that reads Lucky stares back at me. Bile rises into my throat as I bend down to pick it up. The collar is covered in matted fur.

Running out of the bathroom faster than my feet can carry me, I'm frantic to find Lucky and run straight into a solid chest. I'm hysterical and don't realize I'm screaming at the top of my lungs and pounding on flesh until I hear my name.

"Mia! Stop it. Mia, it's Justin. It's okay."

But I can't stop. I need to get away from him. I need to find my dog.

"What the fuck are you doing?"

My body slackens when I hear his voice, and I sag against Justin, who wraps a hand loosely around my waist.

"Get your hands off her!" Quinn snarls, and I'm ripped from Justin's arms and hugged into his familiar embrace.

As I bury my head into Quinn's chest, inhaling his comforting scent, Quinn snarls, "What the fuck did you do to her?"

His hand runs down my back, attempting to calm me down, but the rage seeping from every pore in his body is anything but calm.

"Nothing. She just came running out of the bathroom, screaming. I did nothing!" Justin says, backing away from a livid Quinn, hands raised in surrender.

"Don't fucking lie to me!" Quinn growls, reaching for

Justin while pulling me with him.

I have to stop this, and now that my hysteria has simmered, I can focus on what's important.

"Quinn, stop."

But Quinn continues to stalk toward Justin, deaf to reason.

"Quinn, Lucky!" That's all I say, holding out my fist, his blue collar peeking through my fingers.

That stops Quinn as he reaches for my hand, extending my right palm open.

Gasping when he sees the collar, he quickly asks, "What happened?"

He puts me out at arm's length, waiting for me to explain.

"I found it," I manage to choke out. "In the bathroom, on the floor. And I heard…"

"Heard what?" Quinn asks, his eyes wide, waiting for me to speak.

But when I remain silent, trying to understand how everything has just turned to shit in the span of two minutes, Quinn barks, "You heard what, Red?"

"Hey, man, let her go," Justin says, taking a step forward.

"You take another step, and I'll make sure it's your last," Quinn spits out, never breaking eye contact with me.

"What did you hear?" he asks again, encouraging me to continue.

"*Him*," I reply on a whisper.

That word has never sounded so dirty, and nausea rolls over me.

"We have to find Lucky," I cry, not wanting to imagine what has happened to him.

"Fuck," Quinn curses, grabbing my hand and leading me away from Justin, who looks confused and…angry.

But I don't have time to question why, as Quinn is dragging me toward the front entrance where we left Lucky. But he's gone.

My heart crumbles in my chest, and I choke back a sob. "Where is he, Quinn?"

"I don't know, but we'll find him, I promise," Quinn says with sheer determination as his eyes dart around the courtyard.

I can't help but think, if and when we do find him, what shape will he be in? The sound of barking alerts both Quinn and me, and we turn to see Lucky limp toward us.

"Lucky!" I scream and run toward him. His front right paw hangs at a grotesque angle, hindering his walking.

"Stay, boy!" I yell as he's struggling to move.

The moment I reach his side, I drop to both knees, throwing my arms around his neck. The tears I have been holding on to spill free, and I sob into his soft coat as he collapses onto the cold ground.

My relief is overwhelming, and I pass my hands over every inch of his body, making sure he is real. It isn't until Quinn gasps that I pull away and see what has him winded. My hand pauses, and I notice Lucky's black and white coat covered in smears of red blood.

"Where's the blood coming from?" Quinn asks, dropping to both knees, frantically examining Lucky's body with both hands.

"Oh God," I choke, my hands following Quinn's desperate search to find the wound.

"It's not his blood," Quinn says after a minute of thoroughly examining Lucky, and he turns my left palm over, letting out a tiny gasp.

I hiss in pain as the blood is coming from my hand. I

vaguely remember slicing it open in the bathroom, and now that the adrenaline has worn off, it throbs in severe pain. I attempt to pull it toward me, wanting to cradle it to my chest, but Quinn holds on tight as he tears apart a strip of his gray shirt to carefully wrap it around my hand.

I recoil with the pressure but allow him to tie it tight to stop the bleeding. The sticky blood runs down my arm, and because of my long-sleeved sweater, it concealed the bleeding.

"Sorry," Quinn says, flinching with me when he sees I'm in pain. "I didn't even see you were bleeding before. I just…"

But he doesn't continue.

"You'll need stitches."

"I'll be fine," I reply, nuzzling my face into Lucky's fur. "Lucky is the one who needs stitches. Did you see his paw?"

Quinn nods. "We'll have to find a vet."

"Want to tell me what the hell is going on?" Quinn asks, but I just can't speak, not yet.

A thunderclap alerts us that the heavens are about to open, and I can't help but think, this is just the beginning of a wild storm.

"What are you doing?" Quinn demands, watching me move madly around the room, collecting my belongings in a whirlwind of panic.

"I have to go," I reply, dropping to my knees and searching for my missing Chuck under the bed.

"Red, just stop. You're giving me whiplash with all your buzzing around. Come here," Quinn demands from where he sits on the edge of the bed.

Finding my missing shoe, I back out from under the bed,

puffing my hair off my brow.

"We don't have time."

As I attempt to move to the dresser, Quinn halts my movements by wrapping a hand around my waist and ensnaring me onto his lap.

"Stop," he says, inches from my face, his breath fanning my cheeks. "Tell me what you're thinking."

After we left the gallery, I pretty much remained mute, patting Lucky, lost in my own world. I grunted out bits and pieces of what happened to Quinn so he had an idea of what happened. But I had to be careful because I knew Justin was listening.

We found a vet who took one look at Lucky and confirmed that his front paw was broken by force. He would need to operate and estimated Lucky would be at the clinic for two days after the surgery to recover.

Two fucking days meant Quinn and I were stuck here with my dad and Phil biting at our heels.

I cannot process the thought that my father was breathing the same air as me without feeling sick to my stomach. But what's worse is that he had the chance to end this, all of it, and catch me unawares, but he didn't.

Instead, he opted to toy with me, alerting me to the fact that he's onto me and can strike at any time.

Leaving Lucky's collar was his way of playing with me, sending a message as such, and that message being that he's always two steps ahead of me. He'll always catch up to me no matter how far I run. He'll hurt and destroy no matter whom I bring into my life—Hank, Tabitha, Tristan, Quinn, Lucky.

And I can't live with that on my conscience.

Sitting sidesaddle on Quinn's lap, I wrap my arms around his taut neck. "It would be so much safer and easier for you if I left."

Quinn laughs in response, which is not the reaction I was expecting.

"I mean it."

Quinn nods, his messy hair slipping into his eyes. "I know."

"And you're laughing?"

"It's just funny that you think that's even an option," he replies as he reaches for a roll of gauze sitting on the nightstand.

He uncoils my injured hand from around his neck and unties the bloodied mess of his gray shirt off my palm, which acted as a makeshift bandage.

As I watch his gentle fingers lightly pass over the cut to examine the damage, I ask, "What do you mean?"

But I know exactly what he means because he's right. Leaving Quinn will hurt me more than being captured by my dad.

"What do you expect me to do?" I question softly, sagging in defeat. "Lucky will be at the vet for at least two days. I can't just stay here. We're sitting ducks, and it's only a matter of time until my dad will get sick of waiting, and he'll hurt everyone I love."

"Hey," Quinn soothes, lifting my chin with his fingertips. "I won't let him hurt you ever again, okay?"

"You can't promise me that. And I don't want you to. This isn't your problem. It's mine."

Quinn sighs, the frustration showing in his clenched jaw. We're silent for a few moments, and I watch as Quinn tends to my wound with such care.

His sharp voice breaks the hypnotic stillness of his gentle fingers tending to my wound. "Your problems are *my* problems. I wish you'd get that."

I appreciate his chivalry, but how can I live with myself if anything happens to him? Today was the wake-up call I needed.

"How do you expect me to just sit by and allow you to endanger yourself, Quinn? I can't."

"I'm a big boy. I know what I'm doing," he retorts. He rubs a white ointment into my palm, then unravels the length of gauze around my hand.

"I'm sick of running. It doesn't matter where we go. My dad will always find me."

I'm barely holding back my tears now as the reality of the situation sets in.

Quinn nods, his eyes focused on treating my injured hand. "I know you are. And so am I."

"You are?" I ask, wiping away a rogue tear that has escaped the corner of my eye.

"Of course, I am. This is no life for you to live."

"You either," I add because this is not just about me.

Quinn nods, and his hair slips over his brow, blanketing his narrowed eyes. "No more running, then."

"What?" I gasp because surely, I haven't heard him correctly.

"We stop running, and we figure out another plan. We'll call Abi and get her to talk to her dad tomorrow. This is just too dangerous for you. Today was too close. If anything had happened to you," He pauses before he confesses, his eyes swimming in regret. "I'm sorry I wasn't there to protect you."

"Stop it. This isn't your fault. None of it is."

"I should have been there."

"Well, I shouldn't have let my guard down. There is no point playing the blame game," I state, hoping he'll see reason.

Quinn thankfully nods and lets it go.

"So what do we do now?" I ask, watching as his fingers clasp the bandage together with some tape.

Quinn draws his piercing into his mouth, deep in thought. "Well, we have no other choice. We have to keep a low profile till Lucky recovers."

"So what do you propose we do till then?"

Quinn's sinful mouth tips up into a lopsided smile as he traces over my moon tattoo, which is peeking out from underneath the bandage.

"I can think of a few things," he replies, his eyes lifting to meet my bashful ones, and my pulse quickens at what he's envisioning.

"Oh, Red, you make this too easy."

"What do I make easy?"

"Fantasizing about you in all compromising...positions," he replies, a dimple hugging his cheek.

I almost jet off his lap at his confession, and he chuckles, dipping his head and drawing my lower lip into the warm cavern of his mouth. Moaning at the contact, he pulls away all too quickly, and I pout.

This will be a long couple of days.

I can't sleep.

My hand throbs, and Quinn is right. I think I need stitches because blood stains the white bandage a bright red.

There are painkillers in the bathroom, and I decide to take a couple, hoping to numb the pain so I can catch a few hours' sleep.

Slipping out of bed, not wanting to wake a snoring Quinn,

I tiptoe to the door, wanting to grab a bottle of water from the fridge. With my hand poised on the door, I hear a muffled voice from out in the hallway. I know it's Justin, and I know spying on someone is not polite, but my body acts before my brain can tell me otherwise.

I close the door softly behind me and creep out into the hallway, shrouding myself in the shadows. Justin stands in the living area with his back turned to me, whispering to someone on his cell.

"I know, sorry. I fucked up."

The person on the other end is chewing Justin out, and he rubs the back of his neck in frustration.

"Yeah, well, I'm trying. It's not as easy as you think. Okay, fine. Just hurry the hell up."

I have no idea what Justin is talking about, but it can't be good.

The look he gave me today was one of anger, and I don't know why. Yes, Quinn spoke to him a little harshly, but considering the circumstances, surely Justin can understand? But Justin is hiding something. I haven't forgotten his conversation with me at the bar when he confessed he is hell-bent on revenge.

And I haven't mentioned it to Quinn either.

"Consider it done. Just make sure you bring what I need. Yes, I'm sure. She means nothing," Justin says, snapping me out of my thoughts.

I shiver with the callousness behind his tone and feel for whoever he is speaking of. Suddenly feeling a chill, I creep back into my room. I'm suddenly not thirsty.

Silently slipping back under the covers, I can't kick this feeling of dread because deep down, I can't help but think that my father could have killed me and no one would have known it was him. But I'm alive, and as strange as it may sound, that thought is more troubling than him wanting me dead.

Twelve

My entire body is on fire.

My body is alight from the top of my head to the soles of my feet. And the reason for that inferno is Quinn Berkeley.

The sting of his tongue ring as he licks over every inch of my skin hits me straight between the legs. My back bows off the bed as I fist handfuls of the pressed linen sheets.

But he's relentless, and each moan that escapes my parted lips encourages him to continue.

"Do you like it?" Quinn asks breathlessly, swirling his wicked tongue around my navel.

"Yes, God, yes," I moan my response.

"Do you want me to keep going?"

"Yes, please," I reply, on the verge of begging.

Quinn's dimple appears briefly as he gives me his

trademark lopsided smile and slowly slides down my body, his lips leading the way. As I feel the first wet lick sweep across my sex, I know I'm done for, and I'm his prisoner till the end.

His large hands splay across my ribs lightly, holding my body in place as I'm about to rocket off the bed, and I fear I will never come back down.

"You taste incredible. Feel good, baby?"

"Yes, it feels amazing. Don't stop, please don't ever stop."

I'm almost there. I can taste it, but suddenly, Quinn's mouth is nibbling the crease in my neck.

"Wake up, Red. You're dreaming."

"No," I groan. "Let me finish."

I'm so close; to stop now would just be damn cruel.

But the warm chuckle is like a cold bucket of water, dousing my raging hormones, and my eyes snap open, only to realize I *was* dreaming. I'm panting loudly, and my entire body is on fire. But as I look at Quinn, I turn a beet red.

How embarrassing. I just had a sex dream, and the man smiling smugly at me was the star in my very public show.

Groaning, I throw the blanket over my head, hoping to hide away until my embarrassment fades, which should be in about fifty years.

"Red." Quinn chuckles, attempting to shift the blanket off my face.

But I fight him and hold the fleecy material with no intention of ever letting go. This only has Quinn laughing louder and yanking harder, but I won't budge.

"Please let me wallow in my humiliation alone."

"And miss all the fun?" he replies, slipping under the sheets with me when it becomes clear I'm not letting the blanket go. "If you're not coming out, then I'm coming in."

"You're invading my personal space," I huff, moving back

an inch, but Quinn stops my escape, his hand ensnaring my waist.

"Five minutes ago, you didn't mind me invading your personal space. I think you even begged me not to stop." He chuckles, and I slap him on the arm, mortified.

"Oh, fuck you."

My comment has Quinn raising his eyebrow, and I kick my ass for leaving myself open with such a statement.

"Don't," I caution, pointing my finger at him, warning him not to go there.

With palms raised in surrender, Quinn smirks. "Wouldn't dream of it. Although, you might."

"Kill me now," I groan, tossing my arm over my eyes.

Being cocooned in this tight space with Quinn has flashes of my dream taunting me with visual images I'm ashamed to be reliving. This has never happened to me before. I mean, I know boys have wet dreams, but do girls? Is that even possible? My achy flesh tells me it's *very* possible.

"Let me see those pretty eyes," Quinn says softly, reaching for my wrist and sliding my arm off my face. "Better."

I still don't know what to say, as I have no doubt Quinn heard me panting out his name. There is no way of denying it, so I remain quiet.

"How are you feeling?"

Mortified, humiliated, my brain screams. But instead, I reply, "I'm okay."

"Your hand all right?" he asks, softly reaching for my palm.

The limited light underneath the heavy mass of blankets means he can't see the bandage is stained a bright red.

"I'm fine."

"My tough girl," he replies, the affection clear in his tone.

We remain quiet underneath the blankets, breathing in the same air. And it's perfect.

"Did you still want to call Abi?"

"Yeah. Do you?"

I nod in response.

He surprises me by rolling gently on top of me, ensnaring my hands above my head so they peek out above the sheets.

"First, let's get something to eat." He kisses my neck delicately. "Then we'll call her. Although…" He kisses a path from my neck, over my chin, to my eager lips, sucking my bottom lip in a long pull. "I could just eat you."

I gasp, my body loving his suggestion.

But he shakes his head, his sleep-tousled hair falling over his brow. "But that could take all day." He tosses the blanket off our heads, the sunlight blinding us both. "For now, I'll settle for breakfast."

My lips dip into an involuntary frown because my appetite only hungers for a big portion of Quinn, Quinn, and more Quinn.

Lost in those mouth-watering thoughts, Quinn nudges forward so we are nose to nose, and whispers, "Oh, Red. But make no mistake, I'll be having you for dessert." He kisses my parted lips, leaving me breathless.

"Glad you're feeling better," Justin says, interrupting me from daydreaming about Quinn's kisses.

"Huh?"

Quinn chuckles to my left while digging into his pancakes, knowing exactly where my thoughts were thirty seconds ago.

"You just look better than yesterday," Justin clarifies,

sipping his coffee.

"Oh, right. Yeah, I am."

I have a motive for inviting Justin to breakfast. After last night, I'm onto him. Something about him is not right, and I need to figure out what that is.

I have yet to tell Quinn that I overheard Justin's weird phone conversation because I don't need to add any fuel to that fire. Quinn hates him enough as it is. Telling Quinn I'm suspicious of Justin will only result in Quinn reaching over this table and happily slapping the truth out of him. And I don't think that really qualifies as keeping a low profile.

As I grip my fork, I hiss out in pain, forgetting my injured palm.

"What happened?" Justin asks, gesturing with his chin to my bandaged hand.

Quinn tenses near me, but I use Justin's question as my loophole.

"I cut my palm while trying to protect myself," I reply coolly, sitting backward, attempting to gauge Justin's reaction.

He remains calm and collected as he replies around a mouthful of food, "Oh yeah? From whom?"

"From my father," I state nonchalantly, watching closely for any changes in his expression.

Quinn's back straightens instantly, and his hand grips my upper thigh under the table, obviously questioning my motives.

"Oh? He still a deadbeat?" Justin calmly asks, staring me straight in the eye.

"Something like that," I reply just as casually, crossing my arms over my chest.

Quinn remains silent, watching our exchange with interest.

"Well, if he's anything like I remember, he's a lowlife scumbag," Justin plainly states before popping a strawberry into his mouth.

"Your memory serves you well."

"Why is he after you?" Justin asks after a minute of silence, pushing his barely touched breakfast to the side.

The whole table waits for my answer, and as I take a small, casual sip of my orange juice, I shrug and bluntly reply, "Because I shot him."

Quinn chokes on his coffee, thumping his chest to clear his throat. But Justin and I never break eye contact, nor does his reaction alter at my earth-shattering news.

So he's either not affected that he's sharing his car with a self-confessed criminal.

Or he already knew.

I'm betting on the latter.

Justin is the first to look away, clearing his throat.

"Well, you always were a badass. Looks like some things never change." He reaches for his coffee.

But my gaze never falters. When the server slides us our bill, Justin throws some money onto the table, excusing himself when his phone rings.

As he pushes through the glass door, the bell jingling with his exit, Quinn leans into my ear and whispers harshly, "Care to tell me what that was about?"

"You're right. Something about Justin is off. I was just testing the waters," I reply, matching his low tone.

Quinn pulls back, eyes wide. "What changed your mind? Why don't you trust him?"

"I never trusted him, Quinn. The only person I trust is you."

Quinn's eyes soften, and I can't help myself as I reach

forward, brushing a fallen wisp of hair off his brow. His hair has grown so long that he can now easily tie it back. But stubborn strands keep slipping free, framing his handsome face.

"So what are you thinking?" he questions, turning his cheek into my palm and sighing when I stroke him softly.

"I'm thinking Justin knew I shot my dad. The suburb I grew up in isn't huge, and news like that would have spread quickly."

"So why is he helping you out? What's his deal?"

I shrug, removing my palm. "That, I'm not sure of."

Quinn scratches his whiskered chin. "Well, we'll find out."

"How?" I question, arching an inquisitive brow.

Quinn sucks on his lip ring, his dimple hinting at the wicked plan he's currently conspiring. "We get the fucker wasted and find out what he knows."

Justin has been MIA for most of the morning, which is handy, as we've just got off the phone with Tabitha.

She advised us not to do anything drastic until she talks to her dad because she thinks our idea of staying put is horrible. We're supposed to call her back tomorrow, and hopefully, she'll have some miracle solution because I'm fresh out of ideas.

Running may be the best option, but it's proven not to be the safest. But neither is sitting and waiting to be cornered by two psychopaths.

Quinn has been quiet since speaking to Abi, and I wonder what's on his mind.

"Are you all right?" I question as we stroll toward the

hotel, dodging crazy Christmas shoppers with hands filled with shopping bags.

Quinn shrugs, his broad shoulders rising in uncertainty, which worries me.

"Hey," I say, placing my hand on his bicep, stopping him from taking another step.

Quinn rolls his bottom lip between his teeth, meeting my eyes with a look of dread.

"I've thought of a plan," he finally says, breaking the silence. "But I'm not sure how you'll feel about it."

"Okay, let's hear it."

"We smoke out your dad," he replies, running a hand through his messy hair.

I raise an eyebrow, and Quinn sighs, closing his eyes briefly.

As he opens them, the pain is evident with every deep breath. "Let that fucker find us, and when he does, you let me deal with him…my way."

I know Quinn's *way* entails a lot of violence and murder.

"No, absolutely not. No way in hell are you going anywhere near him. It's too dangerous. You saw what they did to H—" I stop, unable to finish my sentence.

"If we're smart, then the only *death* will be theirs."

"I can't ask you to…" An elderly couple walks past us, oblivious to our poisonous conversation. "Kill my dad," I continue with a whisper when the coast is clear.

"You're not asking me to do anything," Quinn says, hooking his thumb toward his chest. "This is my choice."

"It's not the right choice."

"It's the *only* choice," he spits stubbornly, shaking his head. "Running from those motherfuckers is no longer an option. I don't know how, but they keep tracing our steps. It's only a matter of time before one of us slips up, and I'd prefer it to be them."

By the hard resolve of his jaw, I know he's made up his mind.

Deciding to humor him, I ask, "What do you suggest we do?"

"How do you trap a predator?" he asks, looking as if he is about to be sick, and suddenly, I know why.

"With bait," I reply softly.

In other words…me.

So Operation BAIT sounds like an awful plan in theory, but in reality, it's the only plan we have if we don't run. I know my dad will eventually track me down if we stay put, and I would rather be prepared when he does.

The police will hopefully see reason once I confess my story, but my dad and Phil won't. Therefore, I'm more afraid of getting caught by them than by the police.

There is no other option—my dad and Phil have to die.

That was always the plan, but I hoped it was when I was a little less fugitive. I want to make myself known to my dad but remain elusive to the police. It's hard to do both, but I've been doing a good job of it thus far.

Quinn looks incredibly plagued by his suggestion, but I get it, and I know he has my back. There is no cemented plan just yet, but we've agreed to stay underground from the police, but wave a red flag for my dad and Phil, and hope like hell they'll come charging.

And when they do, Quinn and I will be ready.

And to be ready, we need guns.

And lots of them.

The only problem is, how do we obtain an arsenal with no ID and just a wad of cash to back us up?

We can't. Well, not legally, anyway. And this is where my street smarts come in handy. I know shady when I see it. And a fruit shop that doesn't sell any fresh fruit is shady.

"Let me go in," Quinn says, yanking onto my hand, trying to stop me from waltzing into the alleged fruit shop in a back alleyway downtown.

"No way," I reply with half a chuckle. "Leave this to me."

Quinn sighs, knowing there is no changing my mind.

To ease the tension, I try to make light of what we're about to do. "You do remember what I used to do for a living, right?"

But Quinn's lips dip into a sad frown as he takes a steadying breath. "Every day, Red."

Standing on tippy-toes, I kiss his lips quickly, appreciating the empathy, but it's not necessary.

"Trust me?" I say, resting my forehead against his.

"With my life," he replies without a second thought.

And I smile as I reciprocate the feeling.

Glancing up and down the narrow alleyway to ensure no one is following us, I give Quinn one final, reassuring look and enter through the doorway with Quinn behind me.

The woman behind the front counter eyes us, no doubt committing our faces to memory.

"What you want?" she scowls in broken English, crossing her arms over her bountiful bust.

A few bananas and apples decorate the near bare shelves, hoping to convince any poor soul who happens to make a wrong turn that this is an actual operational fruit shop. But I know I'm right and we have come to the right place.

Looking subtly around the small space, I see the blinking

red lights of four security cameras, filming our every move. And I know if we make the *wrong* move, it'll be the last we ever make.

Wishing I paid more attention in Spanish class, I'm forced to use my street slang.

"Roscoe or gats, you selling?" I ask, looking behind her shoulder to where a beaded curtain sways with the steady flow of the air-conditioning.

Guns have so many street names that it's hard to know which to use. But often when someone wants to use a code for weaponry, so that bystanders don't overhear, they'll pick a word starting with the same letter, and only the insiders know what they're asking for. For example—Roscoe for revolver, gat for guns, and so on.

The lady's brown eyes narrow as she sizes me up, and Quinn is instantly flush against me, letting me know he's got my back if things go south.

"No English," she says, waving me off and shaking her head, her gray-streaked bun bopping from the momentum.

I know for a fact she's lying. So I resort to using the universal language that every individual on this planet understands.

And that is the language of money.

Bending slowly with my hand raised in surrender, I use the other to reach into my boot.

"I'm not carrying," I say, my eyes never leaving hers as I watch her hand dip under the counter to no doubt reach for a piece.

"*Dinero*," I say, giving her a small nod.

I bypass my knife. My fingers twitch for the metal security, but I instead reach for the roll of one-hundred-dollar bills, sitting snugly inside my shoe. Pulling out the cash, I slowly hold it above my head with my hands still raised, indicating I mean no harm.

Taking two cautious steps toward her with Quinn following in hot pursuit, I place the roll of hundreds onto the bench and simply say, "*Pistolas.*"

I step back and lower my hands to chest level as she greedily eyes the money. I can practically see her counting the cash in her head, and I know we're good. With a flick of her head over her left shoulder, she directs me toward the storeroom out back.

"*Gracias.*" I nod, reaching for Quinn's hand and walking slowly but confidently toward the back of the room.

"Why do I have a feeling you've done that before?" he whispers into my ear.

I only smile over my shoulder in response, as I don't care to admit how often I've been involved in such a situation.

Pushing apart the red-and-white-beaded curtain, I take stock of everything in the room, just like I used to when delivering drugs. Old habits die hard.

The storeroom is a smallish, dark warehouse with a roller door as our only other exit if things get dicey. A few dozen wooden crates are stored throughout the warehouse floor, and I glance above me to the second level, scanning the area for hidden men waiting for an ambush. Thankfully, there aren't any.

After a few moments of uncomfortable silence, a man with a curly mustache, taupe flares, and heavy gold chains that decorate his thick neck comes strolling out from an office, approaching us with a cocky, shit-eating grin. This dude is stuck in the seventies and lacks zero balls, as he has six beefy men standing behind him with machine guns strapped over their chests like a badge of honor.

Douches like this act like heavy armor makes a man or gives them the balls to be in this line of work. Little do they know, it's not the gun that makes the man. Instead, it's his honor. And it's his heart.

The man standing behind me perfectly exemplifies what a real man encompasses.

"What you want?" he asks in a thick accent, twirling the left side of his mustache as he eyes me hungrily.

This fucker is making my skin crawl, and the sooner we get out of here, the better.

Without hesitation, I rattle off my list, consisting of a colorful selection of pump-action shotguns, Glocks, Berettas, my all-time favorite Colts, and, just for fun, two AK-47s.

He smiles a reptilian smirk, and I nearly gag.

"A girl who knows what she wants. I like." He licks his lips, making it more than obvious he's ogling my boobs.

Quinn growls, and I place my hand behind me, stopping his retreat, as that's exactly what this scumbag wants.

I want this little league hero out of my life, so I'm direct, ensuring I don't mince my words. "Look, enough with the talking. Do we have a deal or not?"

"Oh, we do." He chuckles, motioning for his goons to bring the goods.

The whole while the dickhead eyes me, attempting to intimidate me. But I just match his stare, defiantly crossing my arms over my chest.

"*Señorita*, you got some cojones," he says with a smirk, then flicks his reptilian eyes to Quinn. "Maybe more than your little *amigo*."

Before Quinn can react, I laugh. "He's got enough cojones for us both." I give him a playful wink.

He breaks out into a raspy fit of laughter, and thankfully,

there's no more talk of cojones.

Waiting while this lowlife checks me out and listening to Richie Valens while he sings "La Bamba" is as clichéd as it sounds, so when the henchman returns, bearing arms, my heart beats in excitement. This is the first step toward taking my life back.

This is the first step toward avenging Hank.

"You know how to handle these?" asks the beefy goon while handing me a Glock 19.

Scoffing, I pull back the hammer, cocking the gun, and let off a round into the far corner of the warehouse, narrowly missing the goon's head. All the men jump, startled, not anticipating me to shoot the gun, but hey, a girl's gotta feel comfortable with her piece.

"I've handled bigger," I joke, slipping the pistol into the back of my jeans and resting it in the small of my back.

All the men, excluding Quinn, chuckle, and I roll my eyes.

Men—tell them a dick joke, and they're putty in your hands.

The henchmen pass Quinn the rest of the guns, and he quickly places them into his backpack, never meeting my eyes. I pull out some bills from my pocket and walk confidently toward the hero, handing him the roll of cash.

"We good?" I ask, watching him mentally count the cash.

"*Si, señorita.* You need anything else, you come see me." He gives me a greasy wink before he whistles to his guards, and they come running like the good dogs.

Quinn straps his backpack onto his shoulders, and I know he is attempting to rein in his temper by the way he clenches his jaw tightly. Reaching for his hand and giving it a light, reassuring squeeze, we cautiously walk backward toward the exit, not stupid enough to turn our backs to these criminals.

Only when we walk through the beaded curtain do we turn around.

"*Gracias*," I tell the store clerk, who is openly counting her cash.

She barely registers our presence, which suits us just fine.

Quinn yanks on my hand the moment we exit and spins me around, forcing me up against a wall, his huge body shrouding mine.

Stunned, I gasp, "What the fu…" Before I can finish, his lips smash onto mine, almost suffocating me with his fierce passion.

I'm left breathless with his fury, but I match everything he gives me, fisting his long hair between my fingers, yanking it to match the insane rhythm of our lips.

We're almost one, as we are pressed chest to chest, and I have no room to move. But I welcome it and lead one hand down his back, cupping his firm ass and squeezing tight.

He moans in his throat with the forceful contact, and I bite his lip, sucking his piercing into my mouth, pulling with force. He melts underneath me, and I feel powerful. I feel alive.

Quinn pulls away, but not before biting my lower lip, and it pops as he lets it go.

"What was that for?" I ask once I catch my breath.

Quinn's eyes are absorbed in black, heated pools of desire, expressing how turned on he is.

He runs a finger down my cheek while toying with his lip ring. "Because I knew you were a badass, but seeing you in action, fuck, Red, that was the hottest thing I have ever seen."

I bite my lip, flushed by his comment and the passionate kiss.

I guess life-or-death situations prioritize what's important.

And what's important to me is Quinn.

"Let's get back to the hotel."

Shaking my head clear of wicked, naked Quinn images, I reach for his hand because that's a very good idea.

As we walk down the alleyway, silent and lost in thought, Quinn smirks. "So you've handled bigger, huh?"

I roll my eyes but can't help the smile that spreads from cheek to cheek.

See? Putty in your hands.

As we hide our weapons in the closet, the front door closes, announcing Justin's arrival.

"You still want to find out what his deal is?" Quinn whispers, jutting his chin out toward the living room.

"You bet."

Quinn sits on the end of our bed, his legs spread out wide.

"If we get nothing out of him, we call it a day, okay? We've got enough to deal with, and some old boyfriend with a raging hard-on for you is low on our priority list."

"Okay," I reply, trying not to cringe at the gross analogy.

"Now, before you start defending him…" Quinn stops, stunned. "What did you say?"

"Okay," I repeat with a smile.

"What? That's it? No fighting me on this?" Quinn asks, arching a brow, watching me as I kick off my boots.

"Nope," I reply because Quinn is right.

With our plan of attack set in motion, finding out what, or if Justin knows anything, *does* fall low on the priority list. But I'll give it one last go, and if tonight nosedives, then so be it. Justin is the least of our worries.

Lost in thought, Quinn leans forward, catching me off guard and scooping me into his arms. I yelp in surprise as he settles me on his lap, turning my face from side to side, his brow furrowing.

"What are you doing?" I ask with a chuckle, convinced he has gone insane.

"You're so obedient, and it's freaking me out. I wanted to make sure it was you."

This man is the only man who would make light of this fucked-up situation, which is our lives.

"Well, I can always argue if that would make you feel more comfortable."

He runs his fingertips along my cheek, the gentle movement causing goose bumps from head to toe.

"I kind of like you submissive," he confesses softly, playing with his lip ring.

My face heats as my mind conjures up how submissive I could be. This really needs to stop, as surely this can't be good for my heart.

"Oh, Red," Quinn whispers, his face inches from mine. "You're a bad, bad girl." He claims my mouth as his.

Our plan to get Justin drunk still stands, but first of all, I want to visit Lucky. It's on the way to the bar, and I figure if my dad is watching me, then he'd be watching this vet like a hawk.

The tension can be cut with a knife between us three, and I really can't wait to get tonight over with and cut ties with Justin ASAP, who begrudgingly agreed to come out with us.

As we enter the clinic, the smell of antiseptic burns my nostrils, and I cannot wait to get Lucky out of this sterile environment. The vet nurse, a young student, offers to bring Lucky out.

The door swings open, and out comes a groggy-looking Lucky with a bandaged paw extending up to his armpit. But he's alive, and that's all that matters. As he sees me and Quinn, his three good legs skid on the linoleum floor, frantically trying to get to us.

The sight warms my heart, and I drop to one knee, opening my arms. "C'mon, boy," I coo, waving him forward, but he stops midway, his hackles rising as he drops low and snarls, looking over my shoulder.

"Lucky?" I ask, looking up at Quinn.

Quinn shrugs, appearing just as confused as I am.

Lucky takes a step back as he raises his lips, showing teeth, and as he commences barking, I notice he's backing away from...Justin.

Justin shuffles uncomfortably behind me, and I don't understand.

"Is this normal?" I ask the nurse. "I mean, he's never done this before."

"I'm not sure. The meds could have worn off, and he's a bit sore and grumpy. I'll take him out back," she says apologetically, yanking on Lucky's lead.

"I'll just wait outside," Justin says and turns quickly, leaving me and Quinn staring at one another, baffled.

I don't want to express the thought churning through my brain because it's too hard to digest without wanting to be sick.

"Those drinks can't come fast enough," Quinn says against my forehead as he wraps me into a tight embrace.

I couldn't agree more.

The random bar we've chosen serves cheap beer, which suits us just fine, as I'm planning on getting Justin toasted so he spills the beans.

Quinn is at the bar, getting drinks, but he's done this so I can milk some information from Justin, who is nursing his sixth beer.

"So you never told me what you did for work." I playfully smile, hoping he won't detect my ruse.

There is *definitely* something up with Justin. After Lucky's reaction to him today, I'm starting to think he may have had something to do with Lucky being hurt. If I find out that's true, then I'll return the favor and break *his* leg.

"Oh, it's boring," he says, waving me off and taking a long sip of beer.

"C'mon, try me," I tease, trying my best to appear flirty without gagging.

Justin laughs, totally buying it. "You could say I'm into repossession."

"Huh? Like cars?" I question, raising an eyebrow.

Justin smirks like a shark and replies, "No. More like possessions. Think of me as a repo agent."

I have no idea what that means, but I'm not stupid, and I know he's lying. I can see Quinn over Justin's shoulder, watching our exchange closely, waiting to attack if I give him a sign that I'm in trouble. But I subtly shake my head because I'm not giving up just yet.

I try another angle and fiddle with the coaster underneath my untouched beer. Justin picks up on my fidgeting and asks, "Everything okay?"

Looking up at him and faking the best innocent look I can muster without looking ridiculous, I say, "I wanted to talk to you."

"What's up?" he asks, giving me his full attention.

Feeling the repulsion slide over my skin as I begin flirting, I purr, "You didn't look too surprised when I told you...about my dad."

Watching Justin under hooded lids, I look for changes in facial expressions, mannerisms, anything. But he has the perfect poker face.

"Yeah, well, nothing you do surprises me, Mia Mouse," he replies, confidently leaning back into his chair.

"What do you mean?"

"You were always a rule breaker."

"Shooting my dad is a little more serious than breaking the rules. I mean, it's breaking the law."

Justin scoots his chair closer to my left, and I can clearly see Quinn watching us from the bar. But he looks like he's seconds away from charging. Again, I subtly shake my head at him, as I'm sick of playing these back-and-forth games with Justin.

I want answers.

"Mia, I'm sure you had a good reason, right? I mean, we do everything for a reason. And at the time, shooting your dad was the right thing to do. I'm not here to judge you...I've got my own demons to deal with than pass judgment over others."

Jackpot.

"What demons?" I question, reaching forward and lightly resting my palm over his clenched fist.

"A man's gotta have some secrets," Justin says, leaning forward, his lips inches from my ear. "And besides, I don't think your *boy* would appreciate me telling you my deepest, darkest secrets."

Quinn takes two furious steps forward, but I gesture with my hand for him to stop, beseeching him with my eyes for him to allow me to handle this. He clenches his jaw, and his nostrils flare in pure rage, but he does as I ask.

"He's just someone to have fun with," I whisper, the words feeling like venom as they pass through my lips.

Justin's breathing accelerates, and as his warm, desperate breath heats my exposed neck, I have to stop myself from throwing up.

"He looks as if he wants to have more than 'just fun' with you," he spits, his lips still inches from my ear as he burrows into my neck.

"Not my problem," I whisper, my gaze never leaving Quinn's.

"Really?" he says, pulling back, and I meet his predatory stare.

"Really. He's just a friend," I confirm with a nod.

"Prove it." Justin smirks, running a hand over his lips and resting his fingers on his chin, deep in thought.

"How?" I question, suddenly not liking where this is headed.

"Come to my room tonight when your *friend* is asleep, and I'll tell you what I know," Justin says, his pierced eyebrow cocked, daring me to accept his challenge.

"So you did know? How? And what do you know?" I ask, kicking my ass when the desperation laces my questions.

Justin tsks me, placing his pointer finger under my chin and meeting my eyes. "You come tonight, and I'll tell you everything."

Trying not to retch, I give him my best seductive smile and nod. "Tonight it is, then."

"No. Fucking. Way," Quinn hisses, his hands threaded through his snarled hair, which he's pulled in fury.

"Quinn—" I press, but he cuts me off, storming over to the edge of the bed where I'm tying up my Chucks.

"No fucking way, Red. No."

This conversation has gone on for the past hour, and looking over at the clock, I dare say it'll continue throughout the early morning hours.

Once we arrived back at the hotel, Justin drunkenly swayed into his room, tossing me a small wink over his shoulder as he shut his bedroom door behind him. As I filled Quinn in on what Justin proposed, the room got smaller and smaller with his wrath. He dragged me into our bedroom, where we have remained, arguing the pros and cons of me doing what Justin has asked.

It goes without saying which side Quinn is arguing for.

"I'm not going to do anything with him. I'm just going to talk to him."

Quinn laughs angrily, pointing toward the door. "You think that asshat has any information? He's just playing you."

"You don't know that!" I retort, standing up.

"Yes, I do. He is full of shit, and he can smell your desperation. He'll tell you anything you want to hear to get into your pants!"

I have seen Quinn angry before, but this, this is taking it to the next level of anger.

"You really think I would stoop to that? I would *never* do that," I cry, trying to keep my voice down.

Quinn's eyes soften as he takes a step forward. "I know

you wouldn't, but he would. He's a guy, and he wants to fuck you. And that makes him a dangerous guy who would do anything to get what he wants."

"Oh please, you think I'm stupid? I can take care of myself!"

I'm livid, but I know what Quinn is saying makes sense. It's just if Justin knows anything that might help us out regarding my father, then I'm willing to make a sacrifice. Quinn will be in the next room, and I know he'll have my back if anything goes wrong.

"Oh, really?" Quinn asks, and suddenly, the room heats up.

"So what happens if he asks you to kiss him?"

"What?" I gasp, stepping back away from Quinn, a slowly moving predator.

"You heard me. What if the terms of him divulging this alleged information is on the proviso of him kissing you?"

Gulping, I shakily reply, "I would tell him to go to hell."

Quinn licks his bottom lip, snickering. "Would you?"

"Of course," I affirm, still walking backward because suddenly, I feel like prey.

Quinn shakes his head, his tousled locks veiling his eyes. "You see, Red, I think your intentions are innocent, but if he gives you an inch, that won't be enough, and I think you would do almost anything to get him to talk."

What is Quinn implying? Whatever it is, I don't like it.

"I would never," I say, insulted he would insinuate something so vulgar.

"Wouldn't you?" he questions, and as the back of my knees hit the edge of the bed, I fall, losing my balance.

Attempting to scramble up the bed proves futile as Quinn crawls on top of me, trapping my body under his massive frame.

"Get off," I snarl, pushing at his chest.

"I plan to." Quinn smirks hungrily, his gaze dropping to my chest as my black camisole has shifted, exposing the top of my breasts.

"Quinn, I'm serious." I sigh, but that sigh transforms into a gasp when he bites me on the chin—hard.

"Stop," I plead, but it's pathetic because my disloyal body writhing underneath Quinn demonstrates I don't want him to stop.

"You don't mean that."

"Yes, I…do," I breathlessly state as his hands begin a slow, torturous journey of my body.

His lips never leave my skin, touching any part of exposed, heated flesh he can find.

Closing my eyes, I tell myself five more minutes, and then I'll fight him off and go see Justin. But as he circles my nipple over my camisole, I know five minutes won't be long enough.

That familiar heat builds in my center, and my traitorous body has ruled over my mind because I know Quinn is doing this as a distraction. But quite frankly, I couldn't care less.

"Beautiful," Quinn whispers against my arched throat, licking down my neck and lazily tonguing the dip between my collarbones.

My legs scissor impatiently, and Quinn removes his hand from my nipple, gliding his fingers to the waistband of my jeans. My camisole has ridden up, exposing my tummy, and Quinn circles his finger around my belly button.

I'm panting, trying to remain quiet, but as Quinn flicks open the button on my jeans, I whimper loudly, knowing what is about to come.

I hear the bedside table drawer open, and my eyes pop

open, wondering what he is searching for.

"Shh, I'll take care of you. Close your eyes."

I nod, my eyes drifting shut, and Quinn's fingers begin sliding down my zipper, stopping about three-quarters of the way.

I want him inside my pants and arch my hips up, urging him to oblige.

"So impatient." He chuckles, and his warm breath tickles my heated chest.

Quinn softly places my arms above my head, and before I can question what he's doing, the cold bite of steel snags my wrists, and I hear the unmistakable click of handcuffs snapped into place.

My eyes pop open, and I arch my neck backward to see my wrists tightly bound to the golden-framed headboard.

"Motherfucker," I curse, pulling on my wrists, which don't budge an inch. "Quinn, let me go."

"No," Quinn simply replies as he pushes off me before I have a chance to bite or kick him.

As I meet his amused eyes, I know I've been played.

Quinn and I are just as stubborn as one another, and he knew that I would go to Justin because, eventually, Quinn would have to sleep. I also know that he never meant all the crass things he said, and I breathe out a sigh of relief.

Looking down at his black jeans, I realize his little ploy has turned us both on. So I lick my lips because it's time to get even.

"Well, the least you can do is finish me off," I say, huffing my loose hair off my face.

"Nope, I think you can just remain cuffed to the bed, thinking about what you did," he playfully scolds, like he's reprimanding a child.

"Really?" I ask, my accelerated breathing pushing out my chest, and I don't miss the way Quinn's eyes flicker with interest as he watches my breasts rise with each intake of breath.

"I think you would much rather punish me." My gaze drops to his jeans. "I mean, you were the one who said you liked me being submissive. And what's more submissive than me cuffed to your bed, a hair's breadth away from coming in my pants at how fucking hot you are when you go all alpha male?" I wriggle my hips because my hands may be cuffed, but my legs are not.

"What are you doing?" Quinn asks with a hiss when my jeans shimmy lower, exposing my lace underwear.

But I don't answer him and continue wriggling, hoping I can yank my underwear down a fraction lower to tempt Quinn back onto the bed. Thankfully, it works, and he places a knee onto the edge of the mattress, lowering himself down onto my body.

"Kiss me," I whisper under hooded eyes, gasping when his nipple ring presses through the light cotton of his T-shirt.

Quinn complies, inching his lips toward mine, and when he's within reach, I rear up…and I bite his lip ring hard.

"Uncuff me," I muffle from around his lip, but Quinn only laughs in response, which infuriates me.

Therefore, I bite harder, sucking his piercing deep into my mouth, my sharp teeth biting into his fleshy lip.

This situation is beyond ridiculous, but I will not let go, and Quinn seems unfazed that his lip is fixed firmly between my teeth. So I guess that means we'll just have to stay this way—forever.

My neck begins to cramp at the angle I'm currently in, and although I can't see Quinn's face as he's suspended above me, I know he is presently smirking his ass off.

"Uncuff me," I murmur again, tugging harder on his piercing, and this time, I taste blood.

The only response I get is Quinn's hips shifting off my body and his hand slipping between us.

I attempt to move my hips, but Quinn is too fast as he slips his hand into my underwear while the other hand slides my jeans down my legs. The moment his fingers touch my bare flesh, I know I'll lose.

There is no foreplay as he inserts a long finger into my hungry body, and instead of crying out, I just bite harder into his lip. I'll try to hold out for as long as I can, which won't be long, as his other hand slides under my camisole, palming my breast.

When he thrusts the bra cup down, pinching my nipple between his thumb and forefinger while inserting another finger into me, I scream, and his lip pops free. But I don't care as I'm about five seconds away from coming.

Sadly, Quinn has other plans as he slows down the tempo.

He is going to make me beg.

His face is hot and wild, and I groan. Lifting my hips, I hope to get faster friction, but it proves unsuccessful, and Quinn only chuckles.

"Beg."

"Never," I stubbornly spit, the cuffs rattling against the headboard as I yank on them, hoping they'll miraculously snap free.

A dimple hugs Quinn's cheek, and my eyes drop to his bloodied, swollen lip. Instead of feeling remorse, I smile, relishing in the fact that I have marred him. This overwhelming, animalistic claim I have over him has a fever burning in me, and Quinn knows it.

"You will." He smirks, and I gasp as he adds a third finger, stretching me further than I thought possible.

A low growl rumbles from within Quinn's chest, and the possessive sound has my back bowing off the bed, my feet pushing into the mattress to arch my hips to deepen the angle.

"Who do you belong to?" Quinn snarls, biting my chin.

"Y-you," I gasp as his fingers twirl deeper within my body.

"Again," he orders, his hand slipping free from my breast as he grips my face, turning my cheek to look at him.

"You," I moan, biting my lip, my eyes never leaving his.

"Who am I?" Quinn asks, his eyes dipping low, mesmerized at how my body responds to him.

"Quinn," I groan loudly as his fingers increase the speed and pressure, and I'm about to become undone.

"Louder," he orders, his breath coming out in labored pants as he watches his fingers pump in and out of my body.

"Quinn!"

"That's right. Say it, Red. Who…do you…belong to?"

As he flicks over my clit, my whole body quivers in unrefined lust. The cuffs bite into my wrists as I tug hard, needing to anchor myself as I'm coming and coming hard.

"You! I belong to you…Quinn Berkeley! I fucking belong to you!" I scream, the intensity of my orgasm bringing tears to my eyes, but Quinn won't stop.

He continues assaulting my body with his skillful fingers, and only when I come again, screaming out his name and whom I belong to, does he stop.

My body shakes, my wrists are raw, and my eyes are filled with tears. But I'm beyond sated that I don't even care.

Quinn kisses over my trembling lips and whispers, "That's right, baby. You belong to me."

I sag under his weight and realize that now Justin also knows who I belong to, which was Quinn's plan all along.

Thirteen

Every part of my body hurts.

But it's a good pain.

It's a deliciously good pain.

I crack open an eye. My hands are thankfully unbound, and my wrists are covered in a white ointment.

Quinn obviously felt bad for cuffing me to the bed. But after the mind-blowing orgasms he gave me, I should anger him more often.

I stretch, my body protesting, needing more sleep, and I turn to see that it's after six o'clock. The bed is empty, and I wonder where Quinn is at such an early hour.

My plan to get information out of Justin was ruined after my orchestral declaration. And if Justin had any doubt of whom I belong to, he and our neighbors certainly now know.

That was Quinn's plan all along because no way in hell

would he allow me within five feet of Justin alone. I should be pissed, but I'm not. We agreed that if he didn't spill the beans, we would cut ties, so I guess last night was me cutting ties. And Quinn made sure Justin knew that—loud and clear.

As the bedroom door opens, I cover the sheet to my chest, but Quinn enters carrying two cups of coffee. He is epic. In the simple attire of blue jeans, a snug white T-shirt, and Chucks, my heart does a tiny flip-flop, and I realize I missed him, which is ridiculous, seeing as I should be mad at him.

I roll onto my side to stop staring and drooling, and Quinn chuckles.

"Don't pretend you didn't miss me," he quips, and I hear him kicking off his sneakers as he lies on the bed.

I remain quiet.

"I brought you coffee," he says, reaching over my body and wiggling the paper cup in front of my face.

Biting back my smile, I roll over to accept his offering. As I raise the cup to my lips, Quinn's eyes drop to my wrists, and he flinches.

"Sorry about the cuffs. I know it was a little extreme."

"You think?" I scoff, playfully rolling my eyes. "Where did you get a pair of cuffs anyway? Actually, I don't want to know."

We remain quiet, sipping our coffees, and I wonder what excuse I can use when I see Justin. Here's hoping he'll still want to talk to me after last night.

"He's gone," Quinn says, leaning back against the headboard.

"What?" I ask, turning quickly to face him.

"He split." Quinn shrugs and reaches into his back pocket, pulling out a white bit of paper.

I unfold the piece of paper Quinn places into my lap, and the messy writing chills me to the bone.

Goodbye, Mia Mouse Wish things could have turned out differently for you and me.

Staring at the note, attempting to decode it, I murmur, "What the hell does that mean?"

"It means he's wishing it was *his* name you were screaming out last night."

"Quinn, you need to rein in this alpha crap."

"I didn't hear you complaining about my alpha crap last night," he adds, turning to look at me with a dimpled smile.

This is true. And I know deep down, I like Quinn's possessive streak over me because I have never had anyone want to possess me the way Quinn does.

"So you don't think there is an ominous message behind this?" I ask, rereading the note.

Quinn sighs, snatching the note from my hand and scrunching it up into a tight little ball. "The only ominous message will be the message I give him if I ever see his face again." He tosses the note into the trash can across the room. "Forget about him."

Nodding, I reply, "Okay, you're right. We've got bigger fish to fry. So what do we do next? Call Abi today?"

I'm hopeful her dad might have some good news.

"Yes," Quinn replies, deep in thought.

Here's hoping that good news is really good news.

I don't realize how much I miss Virginia until I call the

diner.

"I miss you." Abi sighs softly. "Things aren't the same without you."

"I miss you too. Your dad isn't any closer to clearing our name?" I ask, hoping I don't sound ungrateful because I know he's sticking his neck out to help us.

"Nothing yet. Sorry."

"You have nothing to apologize for."

"I just feel hopeless. I wish I could do more."

"Abi, you have done so much for me, and I will never be able to express how much I appreciate it. I will never be able to repay you," I add because without Abi, Quinn and I would not have been able to bribe our way through this god-awful experience.

"I don't expect you to. I just want you home," Abi says, and I can hear the exhaustion in her voice.

Tears prick my eyes, and Quinn brushes my cheeks as he half steps inside the phone booth.

"So your dad still thinks we'd be safer in Canada?" I ask, leaving out that if or when Quinn and I head to Canada, my father will die, as I know Abi will think our plan is a suicide mission.

"Yes. With the laws the way they are, the US government can't touch you without going through Canadian channels. It'll buy us some time," she replies as if reciting her dad's words.

"Okay, Abi. Thank your dad again for me."

"Of course."

It looks like Tabitha's father has no fresh leads or ideas. Therefore, our plan of hunting down my dad and putting him and Phil down, like the sick dogs that they are, is our best plan.

Although I haven't divulged my plans to Abi, I'm certain she knows what Quinn and I intend to do.

"How are you getting around?" she asks, attempting to change the subject of me committing first-degree murder.

I look at Quinn, who clenches his jaw. "We've been hitching a ride with an old school friend, Justin Miller."

Stupidly, I realize I should have had Abi's dad check him out. But he's done enough for me.

"Do you trust this guy?"

I look at Quinn, who seethes at the mere mention of his name.

"I never really did," I confess.

"What happened?"

"Let's just say, Quinn was right about him all along."

"How's he doing? Or should I say, how are you two doing?"

I can tell by her tone that she wants all the juicy details, which I would be happy to share if not for the fact Quinn stands an inch away.

"Okay," I reply vaguely, feeling my cheeks redden.

"Oh, you can't talk?" she says. I wish we could talk, as I have so much I want to tell her.

"Not really," I reply, looking at Quinn, who knows we're talking about him. "I better go. Give my love to Tristan."

"I will. He's still adamant he's coming to Canada."

"I hope you remind him what a bad idea that is," I reply, looking at Quinn, who looks proud that his brother is being as big a pain in the ass as him.

"You know it."

"That's my girl. I'll check in again in two days, okay?" I leave out the part that I'm hoping in two days, my father will be dead.

245

"Okay, be safe."

"You too."

I hang up feeling saddened, wishing we could chat for longer, but Quinn and I need to move.

Stepping out of the phone booth, Quinn asks, "So Canada is still the best plan, according to Abi's dad?"

"Yes. He's no closer to clearing our names; therefore, the police are still hot on our asses. So we've got the cops, my asshole of a father, and Big Phil waiting to catch us unawares," I groan, covering my face with my hands in exhaustion.

"Hey," Quinn says, wrapping his arm around my waist and burrowing my face into his chest. "We stick to the original plan, all right? Lucky should be released today, so we check out of the hotel we're staying at and check in someplace new. We gotta keep moving."

"Yeah, but remain in sight for my dad to find me. How do we remain undetected to the police, but wave a red flag on my ass for my father to see? This is so fucked up, Quinn." I sigh, pulling out of his embrace.

"I know, Red. But it's the only way, right?" he asks, his eyes searching mine, ensuring this is what I still want to do.

"Right."

"Let's get something to eat."

Nodding, we walk toward a diner and take a seat in the booth at the back. We order but are both quiet, lost in thought.

Every time I look at the burger in front of me, my stomach does a backflip, warning me that if I take a bite, it'll just come back to haunt me when I'm throwing my guts up.

Everything plays on my mind. This whole clusterfuck of a situation tests my sanity, but I have no choice but to deal. Thankfully, there is a light at the end of this fucked-up tunnel, and that light sadly ends with my father and Phil being dead.

However, I'm not saddened that their demise results in our freedom. I'm saddened that I've dragged Quinn into my fucked-up life, and now, now he is faced with something I wish he never had to face.

"What's the matter?" Quinn asks, taking a bite out of his cheeseburger.

I shrug, pushing my untouched meal away before I throw up. "I'm just thinking about…everything."

Quinn wipes his mouth with his napkin and nods. "Whatcha thinking?"

Watching the ice blocks swirl in my water while I spin my straw, I reply, "I just wish it was over, all of it."

"I know you do. So do I," Quinn confesses. "But we've come this far, and it's nearly over."

I cringe when I hear the word over because that equates to my dad being over—over and done with, and he deserves it. No one deserves that fate more, but I can't help but wish my life had turned out differently.

I mean, once it's done, what happens then? What happens to Quinn and me? Will Quinn resent me and hold me responsible for something we can never change once it's done? He says he's okay with committing murder, but am I?

The memory of Hank lying in his own blood, watching me with those soulful eyes, replays in my mind, and I know what the answer is.

I know I will never be the same once I kill my father. But the day my father and Phil shot an innocent man in cold blood, a man only trying to protect me, changed me forever.

And I'm ready.

"Red?" Quinn asks, and I snap my head up, as I have totally spaced.

"I'm fine, sorry. I'm just being an idiot," I reply, trying my best to smile.

Quinn reaches for my hand across the table, entwining his warm fingers through mine.

"I'll do it. You won't have any blood on your hands," he whispers, not wanting to be overheard by the patrons sitting around us in the busy diner.

"No," I reply firmly, shaking my head. "I'm doing it. I *have* to do it." Quinn understands I need to do this; otherwise, I will never be able to move on.

"I promise you, when this is all over, you'll live a normal, boring life, gossiping about all the things a typical nineteen-year-old girl should be gossiping about," Quinn says, squeezing my fingers.

Laughing, I reply, "Somehow, I don't see that happening, but one can dream."

Quinn turns serious, his eyes focusing on me. "I want that for you, Red. You deserve that. You deserve to be free," he adds, and I hate that he sounds undeserving of the same fate.

"So do you," I reply softly, and now I'm squeezing *his* fingers.

But Quinn only shakes his head, slipping his hand out from under mine.

"What? You don't think you deserve a normal, boring life?" I question, watching the regretful expression mar his beautiful features.

"My chance at being normal and boring is long gone," he replies, barely audible.

I know he's referring to whatever skeletons he has hidden in his closet. And although I haven't pushed, I wish he'd open up about his past. Deep down, it hurts that he won't trust me enough to tell me what happened to shape him into the man he's become.

The man who has sacrificed everything—for me.

Whatever Quinn has done, it'll never change how I feel about him. Nothing will sway my feelings. No matter how horrifying, I will never stop believing in him.

"So if push comes to shove and your father doesn't make his move, will you be okay if we go to Canada?" Quinn asks, leaving unsaid, *will I be okay if I see my mom?*

I shrug, suddenly feeling claustrophobic at the mere thought of her. Being on the run, attempting to dodge my dad, Phil, and the police, and trying to figure out Justin's angle meant seeing my mom fell low on the priority list. But now that I'm faced with a real possibility of actually seeing her, I realize that no, I won't be okay.

But I put on a brave face and nod, very unconvincingly. Quinn sees through my charade, and I sense he's about to say something I won't like.

"Red…" He rubs a hand down his fatigued face before he continues. "Will your dad figure it out?"

I cock an eyebrow, unsure of what he means.

"What if your dad has figured out we're headed for Canada, and he…goes after your mom?" he clarifies.

The thought has a wave of nausea weighing heavily within my gut, and I cover my mouth, part in shock, the other to stop myself from being sick. I never thought that far in advance, and after the Lucky incident, my dad going after my mom seems very feasible.

He is out to destroy everything I love, and even though I don't know *what* I feel for my mom, I know I would never forgive myself if he hurt her. As it would just be another person I have indirectly hurt because of my choices.

Yes, I'm mad at my mom. And I'm not expecting her to welcome me back into her life with open arms, especially considering my current circumstances. But if my dad gets to her first, then I will never know for sure because I have no doubt he'll hurt her, knowing what it would do to me.

But how do I warn her?

I need time.

I'm not ready to talk to her, not yet.

"We have to warn her," Quinn says gently, sensing my internal war.

"What?" I whisper, shaking my head. "No, I can't."

The walls close in on me.

"I'll send her a letter," I lamely suggest, my body starting to shut down as the fear of talking to my mother takes over.

"It'll take too long," Quinn says, making a sympathetic face when he watches my shaky fingers reach for my glass of water.

He sighs, leaning forward to reach for my hand, but I pull back because I don't want his sympathy.

"If you *are* right, and your dad *is* predicting your every move, then he'll guess we're heading to Canada to see your mom."

"But we're not going there to see her."

"I know. But when we cross that border, you know she's the first person you'll want to see."

"I'm not thinking about a family reunion, Quinn!" I snap, feeling horrible for lashing out, but suddenly, the thought of seeing my mom sinks in, and I'm going to hurl.

"I know this is hard for you. But we have to tell her what's going on. I know you're not ready to talk to her, but—" Quinn says softly, his eyes expressing nothing but genuine concern, and I can't stand it.

I feel like a victim…again.

"How would you know?" I shoot up from the booth,

ready to make a mad dash toward the safety of the exit.

"Red, it's okay to be scared." Quinn stands, and that damn sympathetic look only worsens by the second.

Scoffing and stepping back, I snarl, "I'm not scared."

And it's true. I'm not scared. I'm mad because Quinn is right. I should warn my mother about my father, but a part of me doesn't want to. And that part of me is evil, the part that screams, "Why should I?"

Why should I warn her that a monster is headed her way? She never warned me about the monster. She left me with him.

What kind of person does that make me? To not want to caution my own mother that she is in danger.

All this time, being on the run, I could push my mom to the back of my mind. But now, I no longer have that luxury because Quinn is right. As soon as I step foot into Canada, I will be hunting her down, and I'm not ready for that part of my life. That is the reason I never sought her out when I found her.

I wasn't ready.

But now, now I have no choice, and I'm still not ready.

"I'm not ready to see her." I feel my bottom lip tremble, but I refuse to allow any tears to fall.

"I know, and I'm not saying we have to go see her. I just think warning her is the right thing to do," Quinn states, gently placing his hand on my upper arm.

But I shrug out of his embrace because I don't want his compassion.

"I know," I reply, and suddenly, I can't breathe as the truth right-hooks me in the face.

"Red, it's okay."

"How do you know it will be okay? How would you know

how I feel?" I cry, not caring that I'm causing a scene and have the attention of the entire diner.

Quinn grabs me firmly, drawing me into his chest, not allowing me to evade him as he whispers into my ear, "Because I know how it feels to have a mother abandon you, okay? I know how it feels to be treated like you're nothing but trash. Like you don't matter. I know...because my mother did it to me."

As his bitter words sink in, I feel as if the floor has fallen out from under me, so I quickly steady myself by placing a hand on his taut bicep.

How could his mother do that to him? Are there no good parents out there?

Quinn *is* right; we are cut from the same cloth.

"I didn't know. I'm sorry," I apologize, attempting to envelop him in my arms, wanting to comfort him.

But Quinn flinches.

"I don't want your apologies," he snaps, gently breaking our embrace.

"Talk to me."

But Quinn turns away, looking over his shoulder, his chest rising and falling with harsh, heated breaths.

This is neither the time nor the place. But I guess this scene will surely draw my father's attention if he is indeed watching me.

"Talk to me!" I demand, fisting his shirt in both hands. "Tell me what happened to you."

But he bites his lip angrily and snarls, "So we can compare notes on how fucked up our moms are? I don't think so. I'd much rather forget I have a mother because, in my eyes, my mother is dead."

My eyes soften, and I can't help but sympathize with

Quinn, which is hypocritical, as I hated the same look reflected in his eyes only moments ago.

Quinn suddenly recoils, and I know why.

I hate *that* look. That "sucks to be you" look. It's a look that makes you feel weak. It's a look that makes you feel like a victim. And no one wants to be a victim, especially someone who knows firsthand how that feels.

And now I've gone and given that look to Quinn. But more importantly, I've made him feel like a victim, something he obviously refuses to be.

"Quinn," I say, my voice coated in sympathy for someone who doesn't want it.

"This is why I've never told you about my past. I don't want or deserve your pity."

"I'm sorry, I just—"

"You what?" he snaps, raising an eyebrow, waiting for me to explain, but words escape me.

My heart breaks in half as I watch him fall apart. I don't want to worsen the situation by saying something stupid, so I don't say anything at all.

Quinn reaches into his back pocket, throws a few bills onto the table, and storms off, shouldering open the door with a loud thud with his exit.

I stand frozen for a few seconds, attempting to gather my thoughts because I don't know what the fuck just happened. However, I know this is my fault, and my feet pound on the floor before my foggy brain can catch up.

I can hear patrons whisper under their breath at the debacle they just witnessed, but they can all go to hell. There is only one thing that matters, and that is finding Quinn.

The cool breeze slaps at my cheeks, and I turn my head from left to right, desperately searching for Quinn. Thankfully,

I see him not too far up the street, and my boots pound on the sidewalk as I chase after him.

"Quinn!"

I know he can hear me, but he doesn't slow down. He pushes past a couple of window-shoppers, and he doesn't look like he'll stop as he quickens his pace.

"Quinn! Goddammit! Stop! I'm sorry!" I cry, pushing past people who have stopped and turned to see what the commotion is about.

But he doesn't stop. He just keeps walking, making it clear he needs space. And I owe him that.

Slumping into a wooden bench seat, I drop my face into my palms as my tears bypass through my fingers, running down my cheeks and staining my torn blue jeans. I understand Quinn needs to be on his own because the only time he was willing to let me in, I gave him that damn look, the one I despise more than anything.

The urge to run and purge this shitstorm overtakes me, so I get up, sniffling back my tears, and begin running. I run in the other direction, away from my betrayal of Quinn's trust, and I just keep on running until my lungs burn and my entire body trembles in fatigue. But I can't stop because when I do, reality will catch up to me and remind me of the pained look in Quinn's beautiful eyes.

It's getting dark by the time my body gives out, and I collapse against a wall in a dirty alleyway.

My breath is labored, and the heavy feeling in my chest worsens with every step I take. The marathon run to God knows where has not made me feel better. It's only given me a headache and made me crave a road map.

How will Quinn ever trust me again? His mother, like mine, is obviously a touchy subject for him. And I just hope some groveling and an explanation will make things right between us.

"Idiot," I mumble to myself under my breath.

As a few drops of rain splash against my cheeks, I realize I need to get back. I'm not sure how long I've been gone or where the hell I am. Pushing off the wall, I walk deep in thought and stupidly drop my guard, not taking in my surroundings.

And that irresponsible action costs me dearly.

Suddenly, the hair at the back of my neck prickles in terror, and I hastily reach down, grabbing the knife in my boot. But I don't get there in time.

Someone pushes between my shoulder blades, and I trip, losing my footing, and fall face-first into a stagnate puddle of liquid. The disgusting water, which I'm pretty sure consists of piss and garbage juice, stings my eyes, and I quickly spit out the liquid before I gag.

My hands have broken my fall, which is good, as it gives me the leverage to push off my wrists to find my feet. But the wind gets knocked out of my sails as my attacker forces a knee into my lower back, roughly pinning me to the ground, which results in my face being inches away from the dirty puddle.

My heartbeat begins a steady incline, throbbing in time with my racing pulse, and as my fight-or-flight instinct takes over, I know I need to get the fuck off this ground. I refuse to allow this to happen to me again.

I resist, but my assailant has the upper hand as he deepens the pressure of his knee on my lower back, winding me.

Attempting to turn my cheek to get a look at the motherfucker proves futile as he roughly clasps his fingers around the back of my neck, shoving my face into the filthy ground.

He presses my chin into the ground, but I strain against

his hold, pushing back with my neck muscles, which feel like they are about to snap under the brutal force.

But sadly, that's all I can do, as the weight of my attacker immobilizes my body. But I'll be damned if I don't put up a fight. As I desperately attempt to buck him off, he thrusts his other hand onto my shoulder blade so hard that my collarbone pops as it smashes into the concrete.

With no other choice, I scream, "What do you want? Motherfucker, get the fuck off me!" It comes out muffled because my face is now submerged in liquid.

But I don't stop struggling. I need my face out of this water before I drown. Finally, his hold slackens slightly, and I'm able to turn my head to the right. I take a big breath, and a blood-curdling scream leaves me because I know I'm not getting out of this without help.

However, the louder I scream, the harder he pushes into me, and when I wriggle with all my might, trying to buck him off yet again, he fists my long, knotted hair into his palm, smashing my face once, then twice, into the concrete.

I see stars, but pure adrenaline has taken over, and I know it's now or never as fresh blood rains heavily into my eyes from an open gash in my hairline. The hot, thick blood seeps into my mouth, and I spit it out because with everything that's left, I let out one last scream. But it's a half whimper, half moan as I slowly lose consciousness.

"Motherfuck…" I moan before my head connects with the pavement for the third and final time.

Everything fades to black.

Fourteen

Everything aches.

My body.

My brain.

My heart.

My body feels battered, my brain feels fried, and my heart, well, my heart feels broken.

I don't know where I am or how I got here. But I tell my brain to snap the hell out of it and catch the fuck up.

I need to think.

Thinking back to my last memory, I yelp, which comes out muffled, as a tight gag prevents me from screaming.

Panic engulfs my entire being, and as I attempt to open my eyes to make sense of my surroundings, I realize my eyes *are* open.

So why is everything black?

I realize a scratchy blindfold covers my eyes, preventing me from seeing anything.

A sudden ache stabs me in the heart, and when I try to raise my arms to rub my chest, they don't move an inch because my hands are bound with thick rope.

Taking a calming breath and counting to three, I attempt to kick my legs out, but sadly, they are also bound to the wooden chair I'm sitting on.

I don't know how long I've been out or if I'm alone. All I know is that I need to get the knife in my boot, which will be impossible, but I have to try. I wiggle my fingers, but the rope is wrapped around my wrists so tightly that I'm surprised I haven't lost feeling in my hands.

Now, I really start to panic.

My hearing and sense of smell are the only two things I have to work with, and I plan to exploit the hell out of both.

Inhaling, all I get is pine needles and fast food. But my sense of hearing is quite acute. I will my racing heart to calm the fuck down so I can get some idea of where I am.

There is little to no background noise. No horns blaring, no brakes squealing, no people yelling, no dogs barking, no nothing, which makes me think I'm someplace remote, someplace far, far away from anyone or anything.

My heavy breathing echoes loudly within my chest, and I'm about to hyperventilate because of the stupid gag. But again, I will my breathing to a steady rhythm and use my now semi-clear brain to try to piece together what to do next.

I'm gagged and bound, and miles from civilization. However, I know at least one other person is in the room with me. Looks like my sense of smell came in handy after all, as the smell of fresh fast food is a dead giveaway that I'm not alone. And the pine needles indicate I'm out in the woods.

I pointlessly curse around my gag, swaying the chair, hoping to tip it over so I can slither my way out of here. But I freeze when I hear a tongue clicking because I was right—I'm not alone.

I don't bother to scream for help because I know this person is my captor. Instead, more profanities pass through my bound lips. My captor only laughs, and the tiny hairs on my arms prickle with recognition because I know that laughter.

"Justin?" I gasp around my gag.

The laughing ceases, and I know it's him.

Time freezes, and as hard as I try to make sense of why the hell Justin would do this to me, I come up short. So in its place, I decide to ask the bastard himself.

"Why?" I muffle scream.

Why is he doing this?

"Why?" he angrily asks.

I nod because it's all I'm capable of doing.

"Because you ruined my life, you little bitch," he spits, and I can smell his perspiration, indicating his proximity.

I remain silent, not knowing what to say.

"Not such a smart-ass now, are you?"

His weighty footsteps pound onto the creaky floor, and unexpectedly, he rips my blindfold off my face, strands of hair yanked out from the force. My eyes feel heavy, and as I pry them open, my pupils slowly adjust to the dim light illuminating from the single light bulb hanging above my head.

My squinted eyes take in my bleak surroundings. It looks as if we are in some run-down cabin with nothing but a rusted sink with no taps, a wooden table and chair, a ratty mattress, and two windows covered with black sheets just to set the mood.

I'm guessing people come out here to get their dicks sucked. Or…to torture people.

Justin paces the room like a caged tiger before he pulls the Beretta handgun from the waistband of his jeans.

"Justin," I say around my gag, my eyes dropping to the piece.

"Shut up! It's my turn to talk."

I do as he says because I need to buy some time before he kills me.

He finally stops pacing and pulls up a chair, straddling it so we face one another.

Justin looks like a crazed man. Beady brown eyes narrow on my face, and his lip curls in distaste when I whimper under his cruel stare. He stinks to high heaven, and his dirty, grass-stained white T-shirt, which has a yellow tinge around the collar and underarms, may be the reason.

Overall, Justin is no longer the man I remember him to be.

"It's funny. Seeing you bound and gagged doesn't give me the satisfaction I thought it would," Justin sneers, looking at me with nothing but hatred.

I'm hopeful he has come around, but I know I'm wrong as he rises from his chair and pistol-whips the right side of my temple. Blood trickles from the wound, slipping into my ear. I see stars.

"Better," he says with a smile, retaking his seat.

My head lolls to the side, and I wish I could cover my ears because the buzzing noise rattling around in my head scrambles my already sore brain.

"No passing out," he says, steadying my wobbly head in a

vise-like grip under my chin. "I want you to hear everything I'm about to tell you."

I break free from his hold because his touch makes my skin crawl, but I nod, indicating I'm listening.

"Good girl. What I told you was true. I did have a huge crush on you. All through high school, you seemed so far outta my league, but that time when I found you crying and comforted you behind the gymnasium. You let me in, so I thought maybe you felt something for me too. I was so inexperienced when I kissed you, but the kiss was perfect. And even though I'd kissed a few girls before you, they never made me feel like you did."

I still don't understand what this has to do with me being tied, gagged, and bleeding in front of him.

"Anyway, after that, I thought maybe you'd felt it too, but I was wrong. The next day, you acted as if I didn't exist, and that fucking hurt. I was so lonely, and I knew you were too. So I thought maybe we could fill that void for one another, but you didn't care. You went on like I never existed. And I faded into the shadows, watching you from afar."

That is so creepy. I don't even know how to process it.

"Two years later, you did it to me again when I sat alone on the sofa at that party because no one wanted to talk to the weird, poor kid. Do you remember that night?" he asks, his hateful eyes never leaving mine.

I nod, and my breathing increases as I see a pattern.

"That was the night you tore my fucking heart out. I had finally gotten over you, even dated a few girls, but then you came and sat near me, acknowledging me after ignoring me for so long. And all my feelings for you came rushing back."

I think back to why I sat beside him.

It was because I was waiting for Mickey, the local

quarterback. I only agreed to do the drop-off because he paid good money for a gram of coke. He texted me while I was rummaging blindly through his parents' pretentious mansion, looking for him, and asked that I wait for him downstairs. He was on a beer run and would return in twenty minutes.

I had been bored among the jocks and cheerleaders, and I saw Justin sitting on his own, so I figured I'd kill some time by talking to the only person I could tolerate in the room. But I didn't realize he had feelings for me. I would have pushed him away when he kissed me if I'd known.

"Ah, so you do remember," Justin says, watching me closely as I replay the events in my mind. "Why did you kiss me back, Mia? Why? You should have told me no and not led me on if you never liked me!" He reaches out, slapping me so hard across the face that my head snaps back from the force.

But I push past the pain because I need to know how the story ends.

"After you left me sitting on the couch like I didn't matter…I followed you. I wanted to tell you once and for all that I was sick of being ignored and that I loved you."

My stomach drops as I know what comes next.

"I saw you dealing to Mickey," he snarls, his lip curling in distaste.

I'm not proud of my actions, but I still don't understand why Justin is so mad.

He sees the confusion in my eyes and kicks back his chair, towering over me.

"Do you know why I was the shy, weird kid?" he asks, bracing both hands on the back of my chair so our faces are inches apart.

I shake my head.

"Because my dad was a junkie, Mia. I was so introverted

because my family life was so fucked up, and I just couldn't deal. Then I saw you, and I knew you'd understand because I could see that you were lost, just like me."

I flinch because his next words hit home.

"But I never suspected the reason was because you were a fucking drug dealer. You were everything I hated because your 'career choice' was the reason for my shitty childhood."

I'm sorry for Justin's pain, and I'm not proud of what I did, but it was not a career choice. I knew that what I was doing was wrong. But I just didn't have the balls to stand up to my dad and tell him no.

"But it gets better." He snickers, pulling back from my personal space.

I let out a premature breath because as I watch Justin reach into his pocket, pulling out a ripped, aged photograph, I know the answer lies within this picture.

"Do you know him?" he asks, showing me a picture of a man in his early forties who I don't recognize.

"No," I muffle from around the gag, shaking my head in case he can't understand me, but he does.

"Look closer!" he yells, shoving the photo into my face.

Pulling back to get a better look, I still have no idea who he is.

"Look closer at the life you destroyed," Justin spits, tapping the barrel of the gun against the discolored photograph.

My eyes focus on the picture of the man in blue slacks, watering his rosebush, but still, nothing.

"You filthy whore!" He slaps me again, but this time, my teeth rattle inside my bloodied mouth.

"You can't even remember the face of the person you killed!" Justin screams, his fingers crushing around the photograph in rage.

"What?" I gasp through my gag, my eyes widening.

"Oh, don't play dumb. You dealt this man a bad batch of heroin, and this man was my father!" he shouts, shoving the picture into my face so I can get a clear view of the reason behind Justin's rage.

My stomach burns, and rancid bile creeps into the back of my throat. But I hold back my vomit, as I know I will choke on it if it comes up.

Staring at the photograph with a heavy heart, I can see the resemblance between Justin and his dad, and I don't blame Justin for hating me. He has every right to despise me because I don't remember the face of the man whose life I destroyed.

I deserve this. I knew what I was doing was wrong, but I didn't stop.

I won't fight Justin. If he has to do this to get some kind of peace, then so be it. Revenge is a powerful thing—I should know. And I'm willing to sacrifice myself to give Justin his vengeance. The vengeance he deserves.

"I followed you one day after school because you weren't really around after the party."

That was because I was failing and didn't see the point of attending something trivial like school.

Thinking back, I know the day he's talking about, as it was my last day at school. I was there to collect my shit and drop out. I had a small batch of heroin stashed in my sock that I was to deliver. But I went to school first because the drop-off was about ten minutes from Parkdale High School, which was unusual, as I mainly dealt to people in the city.

That drop-off, I now realize, was to Justin's father. And you know what, I still can't remember his face—but there's a reason I can't.

The faces of the people I've dealt to all morph into one

because I don't want to know what color their eyes are or what they do for a living. I don't want to know because that would make them a person. That would make them someone with a family, which would make them a mom, a dad, a wife, a husband, a brother, a sister, and someone's kid.

It made it easier not to feel guilty when they were just nameless, faceless clients. It made it easier to accept that I was ruining their lives.

"I saw you deal to my dad," Justin whispers, lost in thought. "I always wondered who he got his gear off. I just never imagined the girl I loved was responsible for ruining my life!"

"I'm sorry."

And I really am.

"You're sorry?" Justin asks, his body shaking in fury.

I nod, my eyes filling with tears.

"Are you sorry that you're a fucking drug dealer? Or are you sorry that you got caught?" He pistol-whips me again.

Blood pours into my eyes and trickles over my lips, but I remain still and remind myself that I deserve this.

"That day, my dad died in his car, shooting up the junk *you* sold him. So excuse me if your apologies mean jack shit to me." He slaps me across my left cheek, no doubt leaving a handprint behind.

My cheeks feel swollen, and all I can taste is the unmistakable metal tang in my mouth. But I need him to know that I'm sorry.

"I'm sorry," I spit out again, my eyes widening, needing to express how remorseful I really am.

"Stop apologizing!" he screams into my face, spittle covering my cheeks.

He is beyond reason, and that's okay, so I only nod and

stop with the apologies.

"What are you going to do with me?" I ask, which comes out muffled, but he understands me clearly.

He laughs, and it's not a nice sound.

"This is the best part," he says with a smile, pulling away from me as he begins pacing the room. "You caused quite a scene back home, shooting your father."

Suddenly, the blood drains from my face.

"Finally, I see that you're scared. You're actually human," Justin says in mock horror as he stops pacing and watches me with a predatory grin.

"What did you do?" I spit, but I know the answer.

"When you were accused of shooting your father, I followed your case with interest because, after my dad's death, I wanted vengeance for his murder. He was a bastard and a junkie, but he was still my father."

I nod, understanding his reasoning all too well.

"So I sat and waited, thinking of all the ways I could make you pay for ruining my life because, as they say, revenge is a dish best served cold. But you made it so easy for me. When you shot that lowlife and ran, thinking he was dead, that led me straight to you."

I cock an eyebrow, confused.

Justin smiles, looking pleased with what he's about to reveal. "I visited your father in the hospital, and the moment I saw him, I realized you and I were more alike than I thought. We both had junkies for fathers. And that made me hate you all the more. I just couldn't understand how you chose to live that destructive lifestyle when you knew firsthand how many lives it impacts. How many lives it destroys, and this fact just fueled my need for revenge even more.

"I gave him some sob story that we were dating and that I

wanted to find you, to bring you home, and the stupid bastard believed me. He most likely figured I had more chance of bringing you home than he did, as we were supposedly in love. He agreed, thinking he was in control.

"The police was hot on his ass, so he had to be careful and not rouse too much suspicion. I'm sure he wasn't looking too hard for you since he thought I was doing all the legwork. And that's what I wanted. I didn't want him finding you first because I knew he would kill you before I got my chance at revenge.

"I had to pull a lot of strings, but lucky for me, an ex-girlfriend's dad was a cop. I found the information I needed after I earned his trust, and I located you, trying to blend in, in that pathetic excuse of a town in South Boston.

"But I didn't realize that your father was working with that dirty drug lord. That motherfucker was keeping a low profile, as he too was rousing suspicion among the cops, but he had his sources working on finding you, and unluckily for me, he found out about your whereabouts around the same time as I did.

"It was game on then."

This story gets worse with each passing second, but with no other choice, I listen.

"I followed them to South Boston, but you'd all already split. So I asked around, and there was one blonde bimbo who was more than happy to divulge information on where you were headed. And with little persuasion, I might add." Justin smirks, and I know exactly who he's talking about.

Stacey.

"Her boyfriend's dad was a cop, and he had told his son there was a sighting of you, headed for South Carolina, so I bailed. But I couldn't believe my luck when I bumped into you."

If I had just stayed put and not been jealous, none of this would have happened.

"It was fate. I followed you after our encounter, and then, then I called your dad."

I close my eyes, wanting to shut this horrible reality out.

But Justin continues. "I knew they hadn't found you, because I had the upper hand, thanks to the ever-helpful Stacey. But I was running low on cash, as all my efforts to track you down bled me dry. Then I was struck with a brilliant idea.

"Who has lots of cash? Drug dealers. And who would pay for information of your whereabouts? *Your* drug dealer. I told your dad I wanted fifty grand, and I would tell him where you were. He didn't believe me, but when I gave them the cell number of your little friend, which I knew you were using, *then* they believed me when they called her phone, and her bubbly voice message answered, proving to them I was right. They didn't even know she existed, but after they did their homework, they knew I was telling them the truth."

Shit. That message *was* from them.

"They asked why I would help them, and I told them I needed the cash. They knew they couldn't do this on their own, and with the police also after you, they had no other choice but to trust me.

"Your dad and Phil wanted you so badly, they agreed but said I would get the money *after* I delivered you to them. Alive. I was so fucking happy. I would get my revenge and be one rich bastard after I finished with you. Life was good.

"But then, you just left in the middle of the night, and I fucking lost track of you. But your little boyfriend's romantic gesture tipped off the police, and thankfully for me, little

Stacey knew all the details. But it was pure coincidence I stumbled across you at that rest stop. Once again, fate had a part to play in our meeting."

Justin is the reason my father and Phil were always a step behind us? He's the reason they knew our every move? And he's the reason Lucky got hurt? This son of a bitch has been tipping them off, and I played right into his hands.

"I let your father know we were back in the game, but the stakes had been raised. I wanted eighty grand because we had a complication."

Quinn.

"Your dad asked if he would be a problem, and I told him no."

And how wrong Justin was.

"I told them where we were that first night in Arkansas because they were looking for you in a different direction, the dumbasses. I didn't want the police to find us, so we stayed in that fancy hotel to throw them off our tails.

"Phil deposited a couple of grand in my bank account as a sign of good faith, but because the stupid idiots were on the other side of the damn country, I got paranoid, thinking the cops might be onto us. So we left for Missouri, where I was supposed to wait for them. I was happy to wait out the two days there while I beat, torture, and fuck you, *then* hand you over to them.

"But because of that *motherfucker*, I just couldn't get you alone. And there was another problem. I wanted my damn money. I told your dad I would up and leave if they didn't give me twenty grand as a down payment, and with no other choice, they paid me.

"But when I checked my account, they only paid me half. They thought they were so clever, but I showed them by leaving that early morning in Missouri. That day, that was the day I was going to hand you over, but those fuckers wanted to double-cross me, so I showed them who was in control."

That phone call in Wisconsin, the one I overheard, was to my father. And I have no doubt that *all* the times Justin was on the phone, he was speaking to my dad, updating him on where we were and where we were headed.

Thinking back to all the vague conversations Justin and I had about him running *toward* revenge and being a repo agent, I now get it. He was talking about *me*. He was repossessing me for his personal revenge because my tainted past ruined any chance of him having a normal future.

He *had* done his homework, using Canada as the proverbial carrot. He never had any intention of going there. It was just another bargaining chip, and I fell for it. All those times he was nice to me, it was just a ruse to gain my trust and let my guard down. He was fucking with me, toying with me, paying me back for the times he believed I toyed with him.

He could have let my father have me within the first day of finding me, but now, everything makes perfect sense. We left Missouri because he wanted Phil and my dad to know that *he* had my trust, not them, and that *they* needed *him*. For someone who was never once needed before, the one time Justin was wanted, he played it for as long as he could, as he loved the power. And also, he loved the control.

I have no doubt my dad and Phil were always that step behind us, because Justin eluded them to our exact whereabouts. He was fucking with us all. We were just puppets in his sick little power trip, and he was the twisted, megalomaniac puppet master who loved the control.

I'm so stupid.

As if Justin reads my thoughts, he explains, "But there

were times when nostalgia crept through, and I wished things could have been different for us. Sometimes, I felt like you understood me. So I gave you a chance to be honest when I asked what you were running from. If you could prove that you were sorry for your past, I would reconsider, but then you lied.

"So I knew what I had to do. I played you the rest of the time, trying to earn your trust. I was fucking with you, just as you were with me. Giving you a taste of your own medicine."

"I never fucked with you."

"Yes, you did." He whacks my cheek, stunning me with the force. "You gave me hope that maybe I could be happy. Maybe I could be normal."

My rattled brain can't help but think what a pile of bittersweet irony this is, as we're all trying to find normalcy in a not-so-normal world.

Interrupting my thoughts, Justin continues. "Finally, they paid me my money, and that's when your little puppy paid the ultimate price. I needed an excuse for you to stay put, and what better way to keep you grounded than fucking with your dog. Phil, he is one sick motherfucker, you know that, right?"

I only shake my head because he is absolutely right.

"The morons were about two days away, so Phil told me to hurt you, try to break you down and scare you a little."

So the voice I heard *was* my father then. Justin, the sick fuck, probably had him on loudspeaker because I know I heard his voice.

"Why didn't you just kill me?"

Justin understands my gibberish and replies with a sick smile. "You're worth a lot more to me alive than you are dead. But that night, when you screamed *his* name out, I lost it. You lied to me, pretended that you liked me, and I felt that rejection all over again just because I fell for your fucking lies.

"That night, if you came to me, I was willing to give you one more chance to explain. But then, you made it quite clear that liars never change. I had to leave before I killed you both. And like I said, you're no good to me dead. But in a warped way, that night showed me how my original plan had veered off course.

"Greed was fueling me, but I wanted to bring it back to basics, and the only thing motivating me from that night forward was my revenge. I called your father, told him what happened, and now, now this is the part that gets really good."

Greed and revenge—as simple as that sounds, that was the motivation fueling Justin's rampage. The two most primitive human emotions have turned an already unstable individual into a raging psychopath.

But I don't understand why he would help my dad when he knows Phil is the drug lord. He's the one who supplied the drugs that killed his father.

"I was just the messenger!"

"You're a clever whore. You're thinking how could I tolerate working with your father, who is an obvious drug addict, and Phil, who is the lowest form of scum known to humankind?"

I nod.

"Because, as we know, money talks. Not only are your dad and Phil willing to pay a shitload of cash for you, but so are the police. There is a reward of a quarter million dollars on your head. You're worth a lot of money, Mia Mouse. Growing up where we were so poor that I had to wear hand-me-downs that were basically rags, you surely can understand how that money is motivation to do what I'm doing."

I gasp, and my brain tries to process everything.

"So do you want to hear my ingenious plan?" Justin asks, his eyes lighting up as he sits casually in the chair before me.

I nod again.

He looks at his silver wristwatch and smiles. "Your father will be here very soon to finally claim his prize."

My throat closes over, and a guttural sound gets trapped in my esophagus.

"But that's not even the best part," Justin says happily, rocking back in his chair. "I know Phil is a sick bastard and that he's the supplier of all the drugs. So I'm going to make each one of you who had a hand in my father's death pay, and pay dearly.

"When they collect you, I will get the rest of my money and happily let them drag you out of here without thinking twice. However, once they are gone, an *anonymous* tip will be made to the police with your whereabouts, and I will get that reward too. It's poetic, really. I get money for my revenge, and I also bring down the three people who destroyed my life. Phil for manufacturing those filthy drugs, your dad for creating you, and of course you, for destroying my life," Justin states, ticking his hit list off on his fingers.

Shit, his plan will work. The state I'm in, the police will question Phil and my dad, and Justin knows I will rat them out because that was my original plan all along. That was *my* revenge—to bring those fuckers down for what they did to Hank.

The police will take one look at me and believe me. I'm their perfect witness, happy to confess to everything they did, hoping to clear my name.

And Quinn's.

And to avenge Hank.

Justin is a psychopath, and the saddest part is that I

created him.

Justin could just shoot me, my father, and Phil and still get the reward by reporting it to the cops, saying he stumbled across us. But where's the fun in that? He knows the torment I will suffer, being put on trial and found guilty for my past and watching the people I love suffer with me.

That prospect is far worse than being dead.

Watching the hurt and regret pass over Tristan's, Tabitha's, and Quinn's faces when I'm deemed a criminal would kill me. I would much rather be dead than hurt them in that way.

And Justin knows that.

Killing me would be too easy. Living with regret is the hard part.

And the same applies to my father and Phil.

Once the police start digging around, they will discover just who Phil is, and I have no doubt Phil will take my dad down with him, tying him to Hank's murder.

There is no loyalty.

There is only self-preservation.

And drugs.

And money.

And greed.

"On that note, I better get you nice and docile for when your father arrives." He rears forward, punching me in the guts.

A gush of wind leaves my lungs, and I gag, unable to breathe. But Justin doesn't stop. He stands to his dominating height and sucker punches me in the ribs. I grunt, my body slumping forward, the pain radiating to my toes.

But I don't scream. I remind myself that I deserve this.

"Scream!" Justin roars as he punches me in the nose.

My head snaps back with a sickening thud, and I can feel

hot blood dripping down my face, over my chin, and dribbling onto my jeans.

But still, I don't scream.

As Justin slaps my bloodied cheeks, over and over again, my left eye closes over, and I wish for unconsciousness to overtake me.

Sadly, it doesn't.

It's only when I feel the soiled T-shirt being torn from my body, my bra ripped from my shoulders, my breasts roughly palmed, and my jeans being yanked down my thighs that I make a sound.

"You motherfucker."

Justin merely laughs in response.

My vision is blurry and clouded by my matted, loose hair, but nothing is wrong with my hearing as I listen to the unmistakable sound of a belt buckle being unclasped and a zipper being unfastened.

"I'm sure you had no problems spreading your legs for that asshole!" he yells, his voice shredding my eardrums. "I thought I could sever your infatuation with one another since he has been a pain in the ass from the beginning. I thought this problem would be easily disposed of because, how could you love him and not me?

"You flirted with me to get what you wanted, and I nearly believed you because love is really fucking blind! But that night, it was *my* name you should have been screaming, not his! And that night, I knew it was the beginning of the end for you both because that asshole would die for you, and you will never give him up!"

His words slap me across the cheek because the truth of what he says makes me ache for Quinn.

"I've earned your pussy after you've flaunted it my way

all these years!" Justin spits as his pants hit the floor with a nauseating thud.

His heavy breath whips at my cheeks, and I can smell his desperation as he violently pinches my nipples, laughing when I attempt to pull back from his assault.

My entire body feels like a rag doll as I'm all floppy and have no control of my frame. I tell myself to focus because, in about five seconds, Justin will make good on his word as he skulks behind me.

Justin yanks my limp head backward by my hair and pushes his arousal into my cheek. I'm hoping he takes off my gag and forces that disgusting thing near me because if he does, I will happily bite it off.

He reaches around me, tearing my underwear off. His desperate fingers suddenly push into me with such brute force, I scream out in pain.

Tears I've tried so hard to contain fall as I realize he's going to take the only thing that's mine. The only thing I could offer Quinn that is pure and untouched, unlike the rest of me.

"You think you belong to that fucker? Well, I'll show you who you really belong to," Justin says, inches from my ear, and I close my eye, unable to watch as he brutally takes away my humanity.

However, a loud sound of something being thrown into the wall and sliding onto the floor with an ear-splitting thud has me shakily opening up my good eye to see what's going on.

All my questions are answered when I fuzzily see...him.

As his heavy boots pace onto the wooden floor, murderously calm, I know it's Quinn. I don't know how he found me, and quite frankly, I don't care. I'm just so happy he's here.

What happens next occurs in slow motion, and although I'm seeing it, I don't believe it.

Justin is a pathetic, crumpled pile of moaning, barely clothed flesh slumped onto the floor, where he fell after Quinn threw him across the room. He attempts to sit up while groggily rubbing the back of his head, but Quinn stalks over to him, yanking him up by the collar of his ripped T-shirt.

Justin tries to fight him off, but Quinn is a vision of pure wrath as he smashes Justin up against the wall, once, then twice, pushing Justin's breath out of his lungs in pained exhalations.

The fact that Justin is still breathing enrages Quinn, so he lifts Justin's feet off the ground, his hands still fisted in his collar, and headbutts him, breaking his nose.

I flinch at the sound, but Quinn doesn't stop, nor does he speak, which is scarier than watching him beat Justin with his punishing fists. Justin slumps to the floor, moaning, attempting to curl into a ball to protect himself from Quinn's rage. But Quinn drops to one knee and repeatedly punches Justin, connecting with any and *every* part of his body, until Justin is a bloodied, unconscious mess on the floor.

Quinn never gave Justin a chance to fight back, and like me, minutes ago, I bet he was wishing for unconsciousness to overtake him. The fight lasts for no more than a minute, but I will remember the sound of each brutal strike for as long as I live.

With one final kick to the guts, which echoes off the cabin's walls, Quinn lets out an animalistic yell and slowly turns to face me, his fists dripping in blood.

I wish I wasn't so naked because as Quinn scans my body, his face contorts in pure pain. I know what I must look like, and I close my eye, his pain hurting me more than the physical abuse my body sustained.

He is across the room in seconds, dropping to both knees in front of me. The first thing that overwhelms me is his signature scent. Under the wrath and blood and fear, I can smell him.

I smell home.

Opening my good eye, I see him covering his face with his palms, his shoulders shuddering in rage. I want to comfort him but can't because I'm still tied. So I sit and allow him to grieve because we will never be the same after this.

After a few moments, Quinn raises his pained eyes, his long hair sticking to his bloodied cheeks, and to me, he looks like a warrior. My Prince Charming, who slayed the dragon.

"Oh God, Red," Quinn says, his voice wavering, his eyes filled with unshed tears.

He reaches for the gag in my mouth, untying it softly, not wanting to tear my matted hair out, and throws it to the floor.

Wincing as I move my jaw from side to side, I hope to soothe my sore facial muscles. It hurts like a bitch, but the pain is welcomed as I'm grateful to have the stupid gag out of my mouth.

Quinn slowly reaches behind him, pulling out a knife from the small of his back, and begins carefully cutting through the ties that bound my injured wrists. As soon as the pressure releases, a sigh passes through my cracked lips, and Quinn's warm hands rub my numb fingers, attempting to get the circulation flowing through my cold digits.

"My feet," I croak, my throat hoarse and sore, my arms hanging limply by my sides.

I can't stand to be bound for a second longer.

Quinn nods and goes to work, cutting through the rope at my feet.

The moment I'm unbound, I slump forward with a sigh of relief, and Quinn catches me. He slips off his black sweater and bundles me up into it. He does all this while still on his knees before me, and I don't miss the gesture behind it.

"Forgive me, Mia," he cries softly, his face twisting in pain.

That's the first time he's ever used my name. And I like it.

Shaking my head, I don't accept his apology, as he has nothing to be sorry for. I realize I want to stand, but I don't think I can.

Quinn wraps his hands around my waist, slowly helping me up, and he makes a pained face as I cringe because my ribs feel battered and bruised.

"I'm so sorry," he says as I steady my hands on his shoulders for support, thankful my legs don't give out.

"Not your...fault." I pull up my jeans. "Let's go. Dad... coming," I say, each word pained.

"Your dad?" Quinn asks as I lean onto him, insisting I walk.

I nod, biting my lip in pain as I take my first baby steps, my feet stinging with pins and needles.

"How?" Quinn asks, steadying me when I almost fall.

Gesturing with my chin toward a moaning Justin, who is slowly waking up, I reply croakily, "He was working with my dad and the police," I mumble and whimper when my feet give out.

Quinn catches me, supporting me against his warm body, and I groan softly, the contact warming my broken soul.

"He was going to turn me over to the police for money and revenge."

I know I'm not making any sense, but I'm starting to feel faint. I'm pretty sure I'm on the cusp of passing out.

"He sold you out? For money?" Quinn asks, lightly

running a hand down my cheek as he turns me to face him.

I nod, and my head feels like a bobblehead toy.

"Motherfucker," he snarls, and without warning, he gently places me onto the mattress and walks over to a moaning Justin.

My eye widens as I watch Quinn kick Justin over until he's lying on his back, helpless and afraid. I internally celebrate when I see the damage Quinn inflicted on him as he moans and splutters up bloodied spittle. But that celebration turns to shock as Quinn reaches for the knife in the waistband of his torn jeans, his expression unreadable. Flipping it over once, he drops to one knee and plunges the knife upward, straight into Justin's side.

The astonished breath catches in my chest because I'm pretty certain Quinn just stabbed through Justin's rib cage, puncturing a kidney or lung.

A pool of blood seeps through Justin's shirt, staining the white material a bright red as Quinn yanks out the knife, which makes a sickening, sucking sound at the withdrawal. Justin gurgles from the pain while his broken body writhes from side to side as he blindly reaches for his torso, attempting to put pressure on the gash.

My eye zeros in on his wound because, unattended, Justin will die. But that was Quinn's intention all along. He rises to his full, towering height, and I'm stunned into silence.

"C'mon, Red," Quinn says. Leaning down, Quinn wraps his bloodied hands under my knees and lifts me into his chest.

Wrapping my shaky arms around his neck, I allow Quinn to carry me away from the horror that will never leave my memory.

He kicks the door open, and the bright moon is our only light. The trek through the forest is long, but I don't mind since I'm in the arms of my savior. Quinn leads us to an old, beat-up Dodge and opens the door for me, placing me along the bench seat, softly rearranging his sweater so I'm covered.

My open eye closes as soon as my head rests on the leather seat.

The engine roars to life, and Quinn reverses out slowly.

"Sorry," he tenderly apologizes when I hiss in pain as he drives over a bump.

He brushes the hair off my sticky brow, and I cry out when he passes over my temple, which is caked in coagulated blood.

"Fuck, I've got to take you to the hospital."

Curling myself into a ball, I groan, shaking my head. "No, Quinn," I choke out, turning toward him. "You look after me. No one…but you. Promise."

Warm fingers barely stroke my cheek, but I sigh, comforted by his tender touch.

"Okay, I promise," Quinn whispers. It's all I need to hear because, with that, I slip into a black abyss and stay there for days.

Fifteen

I know I'm not awake, but I'm also not asleep. I'm just here and there, floating in and out of consciousness.

But it's better this way, as every time I come to, my body aches, and it's better not to deal with the pain—just yet.

Because I know when I do, nothing will ever be the same.

I never knew you could float among the clouds. But here I am, doing just that.

I jump from cloud to cloud, laughing because the texture feels like marshmallows between my toes. I know I'm dreaming…unless I'm dead? But I doubt Quinn would let me go.

"Hello, child."

My movements are in slow motion as I spin in a circle, attempting to find the owner of that voice.

Everything here is different.

When I finally see him, my eyes fill with tears. But my tears are the color of rainbows, not clear or translucent.

I guess in my dreams, I cry colorful tears.

"Grandpa?" I gasp when the form of the man who died for me comes into view.

He looks just as he did the day that he died. Brown slacks held up by black suspenders and a white cotton T-shirt.

God, I miss him.

I reach out, but my feet won't move since they're glued to the marshmallow floor.

"Are you okay?" I cry, my colorful tears slipping into my lips.

Hank nods, his warm eyes smiling brightly. "I am, child. Are you?"

Shrugging, I reply, "I'm not sure."

The last thing I remember, I was on the run with Quinn.

Quinn.

I really wish he was here with me, as he makes everything okay.

"You love him, don'tcha?" Grandpa asks, looking carefree and happy.

"I don't know what love is. But I think I do," I reply, turning to my left and scrunching up my face when I see a winged cherub playing a song on a polished piano.

"Are we in heaven?" I ask as the cherub plays "November Rain" by Guns N' Roses.

"I don't know, child. Heaven, hell, it doesn't matter. I'm up here in the clouds, looking down on you. Let go of your vengeance. You can never win," a voice unexpectedly whispers, but that voice morphs into three different tones.

"What?" I ask, my skin prickling in fear. "But…they killed you."

"I deserved it because I was a stubborn fool. Fool. Fool," he says, which echoes deeply around me.

Suddenly, Hank transforms into something that is not him.

"Grandpa?" I question as his face begins whirling and pulsating into a swirl of blackness.

This isn't Hank.

I try to move, but my feet are still glued to the floor. Dropping to my knees, I begin dragging my body away from the man cackling with that sick laughter.

My dad.

"You can run, Mia, but you can't hide. I *will* find you, and when I do, you'll wish you had killed me."

My eyes meet the spiteful gaze of my father, and I wish I could move or fight, but I can't. I'm frozen solid because I'm afraid. I try to scream, but my mouth is glued shut, and everything melts around me.

The marshmallow clouds have turned into sludge, and I sink farther and farther until I'm submerged up to my neck. My father slowly turns his face, and I scream, as the right side of his face has distorted into Phil's.

"I'm going to enjoy killing you, over and over again," Phil/Dad crows, aiming the gun that killed Hank against my temple.

As I hear the gun cocked, my eyes pop open, and I scream. My body thrashes around on the bed, desperately attempting to escape my demise.

"Red! Red, shh…you're dreaming."

I know that voice. Focus on that voice.

However, I can't shut up. No matter how hard I try, I just keep yelling. I feel like absolute shit, but screaming makes me feel remotely better.

"Mia, stop it. It's Quinn."

His soft breath warms my tender temple as his lips press over my sweaty brow.

"Mia? You called me Mia," I whisper gutturally, my eyes trying to make sense of where I am, but it's pitch black.

"Yes, because that's your name," Quinn explains, bundling me into his chest.

"It's not Paige?"

Why am I so damn confused?

"No, that's not you anymore."

And he's right. Paige died the day Hank did.

"Hank," I sob as the dream slams into my brain, reawakening my fear. "He's dead?"

"Yes, he is. I'm so sorry. It's okay," Quinn coos, his voice breaking with his pain.

Clawing onto his arms, I inhale deeply, and his warm scent calms me.

I feel like I'm going crazy because everything is so fuzzy and sore, and I'm just so tired. It hurts to think, and I want to switch it off.

I don't want to think or breathe.

"Sleep, Red. Go to sleep. I'll be here when you wake."

And I do.

Birds chirp.

I try to turn, but it hurts to breathe.

Open your eyes! I yell at myself, but my eyes feel like they've been hinged closed with concrete.

"Red…are you awake?"

His soft voice is like music to my buzzing ears, and

suddenly, my eyes desperately want to open and see the man before me.

"Quinn?" I croak, barely audible.

"Oh, thank God," he says, a relieved breath whooshing from his chest. "Can you open your eyes for me?"

After a few moments of desperately trying to pry them open, they finally peel apart, but my vision is blurred as dried gunk sticks to my lashes, hindering my vision. However, I try to focus on the one important thing—Quinn.

Holy shit, he looks horrible. His untidy hair is tied back at his nape, but most of it falls around his weary face. His eyes are bloodshot and lined with fatigue, and he desperately needs to shave.

"You look like shit," I say, my voice sounding like I swallowed a grater.

Quinn's mouth tips up into a small smile as he kneels by the bed, softly grasping my hand.

"Where are we?" I ask, looking around the dimly lit room.

"Just outside of South Dakota," he replies, his thumb rubbing over my tattoo softly as his eyes never leave my face.

"South Dakota?" I choke out, attempting to sit up, but Quinn's fingers tighten around my wrist so I remain prone. "Shit, how many days have I been out?"

Quinn sighs as he closes his eyes briefly before opening them and replying, "Four days."

"What?" I ask, wincing when I attempt to sit up again.

I now understand why Quinn wants me to stay horizontal. My entire body aches.

"Yeah." He nods, his face pained as he fills in the blanks. "You were in and out of consciousness, and I tried to take you to the hospital. But you asked me not to, so I looked after you as best I could."

My head aches, and without thinking, I raise my hand to my forehead, attempting to soothe my pounding temples. But as my fingers pass over a bandage, I realize my entire frame seems covered in gauze.

Quinn must have attended to me when I was unconscious, and I know he looked after me with the utmost care because I'm not dead or missing a limb.

"Thank you," I say, wishing I could move because I really want to throw my arms around him.

He nods, his eyes softening when I shakily reach forward, pressing my cold palm against his cheek.

"So what now?"

Quinn smirks, leaning into my touch. "Well, first things first. You need to shower because you look like hell."

I can't help the croaky laugh that escapes my chapped lips, and it's the best sound I've heard in days.

Twenty minutes of arguing with Quinn has paid off because he's finally allowed me to shower by myself. Of course, he insisted he bathe me, which was so not happening.

But in all honesty, I crave some alone time. I need to process everything because *a lot* has happened.

My life has finally caught up with me, and no matter how many miles I put between me and my past, it just keeps popping up, haunting me with memories I wish remained dead and buried.

I deserved everything Justin did to me because he, too, needed vengeance on the person who ruined his life. The look of rage and hatred reflected in his haunted eyes is a look I know all too well. But it also confirmed what I have always known—that I'm a bad person.

I have ruined countless lives, and I deserve no happiness. All I seem to do is leave pain, death, and destruction in my path, and I need it to stop.

As I look at the beaten girl, staring back at me with a puffy and unrecognizable face, I realize I need this to change. I can't live my life like this for a second longer. And I don't want to.

But I don't know how to make it stop.

Lifting my legs over the tub and turning on the shower is an effort since it aches to move. But I don't care because it warms my broken body.

I look down and cringe at the purple and blue splotches covering my ribs, but I can see the faint yellow tinge beginning to appear as I slowly heal.

Suddenly, I realize I got off lucky. Justin, however, didn't. I'm pretty sure Quinn killed him when he jammed the knife straight into his side. Quinn committed the ultimate crime, and he did it…for me.

The thought has my teeth chattering, and I switch off the shower before drying off. I need to talk to Quinn.

I feel semi human as I make my way into the bedroom in a white robe, feeling clean and warm since the hot water thawed out my aches and pains.

My eyes fall to Quinn. He's propped up against the headboard, watching TV, topless.

"Hey, how are you feeling?" he asks, pressing mute on the remote.

"Human," I reply, tying back my wet hair.

He chuckles and pulls back the comforter, gesturing for me to sit. As soon as I slide under the covers, Quinn softly bundles me against his chest, my head resting against his shoulder.

"You scared me, Red," he confesses into my hair after a minute of silence.

"I'm sorry," I whisper, closing my eyes and basking in his warmth.

"No," he rebukes. "I'm the one who should be sorry. If I hadn't lost my temper and left you alone, none of this would have happened."

"None of this is your fault, Quinn. It's all mine. Everything that's happened, I have no one to blame but myself," I declare. Snuggling closer and touching him gives me the strength not to break down.

"How did you find me?" I croak after a minute of silence.

Quinn sighs, the deep sound resonating in his chest. "Abi."

"What do you mean?" I ask, confused.

"After I calmed down, I listened to my gut. I just knew we hadn't seen the last of Justin, and the more I thought about it, I realized his note was some fucked-up forewarning of things to come. I just had a bad feeling, and that bad feeling told me he'd come back for you." He grinds down on his jaw.

"So I called Abi and asked if her dad could pull some strings with the cops. I had Justin's license plate and asked if Abi's dad could trace him. And they did.

"I don't know just who Abi's dad is, but he's one powerful man. He has connections everywhere."

When Quinn frowns, I understand why.

Even with his connections and power, he still can't clear our names. We're in so deep.

"The moment she told me where he was, I stole a truck and broke every traffic law to get to you. But I still didn't get there in time."

"Hey," I say, not liking the guilt I see. "If it wasn't for you…"

But I can't finish.

We both remain silent, no doubt processing what would have happened if Quinn had not found me.

"Tell me what happened."

He has every right to know, but when I tell him, will he think differently of me? I guess there's only one way to find out.

"I dealt to Justin's dad." I sigh, the truth burning an acidic hole in my throat.

When Quinn remains quiet, I continue. "Not that it makes it right, but I didn't know it was his dad. His dad…he died because of the drugs I sold him."

Quinn is silent, his heavy breathing echoing throughout his chest.

"Justin and I, we kissed twice in high school."

As Quinn's body tenses under me, I quickly add, "But that's all we did. He told me he loved me, and I didn't even know he existed." I come clean with a hint of remorse in my voice. It's a horrible reality knowing your feelings aren't reciprocated.

"He saw me dealing to a classmate and figured out I was dealing to his dad," I say, leaving out the irrelevant details.

"So he wanted revenge on you?"

"Yes."

"Motherfucker," he utters under his breath.

"I dropped out of school and never saw Justin again. The whole time, however, he was scheming ways to pay me back for what I did to his dad. I gave him the perfect opportunity when I drew attention to myself by shooting my father."

"He knew my dad would be looking for me, so he made a deal with him and Phil. For information on my whereabouts, they would pay him fifty grand."

"How did he know where we were in the first place?" Quinn asks. I know I'm leaving out a big hunk of the story, but I want him to know the essentials before I pass out.

"Stacey. He came looking for me in South Boston, but we had already split. Stacey was more than happy to rat us out since she had all the info from Brad."

Quinn's chest expands as he takes a lungful of incensed breath, but he allows me to finish.

"The day Justin ran into us was his lucky day because he'd made another deal with my dad. They were supposed to give him eighty grand for information on my whereabouts. And of course, my dad agreed. But Justin was a fool for ever believing he would see that amount of money. I have no doubt they would have killed him before we left the room.

"But it wasn't enough for Justin because as much as he wanted the money, he also wanted his vengeance. He toyed with Phil and my dad. That was why he didn't turn me over right away. He wanted power and control, and he wanted to fuck with me for as long as he could. However, things turned sour when his plan backfired."

And by backfire, I mean he tried to come between Quinn and me, but when he saw he couldn't break the foundation of our strange but solid relationship, he'd had enough and wanted his money and his revenge.

"But there's a catch," I whisper, and Quinn tenses again.

"He was going to rat me out to the police because there is a quarter-million-dollar bounty on my head. He planned to make an anonymous phone call and tell them where I was, resulting in Phil and my dad also getting caught. He knew I'd tell the police everything, therefore bringing my dad and Phil down with me.

"And he, in return, gets the reward and is deemed a hero

for trapping three wicked criminals. It's actually quite clever. Too bad it was happening to me."

And only then do I take a breath.

I don't realize I'm crying until the tears sting my eyes, but these tears remind me that I've lived through this and I'm alive.

Quinn is deadly silent as he mulls over my revelations, and I understand he needs a moment to process everything.

But when that moment becomes a heavy, lengthy silence, I quietly ask, "Quinn, are you okay?"

I attempt to look into his face to read what's going on behind those intelligent eyes, but his grip on me tightens, halting my movements.

"That motherfucker," he finally sneers, his chest rising quickly. "He was going to rat you out...twice and get a fucking reward for your capture?"

I nod, my finger inadvertently tracing his nipple ring because I need something to do with my hands. Quinn's breath hitches in his throat, but it's not from pleasure.

Thinking back to what he did to Justin, I realize I don't regret his death. I only regret that Quinn has to live with a murder on his conscience. Although I don't have proof that Justin's dead, I'm damn sure he is.

"What do you think happened to him?"

Quinn rubs his lips atop the crest of my head, contemplating his response.

"I left him as a message for your dad. So if I didn't kill him, then I have no doubt your father will. Either way, he got what he deserved."

Quinn did this for me. He's got blood on his hands because of me. How can I live with myself, knowing what I made him do?

"I'm sorry," I say into his neck, burying my face into his warm embrace.

"*You're* sorry?"

"Yes. I have brought you nothing but trouble. How can you still be here? How can you still want me?" I ask, my throat beginning to close over. "I'm a fucking mess. I should just do everyone a favor and turn myself over to my dad or the police. I'm nothing but trouble, and I will do nothing but bring you down with me.

"I need to let you go, Quinn. You deserve better than this!" I cry, spreading out my hand to gesture to the shitty hotel room we're sitting in.

And with one final plea, I whisper, "And you deserve better than me."

"Stop it! I'm not going anywhere!" he says angrily, pulling me out of his embrace to meet his wild eyes.

"It's true."

He attempts to calm me down, but the past nineteen years come crashing down, and I can't stop.

The fact I was bound and gagged, about to be raped by a severely disturbed man, isn't why I'm crying. The fact my father and his drug dealer are out for my blood isn't the reason either. And the fact I'm on the run doesn't even skim the surface.

I'm crying because of Quinn. I'm crying because he still won't leave me despite everything I've put him through.

He still looks at me like I'm the most beautiful thing he's ever seen. He still looks at me like I'm pure and worth all this bullshit I've dragged him through.

"I don't deserve you. No one in my entire life has ever thought I was worth anything."

"Listen to me, Red. I'm not leaving you. Ever. You hear

me? You're my girl, and I will protect you until my last dying breath. I'll happily kill for you, again and again, and not lose a night's sleep if it keeps you safe. You're all I care about." He takes a deep breath before he confesses, "And you're all I fucking want."

Before I have time to respond, he sets me free and yanks me forward, settling me onto his lap as he smashes his lips to mine. My body protests since everything hurts, but Quinn feels too good, and I'd rather hurt than pull away.

"Oh fuck," he groans between frantic kisses, his hands fisting in my hair.

I whimper as the feeling blurs that fine line between pleasure and pain, but pleasure is currently setting pain on fire. And before long, pleasure hums through my body like a live current of electrified desire.

"I want you," Quinn says as he slides a hand up my leg, stopping mere inches from the apex of my thighs.

"I want you too," I choke out as I gasp for air.

I'm well aware that I'm naked underneath my robe, and so is Quinn as he skates his fingers higher up my thigh, hissing as his fingers skim over my sex. He's being a gentleman, so I reach down, untying the belt, and I do what we both want— remove it so we're skin to skin. The robe falls open, and this is the first time I've been totally bare. The feeling is like nothing I've ever known before.

I rub myself against Quinn's naked chest, and it feels better than I could have ever imagined, and we both moan at the contact. He runs his fingers along the length of my spine, and the sensation sends my skin alight.

I begin softly rocking against him, and Quinn pulls away when he sees the bruising on my ribs.

"Shit, sorry, I didn't think," he apologizes quickly as he

reaches for the lapels of the robe to cover me up, but I secure my hands over his.

"Don't stop. I want this. I want you." I lean forward, sucking on his nipple and drawing the piercing into my mouth.

Quinn groans as he threads his fingers through my hair and bows backward as I busy myself with tonguing his nipple. The metal instantly warms the second my lips wrap around the piercing, and as I draw it into my mouth, I realize I could do this all night.

Getting Quinn off and having the power over his willing body is far more of an aphrodisiac than him making me come, and I suddenly love being in control.

Letting his nipple go, I push on his bare chest, and he falls backward, his hands settling low on my hips as I straddle him.

My eyes feast on every inch of the breathless man underneath me, and I need his hands on me like I need oxygen to breathe. With our eyes locked, I slowly wrap my fingers around his right wrist and draw it up to my chest, silently begging him to touch me.

Quinn pulls on his lip ring, his entire face flushed and filled with nothing but red-hot desire.

"Touch me," I whisper, and he hisses as his fingers embark on palming my breast with slow, deliberate movements.

With our fingers entwined, I can feel the way my nipple instantly peaks, aroused by his gentle touch, demanding more. I can also feel my heart pounding against my rib cage, and it only beats faster as Quinn's skilled finger circles my areola, which sends a shooting pain of need straight to my center.

My grip over his hand slackens, and I arch into his touch as his movements become a little harder and a little faster, and it's exactly what I need.

As I begin grinding my hips on his cock, matching the torturous strokes on my breast, I can't take it any longer. Blindly reaching for the top of my robe, I push it off my left shoulder, but suddenly, Quinn stops me, his fingers overlapping mine.

My confused eyes meet his, and I gasp, suddenly feeling like a fool. "You don't want to?"

The thought has me quickly reaching for the lapels to tug them over my nakedness, but Quinn ceases my movement.

"Of course, I do, but just...not like this," he replies, ensuring his response is measured.

"I don't understand." I'm feeling self-conscious.

Quinn releases my hand, and as he sits up, his fingers gently draw the lapels of my robe together, covering me from his heated stare.

"Seeing you beaten, gagged, and almost raped is an image that will haunt me for the rest of my life," he whispers, gently tying the belt around my waist. "When the time is right for us, I want it to be perfect."

As I cock an eyebrow at him, he chuckles. "Well, something like perfect."

He takes a shaky breath before he continues. "Nearly losing you put everything into perspective, and when I possess every single part of you..." I gasp, aroused by his dominance. "It won't be in some shitty motel where I can hurt you more than you already are."

I'm about to rebuke, to declare he never could. But Quinn stops me, his fingers tightening around my waist.

"Red," he says huskily, mere inches from my lips. "With you, I have no control. And I know it won't be enough when I'm buried deep inside you and you're screaming out my name. I won't be satisfied till I own every inch of you...inside and out."

My body undulates at his confession, and I remind myself to swallow.

"So until then, let's just enjoy this." He wraps a warm hand around my nape, capturing my lips to his, and kisses me until I'm gasping for breath.

For now, this will do. But tomorrow, tomorrow is a brand-new day.

Sixteen

The veil of darkness lifted, the harsh light of day blinds me, and I realize it's time we make our move. I'm not feeling as rough as yesterday, but I want to leave because I have no idea where my father and Phil are.

"You're feeling better."

I jolt, startled that Quinn is awake.

I look over at him and can't believe how someone so beautiful, inside and out, could want me. And risk his entire life to protect me.

"How do you know I'm better?" I ask, shuffling closer to him so we're sharing the same pillow.

"'Cause I can hear you thinking," he says with a dimpled smirk.

I can't help the chuckle that escapes my lips, and it's nice to be laughing again.

"What were you thinking?"

"We need to make a move," I reply with a sigh, wishing we could stay in our protective bubble forever.

Quinn nods, his sleep-rumpled hair slipping into his eyes. "Where did you want to go?"

He watches me closely, and I know that if I told him I wanted to hitch a ride to the moon, he would follow me. But in a way, I'm traveling to outer space. I'm traveling to a land with the power to change me forever.

"Canada," I reply, and who would have thought one word could feel so claustrophobic?

"You want to stick to the original plan?"

"Yes. I'm mentally and physically fatigued, and if I were to fight my father and Phil, I know I would lose. We stick to Tabitha's dad's plan; at least this keeps the cops off our asses."

"You wouldn't have to fight them," Quinn states, reaching forward and running a finger down the length of my nose.

"What do you mean?"

"I would do it. We still have the guns. I could arrange a time and—" I silence him by placing a finger over his lips.

"As much as I appreciate the offer, no. We finally have the upper hand because they don't know where we are. Let's make a run for it, and then we'll figure out what to do next."

At the start of this journey, it was all about revenge and vengeance, but now, it's about survival. To survive this in one piece—physically and also emotionally—is all I care about.

When I think the coast is clear, I remove my finger, and Quinn's mouth dips into a small frown.

"When the time comes, I'll do it for you."

I don't need to ask what he's referring to, as this experience has shown me that I can run but can't hide. Sooner or later, my father *will* catch up to me, and when he does, one of us will die.

There are no compromises or happy reunions. The ending of this story results in someone's death. And I'm just hoping it's not mine.

"I can't let you do that," I say, shaking my head. "I can't let you kill for me…again. With each life you take, Quinn, a piece of you dies with them. Believe me, I know."

"I don't care," he replies. "I meant what I said. I'd do anything to keep you safe, and you're not safe while your father is still alive."

"You're so stubborn."

Resting my palm on his stubbled cheek, he turns into my caress and kisses over my moon tattoo.

"What does this mean?" he asks, gently holding my wrist while kissing over my ink again.

I'm hypnotized, watching Quinn's lips lightly press over my skin, and think back to the day I got it.

"It was one of the worst days of my life. And still, to this day, thinking about it makes me sick. It was Wednesday, and I was making my last drop-off. This customer was a regular, and she always ordered a hit of heroin every second Wednesday of the month.

"Nothing was extraordinary about this woman. She looked like an average junkie mom, but unlike other junkies, she was always punctual. She would stand by the back door at exactly six o'clock in her pink fluffy robe and Bugs Bunny slippers, biting her nails, awaiting my arrival.

"Six o'clock rolled around, and she wasn't there," I say, my mind lost in the past. "I noticed the back door was unlocked, so I thought maybe she had passed out inside. I let myself in, but as I opened that door, whatever innocence I had left died with her on that filthy floor."

Quinn's captivated eyes, which watch mine closely, are the only reason I go on, as this memory is one better left buried.

"She was lying on her kitchen floor with a fucking needle hanging out of her arm, the tourniquet still wrapped around her bicep. She looked dead, but her chest was rising and falling. My brain told me to run, but I couldn't leave her there if she was alive.

"I don't remember the smell because the closer I got, all I could focus on was her chest, which was rising abnormally fast. When I was a few feet away, I toed her with my boot and asked if she was okay. She didn't answer, and I couldn't see her face because she was turned away.

"I asked her again if she was okay, and I crouched low, attempting to turn her face. But suddenly, all I could hear was a whisper of...scurrying. I could hear millions of legs scampering all around me.

"I listened intently because I couldn't figure out the sound. And that's when a fucking cockroach ran up my arm. As I looked down, the entire floor swarmed with bugs of all different shapes and sizes, and I realized the noise was coming from her. It was coming from *inside* her."

Quinn gasps, and I conclude my gory tale. "They were fucking eating from her like she was a buffet. I stood so quickly, I lost my balance, and I fell...on top of her. On top of them. It was like a bomb of every type of bug went off, and that's when the smell hit me.

"In my panic of getting the fuck up, I somehow moved her, and she was staring at me, with only one glassy eye, as the other was an empty socket, eaten out by the spider using her skull as a nest. The louder I screamed, the more bugs emerged from her body. It was an endless sea of bugs coming out of every orifice," I whisper, almost gagging at the memory.

"And that's why you hate bugs," Quinn finishes.

I nod in response.

"So I got this tattoo because if a man can walk on the moon, then anything is possible. I would look at it in my darkest hours and know I would be free one day.

"If a man could do such an amazing thing like walk on the moon, then I could do the simple thing of leaving my dad and live a normal life. Well, something like normal. And it's better than getting a tattoo of a bug," I add with a gasp as Quinn kisses up my arm, licking along the crease in my elbow.

"You're right. Anything is possible," he says. "And you're proof of that."

I raise my eyebrow, about to ask him what he means. But he presses his lips to mine, silencing me and my memories.

We drive through the night, stopping only when imperative, as getting to Canada is more vital than ever. I try my best to remain awake, but sadly, my beaten body is still healing, and sleep overcomes me often.

The sound of tires crunching over the open road and the low hum of the talk radio is my background noise for the next couple of days as Quinn allows me to sleep off my injuries. However, I think he also needs the silence to process everything that's happened over the past couple of weeks.

From where we started to where we are now seems like a lifetime ago. But after this is over, I know things will never be the same. I know something *big* is just around the corner. I just don't know what.

"Red, are you awake?"

My sleep-induced brain recalls the significance of that

phrase, as those exact words were spoken to me all those weeks ago. We may still be on the run, but so much has happened since then. And I know this is only the beginning.

"Where are we?" I grumble, rubbing the sleep from my eyes with the heels of my hands.

"Just outside Canada," Quinn replies with a yawn. "I thought we could get some clothes and other stuff, seeing as we both need supplies."

I open my heavy eyes, and thankfully, it's the cusp of dusk because my irises can't handle any sunshine.

"Good idea," I say, looking up at Quinn since I have used his lap as a cushion. "Sorry." I quickly jump up. I can only imagine how hard it must have been to drive with my head in his crotch.

"It's okay," he replies with a wink as he climbs out of the truck. "I like having your head in my lap."

I smile and stifle a yawn behind my hand as I lock the door behind me.

"I so should not be tired," I declare, and Quinn chuckles, reaching for my hand as we enter the department store.

The simple gesture of handholding shouldn't give me such a rush, but it does. Quinn and I have come so far, and I just hope we keep moving forward.

"I'm just going to get some girlie things. Gimme five?"

Quinn nods, and we go our separate ways.

I head to the cosmetics section and throw some foundation into my basket because I bet I look like shit. As I pass a mirror, my fears are confirmed. Yellowish-blue bruising covers my face, and my hair sits in dreadlocked clumps. I won't even touch on the topic of my clothes.

As I'm throwing in some other face products to make me appear a little more human, I pass an elderly shopper who suddenly stops and stares, her face paling to an ashen white.

From her reaction alone, I decide to throw in some toothpaste, shampoo and conditioner, and some extra toiletries. Warmer clothes are also definitely in order, as I've heard Canada is freezing this time of year.

While I'm blindly tossing items into my basket, I notice a mother ushering her children away from me with a horrified look on her concerned face.

What the fuck is going on? Surely, I don't look that bad, do I?

Just as I'm about to go in search for Quinn, a hand clutches onto my arm, startling me, and I yelp in surprise.

"We have to leave. Now."

I don't understand what's going on until I look around the store and notice that *everyone is* looking at us.

"Quinn?" I ask, my eyes taking in everything around me.

"Just walk," he demands, ushering me toward the door.

Nodding, I lower my basket onto the floor and latch onto Quinn's hand as he leads the way toward the exit. A few shoppers turn away frightened, while others hide with fear apparent in their wide eyes.

I don't understand what's going on, and as a mother turns her child's face away from me like I'm a monster, I trip over my feet, stunned. Quinn all but drags me toward the door but halts when we see the shop front lit up by red and blue flashing lights.

At this moment, my heart drops to the floor.

"Fuck!" Quinn snarls softly as he stops in his tracks at the sight of five police cars surrounding the front of the store.

I see a dozen policemen armed and suited up with bulletproof vests, ready to take us down.

"We called the police!" a pimpled clerk yells, hiding

behind the register. "She's worth a quarter million dollars."

His words resonate in my brain, reminding me of Justin. Is that all I am to people? A fucking reward?

Quinn curses before whispering in my ear, "Forgive me."

Before I have time to react, he roughly seizes my bicep and spins me around, holding me prisoner as he wraps his arm around my neck, crushing my windpipe.

"What the fuck? Quinn!" I choke out but freeze when the unmistakable metal of a gun barrel presses into my temple.

The whole store gasps, and I watch them all duck for cover or raise their hands in surrender.

"She's not worth anything if she's dead. Where's the back door?" Quinn shouts at the not-so-confident clerk as he steers us out of sight of the police.

"It's—it's—that way," he stutters, pointing behind us before dropping to the ground.

Quinn's smart. He's ensured the police can't see us, but he wants everyone inside this store to witness him holding a gun to my head. And he's done this with intent. He wants the onlookers to believe that I'm *his* hostage, and *he's* the guilty one. He's taking the blame—just like I was going to do for him.

My hands clutch at my throat, desperately attempting to pry him off me, but as I struggle, Quinn's hold only gets tighter, and I know he won't let me go.

"Quinn!" I yell, but he hushes me by pressing harder onto my windpipe.

Tears roll down my cheeks as Quinn sacrifices himself for me. When the police question everyone in the store, they will recount seeing Quinn pull the gun on me, making it appear that I'm innocent, confusing the police.

He'll be in so much trouble for this. I know if we get

caught, he'll say he forced me to do all the illegal things we're accused of, including killing Hank.

If anyone is going down, it'll be him. His words take on a whole different meaning when I asked him, "How did you know I was going to the police?" And he replied that he would do the same for me.

He's taking the blame—all of it. But I can't let him.

I try to reach for the knife in my boot, which is near impossible, as his strong hold around my neck allows no movement.

"Don't even try it," he orders, slowly walking me backward toward the back door as he takes in everything around him.

Some onlookers appear utterly confused, while others are staring at me with nothing but sadness in their eyes.

"It's okay, sweetie," the grandmother says, who eyed me earlier.

I want to scream that Quinn is no monster. But I am.

But I only sob, unable to speak, making me look all the more the victim.

"You won't shoot me," I cry when I make another fruitless attempt for my blade.

"No, but I have no qualms shooting any of these assholes," he says as he tightens his hold around me.

I hope he's not serious, but I don't test him.

We arrive at the back of the store, and I watch in horror as shoppers stare at me, hands raised in surrender. My tears stream down my cheeks when someone records a video on their cell, which will undoubtedly be up on YouTube before we leave the store.

"Let me go!"

"No. You're mine. And I protect what's mine," he whispers inches from my ear.

As Quinn fumbles blindly for the door handle, I attempt to set myself free by throwing my head backward and connecting with his nose, knocking him off balance. I frantically reach for my knife but am stopped, dead in my tracks, when I hear a gun being cocked.

"You take another step, and I'll blow your fucking head off," Quinn warns.

I look up, mid-crouch, to see a middle-aged man stepping forward in an attempt to help me. The guy freezes, hands in the air.

"Let her go, son," he says softly, stepping toward me.

"No!" I shout, but Quinn slaps his hand over my mouth.

"Move, Red," he snarls, picking me up from around the waist as he shoulders the emergency door open, an alarm blaring as soon as it's triggered.

The moment the breeze slaps my cheeks, I desperately try to break free, but Quinn holds on tighter and breaks into a dead run, away from his undoing.

After a few blocks, Quinn sprints down a deserted alleyway as he can no longer contain my frantic flailing. As soon as my feet touch the ground, I slap him across the face with an ear-splitting whack. And then I do the same with the other cheek.

"Why?" I scream, incensed as I push with all my might into his chest. "Why would you do that? Why!" I shove against his chest again and again, but my laughable strikes are not even making a dent.

Quinn allows me to hit him, my tears blurring my vision until I'm bundled up, sobbing into his chest. I hold on tight as I can't let go because I'm afraid he will leave me.

His lips caress my temple as he coos, "Because now, you're free."

"No! I will not allow you to take the blame for this!" I sob, resting our foreheads together. "The plan was to go to Canada!"

"And then what?" he whispers, regret clear in his eyes. "We wait it out till your dad kills you. No fucking way! You're not running anymore. This way, you turn yourself over to the police and say it was my fault. I will head to Canada and wait until Abi's dad can clear my name. I will probably do some jail time, but if it means you're free, then I would happily serve a life sentence."

"No!" I pull out of our embrace. "The only people doing time are those motherfuckers!"

"And what if they catch us before we can clear our names?"

I stare him straight in the eye, and my voice never wavers as I reply, "I hope they fucking do."

Quinn shakes his head, his long bangs covering his brow, but he's done enough talking.

"I *will* fight for your survival, Quinn. Whatever I have to do, I *will* do." And I mean every word of it. "We're doing this together."

"I've just given you a get-out-of-jail-free card, and you're going to throw it away?"

"I'm done cheating," I reply, wiping my tears.

"Then what do you suggest?"

"I don't know yet. But we'll figure it out. *Together*," I press, emphasizing the word. "We're a stone's throw away from Canada. We'll cross international waters when we get there, and the police can't touch us." I latch onto Quinn's hand, begging him to listen.

"Abi will come through for us. I know she will. When we get to Canada, we won't be running. We can stay put and lay low until we figure out what to do next. But I can't let you turn yourself in for me. Please, Quinn, don't fight me on this. I would rather die than have you take the blame."

I hold his hand over my beating heart, squeezing his fingers, hoping he sees reason.

"Okay?" I ask, waiting for his response.

Quinn nods, drawing me flush against his chest.

"Okay," he replies.

"You're crazy," I whisper, shaking my head, our breaths mingling into one exhalation.

Quinn smirks. "I stick to my word, Red. I would kill for you."

And I know he means every word.

I've never felt so many raw emotions as I do now.

You'd think crossing the border would equate to feelings of freedom and emancipation, but they don't. In a way, I'm caged in another manner. I'm encaged in my past, and now that past is about to become my present.

"Are you okay?" Quinn asks as we drive our stolen pickup into Alberta.

"Ask me tomorrow," I reply honestly, my eyes focused on the minivan in front of us as I blindly pat Lucky.

Quinn looks over and nods. Thankfully, he doesn't push.

As we wait for the light to turn green, my eyes never waver from the bumper sticker in front of me.

"It is not in the stars to hold our destiny but in ourselves."
William Shakespeare

I've heard this quote before, but now it sings to me differently.

My quest for redemption has taken on so many different

meanings. But now I realize I need redemption after all this is over. I want to redeem myself from all the awful things I've done in the past, and *I'm* the only one who can deliver that salvation. Finding that new beginning is not in the stars but within me.

And that redemption starts now.

My heart begins beating frantically as we pull onto the street I've memorized by heart.

"I once heard this story," Quinn says randomly as I twist my hands in my lap.

I look over at him, waiting for him to continue.

"About a little boy who just wanted to belong," he continues as he chews on his lip ring.

"His whole life, he just wanted to be part of something humble, something good. And he couldn't understand why his life wasn't like everybody else's. But the older he got, he realized that life isn't anyone else's to own. Life is what you make it. Family is what you make it," he concludes, his eyes never leaving the road.

I know the little boy is Quinn, and I listen intently because this is the first insight he's given me. Vague or not, I give him my full attention.

"What happened to the little boy?" I ask, realizing we've stopped in front of the place I've dreaded seeing.

Quinn turns to me as he shuts off the engine. "He grew up and realized that it's okay to make mistakes because you've always got tomorrow to make amends."

I swipe the tears from my eyes as I crawl over to him, wrapping my arms around his neck.

"Thank you."

Whatever Quinn's story, we will deal with it together, just like we always do. We are both scarred souls, drawn together by tragedy, but we're trying damn hard to break the binds of our past.

"You ready?" Quinn asks as we stare at the mansion before us.

"Ask me tomorrow," I reply again.

Quinn kisses my temple, and I take that as my cue.

"Will you come with me?"

"Try to keep me away."

As I set my feet on Canadian soil, I feel like I've just stepped in quicksand. And if it weren't for Quinn's warm hand in mine, leading me toward my future, I would have crumpled onto the ground.

This is another crossroad in my life that will shape me into who I become. This moment will either make or break the connection I'm so afraid to make.

As we walk up the stairs of the extravagant home, I feel underdressed and unprepared for what I'm about to face. I try to smooth out my sleep-rumpled locks, but my fingers snag, and I give up. Quinn presses the doorbell for me as my shaky fingers fiddle with my frayed sweater.

As the sound resonates inside, I jerk and turn on my heel. "I can't do this," I cry, descending the first step faster than the wind.

But the door opening stops my retreat, and I turn slowly, seeing a sight I did not expect to see.

A girl with eyes just like mine looks at me with an arched, sculptured brow. "Can I help you?" asks the bored teenager, looking at me with obvious distaste, but as her eyes fall to Quinn, they pipe up in interest.

"Hi, sexy," she purrs, leaning against the doorjamb.

If I could speak, I would rip out her eyes, but I can't. Nor can I move.

The teenager licks her glossy lips as she concludes undressing Quinn. She then narrows her eyes at me, waiting for me to speak.

However, when I remain mute, gaping at her familiar appearance, she barks, "Look, go bother someone else," and she flicks her long, black hair over her shoulder.

"'Cause whatever you're selling, we're *definitely* not interested in." She scoffs and is about to slam the door shut when my legs finally move, and I launch up the stairs, placing my boot in the doorway.

"Gee, rude much?" she taunts, and this close to her, I can see why Quinn stares, mouth agape.

"Is…is Cynthia Lee home?" I finally get out without choking on my tongue.

She tilts her head to the side in interest. "How do you know her?" she asks, crossing her arms over her chest.

"I just…is she home?" I stutter, looking at this stranger who can't be who I think she is.

"Fine. Whatever… Mom!" the teenager screams over her shoulder.

Mom?

Oh my God. Is she? But surely, she can't be. But as I look at *my* expression mirrored on this teenager's face, I know it's true.

"Who's at the door, darling?" I hear a sweet voice ask before the door opens wide, and a middle-aged woman with black hair and bright blue eyes comes into view.

She's wiping her floured-covered hands on a frilly red apron. But as soon as her eyes fall on me, her hands cease all movement, and she gasps.

At this moment, everything is heightened. The harsh sound of my breathing, the frantic beating of my heart, but most of all, my brain is stuck on repeat, screaming, *This can't be her! This can't be her!*

"M-Mia?" she chokes out, her trembling hand covering her gaping mouth.

But I know with every fiber of my body that this woman abandoned me, leaving me alone with a monster.

And this woman ruined my life.

"Hi…Mom."

Subscribe to my Newsletter:

https://landing.mailerlite.com/webforms/landing/b4j1v6

Something Like Normal Playlist:

https://tinyurl.com/bddea5bp

About the Author

Monica James spent her youth devouring the works of Anne Rice, William Shakespeare, and Emily Dickinson.

When she is not writing, Monica is busy running her own business, but she always finds a balance between the two. She enjoys writing honest, heartfelt, and turbulent stories, hoping to leave an imprint on her readers. She draws her inspiration from life.

She is a bestselling author in the U.S.A., Australia, Canada, France, Germany, Israel, and The U.K.

Monica James resides in Melbourne, Australia, with her wonderful family, and menagerie of animals. She is slightly obsessed with cats, chucks, and lip gloss, and secretly wishes she was a ninja on the weekends.

Connect with Monica James

Facebook: facebook.com/authormonicajames
Twitter: twitter.com/monicajames81
Goodreads: goodreads.com/MonicaJames
Instagram: instagram.com/authormonicajames
Website: authormonicajames.com
TikTok: @authormonicajames
BookBub: bookbub.com/authors/monica-james
Amazon: https://amzn.to/2EWZSyS
Join my Reader Group: http://bit.ly/2nUaRyi

www.ingramcontent.com/pod-product-compliance
Lightning Source LLC
Chambersburg PA
CBHW070533120726
47909CB00007B/2123